'What is mine stays mine.'

A muscle jumped in Ash's jaw as he continued. 'I trust Valdar the Steady and everyone else understand that now.'

Kara's mouth went dry. 'Does that include people?'

'I look after my own.'

Kara straightened her back and dug her heels into her horse's flank. 'Then I was never yours. Seven years you've been gone, Ash—seven long years.'

AUTHOR NOTE

For many years one of the stories I wanted to write was a 'returned from the dead' story. It has always intrigued me, the way people cope when a person has been through a life-changing experience and has to go back home—only to discover home is not the unchanging place he or she thought it was.

I thought about writing it as a Roman-set novel, then a Regency, and finally knew I had to write it as a Viking story. The characters and their situation really came alive in my mind and it was a relief finally to do justice to a story which I have wanted to write for a long time. Sometimes ideas scream to be written, and sometimes you have to wait until the moment is right to write an idea.

I do hope you enjoy Kara and Ash's story.

As ever, I love hearing from readers. You can contact me through my website www.michellestyles.co.uk, my blog www.michellestyles.blogspot.com or my publisher. I also have a page on Facebook—Michelle Styles Romance Author—where I regularly post my news.

RETURN OF THE VIKING WARRIOR

Michelle Styles

Published in Great Britain 2014
by Mills & Boon, an imprint of Harlequin (UK) Limited,
Eton House, 18-24 Paradise Road, Richmond, Surrey, TW9 1SR

© 2014 Michelle Styles

ISBN: 978 0 263 90959 3

Harlequin (UK) Limited's policy is to use papers that are natural,
renewable and recyclable products and made from wood grown in
sustainable forests. The logging and manufacturing processes conform
to the legal environmental regulations of the country of origin.

Printed and bound in Spain
by Blackprint CPI, Barcelona

Born and raised near San Francisco, California, **Michelle Styles** currently lives a few miles south of Hadrian's Wall, with her husband, three children, two dogs, cats, assorted ducks, hens and beehives. An avid reader, she became hooked on historical romance when she discovered Georgette Heyer, Anya Seton and Victoria Holt one rainy lunchtime at school. And, for her, a historical romance still represents the perfect way to escape.

Although Michelle loves reading about history, she also enjoys a more hands-on approach to her research. She has experimented with a variety of old recipes and cookery methods (some more successfully than others), climbed down Roman sewers, and fallen off horses in Iceland—all in the name of discovering more about how people went about their daily lives. When she is not writing, reading or doing research, Michelle tends her rather overgrown garden or does needlework—in particular counted cross-stitch.

Michelle maintains a website, www.michellestyles.co.uk, and a blog: www.michellestyles.blogspot.com. She would be delighted to hear from you.

Previous novels by the same author:

THE GLADIATOR'S HONOUR
A NOBLE CAPTIVE
SOLD AND SEDUCED
THE ROMAN'S VIRGIN MISTRESS
TAKEN BY THE VIKING
A CHRISTMAS WEDDING WAGER
  (part of *Christmas By Candlelight*)
VIKING WARRIOR, UNWILLING WIFE
AN IMPULSIVE DEBUTANTE
A QUESTION OF IMPROPRIETY
IMPOVERISHED MISS, CONVENIENT WIFE
COMPROMISING MISS MILTON*
THE VIKING'S CAPTIVE PRINCESS
BREAKING THE GOVERNESS'S RULES*
TO MARRY A MATCHMAKER
HIS UNSUITABLE VISCOUNTESS
HATTIE WILKINSON MEETS HER MATCH
AN IDEAL HUSBAND?
PAYING THE VIKING'S PRICE

*linked by character

And in Mills & Boon® Historical *Undone!* eBooks:

THE PERFECT CONCUBINE

**Did you know that some of these novels are also
available as eBooks? Visit www.millsandboon.co.uk**

DEDICATION
For my eldest son, William

Chapter One

Early autumn, AD 793—Sand, Raumerike, south-eastern Norway

Seven years and Ash Hringson refused to think about how many thousands of miles it had been since he last set foot in Sand, the capital of Raumerike. He would have preferred to go straight home to Jaarlshiem, but he had a duty to inform the king of his travels and his plans for the future.

Ash rubbed a hand over his chin, fingering the small half-moon scar there. He had seen over thirty battles and minor skirmishes since he'd left. His face might be clear of all but the most minor scars, but he walked with a distinct limp, the legacy of a battle three years ago, which aggravated the injury he had received in a Frankish dungeon. He knew that he was not the same carefree youth who had left Raumerike's shores, with a thirst for adventure and the certainty of a glorious future. In his mind, Raumerike and all he'd left behind remained the same.

A great unexpected feeling of long-awaited belonging rose up in his throat. He was in his home country. On his native soil. A foreigner no longer.

Ash gave a wry smile. He must have done enough to regain some measure of his father's respect. Hanging his head in shame or walking in the shadows of life was no longer his destiny. He'd become a leader of men rather than a coward who left others to die in a fiery inferno.

The town had seen a few changes over the seven years he'd been gone, expanded with an air of bustling prosperity, but the streets were laid out the same. The blacksmith where he'd purchased his first sword looked to be under different management and the king's hall appeared to have been rebuilt. The market by the quayside was larger with a broader range of fabric and fur, but the fishmonger still traded in the right-hand corner, calling about fresh herring and salted cod.

Several market dwellers gave him sideways glances, paled slightly and turned away the closer he came, hurriedly pulling the shutters down. Ash's hand tightened instinctively on his sword's hilt. He forced it to relax.

Did they remember the shame he had brought to his father and the country? The brothers, friends and cousins who had died because of his recklessness on that fateful night? Was that why they looked at him as if he were one of the walking dead? Or was it the typical Raumerike distrust of an outsider?

He might be dressed in Viken clothes, but his heart beat with a love for Raumerike. He'd always remembered where he came from. It was why he'd returned—to make peace with his father if he could and to offer young Raumerike warriors true opportunity for advancement, rather than facing likely death on an unfriendly sea.

A temptation filled him to shout to the curious, doubters and naysayers that shame and coward were no longer carved on his chest. The youth who had run his ship aground in a storm because he was far too eager for wealth had learnt his lesson. A man's life was more precious than objects or gold. He kept his mouth shut, his hand firmly at his side and strode silently on.

Ash set his jaw and turned his feet towards the king's hall. First the king, then his father and finally his wife. He knew the proper order of things. Now.

Kara would understand. He remembered that about her, even if he could not conjure up the exact tenor of her quiet voice or the precise colour of her golden hair. She'd always been his most loyal supporter since they had first met when they were children and she'd bound his falcon's broken wing. His last memory of her was her head held proudly aloft and a single tear trickling down her cheek as she begged him to return a hero.

Ash pushed the thoughts about Kara away, just as he had done for the last seven years. Soon, soon he'd be able to remember. First he had to do his duty to king and country.

'Why are you walking amongst the living, Ghost?' an elderly voice called out from a stall hung with cooking pots. 'Today of all days?'

Ash winced as he mistimed his step, and put all of his weight on his bad leg. Of all the people to greet him first, it would have to be this woman. He forced himself to recall each of her sons' deaths before answering. The elder two had died in the storm, but the youngest had endured captivity with him, keeping him alive with his tales of long-ago bravery. He had wept when his last friend died. For a day and a night, he had lived in that hell hole with the body. Eventually, he'd been able to overpower the Frankish guard who had been sent to check on them and escaped through the narrow stinking drain.

Even now, after more than six years, he found it impossible to sleep inside or to go underground.

For the first time in that cursed journey, the gods had been with him. After he'd pulled himself from the drain, he had found a Viken ship in the harbour, signed on and had begun life as a sell-sword.

'No ghost walking. I am real, Hildi, the mother of warriors and a pearl amongst women.' Ash named her three sons who had sailed with him and all of whom had perished. 'I have come to give you the tribute for the lives of your valiant sons. All three sup with Odin. Feel my hand. I am real.'

She poked him with a bony finger. 'Bah. Your tongue still runs with silver, Ash Hringson. Let's hope there is some truth in your words this time. Alive and not drowned. This is indeed something new.'

'I survived, but know I will atone for their deaths. I give my promise, Hildi, as I once promised all those who followed me.' He looked into Hildi's eyes. 'Your sons now reside in Valhalla, instead of sharing the deep with Ran. What more could you ask for?'

'That I never doubted.' The woman barked an order and came out from behind the market stall.

Slightly more bent and a few more wrinkles, but essentially the same woman who had wept when she waved her boys goodbye. Her three sons had gone on the journey so that their mother would not have to work at the market, selling fish. Ash bowed his head.

The familiar tang of regret filled his throat. He'd lost count of how many times he'd wished that it had been he who had died rather than worthier men like Hildi's sons. Silently he added more to the amount he owed her. It wouldn't bring her sons back, but it would make her life easier.

'The king remains the same?' he asked when he trusted his voice.

'Aye, King Eystienn clings to the throne. His eyesight fails and his sword arm is not as strong as it once was, but his mind is as sharp as ever. It remains to be seen if he dies in his bed or with a sword in his hand.'

'He should be the first to hear the tale before I pay the tribute. I want no one to question. Does he sit or hunt today?'

She gave him a curious glance and cackled. 'Neither. Today he attends the wedding.'

'Whose?'

The elderly woman looked over her shoulder and tightened the shawl about her shoulders. 'Your wife's. She is marrying again with the entire court in attendance.'

'Kara Olofdottar remains my wife.' Ash

squared his jaw. 'There has been no divorce. There will be no divorce. She is mine. What is mine stays mine. My father's motto and therefore mine.'

'Then you had best claim her, Ash Hringson.' The old lady paused and gave a toothless smile. 'Before someone else does. Next time, return sooner if you wish to keep the things which are rightfully yours.'

A prickle of unease coursed down Kara Olofdottar's back. She wished she hadn't given in to Valdar's plea to marry at Sand with everyone watching their solemn oaths before Var's high priest. Life would have been much simpler if they had married at Jaarlshiem beneath the spreading branches of the *tuntreet* as she'd suggested. She'd grown to love that old tree, the gnarled guardian of the estate who kept everything safe and prosperous.

Following the example of her late father-in-law, Kara told the tree all the news. Always. And thereby ensured that her undertakings benefited the estate. Her late husband had failed to tell the tree he was leaving on his ill-fated expedition and he'd also failed to return. She liked to think it made a difference.

She understood why Valdar wanted this very

public declaration, but she hated crowds, always had done.

'Are you all right, Kara?' Auda, one of her closest friends, asked, giving her a searching look. They had met when Auda had first come to court, shortly after Ash had left on his ill-fated journey. Auda's eldest was about the same age as Kara's son. And her husband had died of a fever last spring shortly after Kara's father-in-law's funeral. 'You appear lost in your own world. Still thinking about the horse my uncle forced you to examine when you arrived? It will recover. Horses always seem to after you have examined them. You have the knack.'

'I'm merely about to get married in front of what feels like the entire kingdom.' Kara smoothed her blonde hair back from her shoulder. It had been so long since she'd worn it loose that she'd forgotten what a nuisance it could be, constantly tangling and blowing in her mouth.

'Everyone is interested in the beautiful widow from Jaarlshiem and what happens to her. It gives me hope that some day I'll find another man.' Auda clicked her fingers. 'You and your bridal finery will keep the tongues wagging until it is Jul-time. No one will speak against this marriage or say that it was not done properly, if that is what you are worried about.'

Kara wet her lips. 'Why would any speak

against the marriage? We are both free to marry. Or do you know something about Valdar?'

'My brother-in-law remained single until you came into his life.' Auda laughed. 'It is your uncle by marriage, Harald Haraldson, who concerns me. He plays more tricks than Loki, as my late husband used to say. He never forgave Harald for the diseased sheep he traded.'

'Harald Haraldson is powerless to halt this marriage!' Kara forced her hand to stay in her lap and not tuck a strand of hair behind her ear. She was determined her hair would be beautiful and not hanging like a witch's for this marriage. 'The king approves of the marriage. I'm hopeful the king will finally confirm my son as the rightful jaarl of Jaarlshiem once he sees that Valdar will protect Rurik's interests.'

'How can I help you to finish your preparations? It wouldn't do to keep your new husband waiting. These Nerisons can become impatient when they want something.'

Right now, she wanted to run back to the security of Jaarlshiem; she wanted the nausea to retreat back down her throat and the panic to recede. She wasn't a naïve bride of sixteen any more. She was a widow of twenty-three. She couldn't afford the luxury of being unwed any longer. The very public marriage would show the entire kingdom, indeed the entire North lands, that she'd chosen a strong warrior to guard the estate until her son came of age.

While her father-in-law had lived, there had been no need to remarry as he had still commanded all of Raumerike's respect. But now that he was dead, she knew she could not hold the lands without help. She had no choice—she had to remarry or risk losing everything she had worked so hard to keep these last few years. She had promised herself on her father-in-law's deathbed that it wouldn't be as he predicted with his final gasp of breath—that as a lone woman, everything would slip from her grasp and Rurik would inherit nothing when he came of age. She would succeed and prove him wrong.

'Unpack my mother's bridal crown. I should have done it before now, I know, but I had to look at that horse and then there were the final preparations for the feast and...'

'Old crowns are the best. I had to make do with a simple wreath of flowers when I married.' Auda clapped her hands together. 'In a few days' time you will wonder why you ever hesitated, Kara. Valdar confessed how many times he asked you. Was it fifteen or twenty?'

'Seventeen—not that I kept track.'

The marriage made sense. Valdar was kind, steady and dependable. He never had any inclination to go Viking or even on long, distant voyages for trading purposes. Her father-in-law had proclaimed Valdar to have been born under a steady star, unlike Ash's wandering one. He would be the right sort of father for Rurik—patient and caring, present instead of risking it all many leagues away. A man to lean on.

'A pity Rurik isn't here.' Auda fastened the white cloak about Kara's shoulders. 'He would have loved seeing his mother looking like a goddess. And his first opportunity to see the capital.'

'Jaarlshiem is safer. Fewer opportunities for mischief. My nerves are in shreds enough as is.' Kara firmed her mouth and ignored Auda's remark about looking like a goddess.

If she'd been more of a woman, Ash would not have gone. Ash would have stayed and made sure that he had a healthy heir. Her father-in-law's bitter words just after he found out about Ash's tragic death still had the power to hurt. Kara shook her head. Her late husband was the last person she wanted to think about today of all days. It was her wedding day.

A new start. A new chapter to ensure that Rurik grew up without fear. Jaarlshiem had been without a strong warrior at its helm for far too long. Ash Hringson belonged to the unremembered past and the girl she had once been. If she had been the one to die instead, her ashes would have barely been scattered on the *tuntreet's* roots before Ash found another to warm his bed.

'What has Rurik been up to?' Auda gave an indulgent smile. 'Surely he learnt his lesson after being caught out in that thunderstorm with a horse he could barely control.'

'Trust me, you don't want to know.' Kara held up her hand. 'But he worships Valdar. I hope he will be a calming influence.'

She refused to think about the narrow escapes her six-year-old son specialised in recently. The incident with the horse had been enough, but he had taken to defying her at every opportunity. Leaving him with Gudrun, Ash's old nurse, had seemed like the best option. Gudrun was used to such behaviour. She often proclaimed how like his father Rurik was, particularly around his ears and nose.

Ash's many scrapes were the stuff of legend. They first met because he had fallen while trying to recapture his falcon. The falcon suffered a hurt wing and Ash had brought the falcon to her mother rather than wringing its neck as his father had advised.

Her mother's skill as a healer had been second to none and it had been the first time Kara had been allowed to bind up a bird's wing while her mother had attended to Ash's twisted ankle. Five months later her mother had died in an accident. Ash had spoken to Kara during the funeral, taking the time to discover her hiding place behind the iron trunk and bring her a sweetmeat. Instant adoration had followed and when he'd asked her to marry him, all of her girlish dreams had come true.

Until it was too late, she had never considered that he might not feel the same way about her. Foolishly she'd failed to realise her hero was a selfish man, not a god.

A sudden shiver coursed down her back. Rurik might look like Ash, but she was the one raising him. She refused to make the mistake Ash's father had with Ash—spoiling him when he showed prowess at being a warrior or did something which pleased him and abandoning him to his fate if the challenge proved impossible.

'Kara, you've become very quiet.'

'I'm always quiet, Auda.'

'Only when people don't know you or if you are upset. When you are comfortable, you talk all the time.'

'I'm trying to get my eyeliner right. Why I have to wear it is beyond me.'

'A bride needs to make sure she is well painted. Everyone knows that. You don't want to risk Freya's displeasure. You do want the goddess's blessing for this union?' Auda started chattering like a magpie about various weddings and how the recent brides had looked and whether or not Freya had been pleased. 'You've smudged it. Start again and keep to the corner of your eye, rather than trying to draw a line under it.'

Kara picked up the small brush and started again. This time, she was going to be a bride to be admired, rather than laughed at or pitied. She shuddered, remembering how the liner had run down her cheeks at the last wedding. Ash had cleaned it off with his handkerchief with an indulgent smile.

Auda held out the gleaming crown. It was even more ghastly than Kara remembered. The last time, she had worn it with such pride, thinking Ash would want her to look radiant. But she'd heard the whispers and catcalls of 'witch's child' which had followed her progress.

'You do agree, Kara?'

Kara started and realised she was expected to say something. 'I missed that, Auda.'

'I merely said that the women will now have several more things to envy you for—a gorgeous bridal crown and a handsome warrior in your bed.'

'How could anyone envy me?' Kara forced a laugh. The thought of sharing a bed with Valdar left her cold. She'd do her duty, but ever since she had learnt of the truth about her marriage with Ash, she had felt entombed in ice. Despite his looks, Valdar's kisses chilled her. Even the simplest touch from Ash had been enough to send her up in flames during that long-ago spring.

'You'd be surprised. There are rumours about Valdar's exceptional good fortune in bed. Many have hoped to capture him, but thus far he has only wanted one woman for his wife—you.'

'The rumours failed to reach Jaarlshiem.' Kara kept her back stiff. She knew Valdar could have had his pick of the women, but he'd chosen her. His many proposals had emphasised his growing friendship with Rurik, the nearness of their estates and the compatibility of their natures rather than her golden hair or the curves in her bottom lip as Ash's had done. 'The bedsport will be what it is.'

'You should see your face, Kara. Redder than a beetroot. Anyone would think you a maid of sixteen rather than a widow.' Auda tapped a finger against the crown. 'Is the bedsport with Valdar not to your liking? Surely you sampled him before you agreed to this match.'

'Auda, stop teasing. When would I have had time to enjoy Valdar? I am a mother and I run Jaarlshiem. Valdar and I have barely had an hour alone since the match was agreed.' Kara reached for the crown and jammed it on her head.

Her doing, not his. It hadn't felt right dishonouring Ash in that way. Once the ceremony was over and she no longer belonged in any way to Ash, everything would be different.

Seeing her friend's increasingly troubled expression, Kara relented. 'I just want this ceremony over and done with. The whole day, in fact.'

'You look exquisite, you know that, Kara.' Auda laid a gentle hand on Kara's shoulder. 'Anyone looking at you now will understand why one of the finest warriors in the land chose you for his bride and why he laid his heart at your feet. All you have to do is see the way his face lights up when he spies you.'

'Sweet Auda.' Kara gave her friend a quick kiss on the cheek. 'But I do know my limitations. Shall we get this ceremony over with? Before Valdar realises the sort of woman he is marrying and changes his mind?'

'He won't. Once my brother-in-law has made up his mind, he stays the course. He is exceedingly stubborn.'

'Steadfast, I know. You've said.' Kara gave one last despairing look in the small mirror. She repeated the words she had taken to saying over the past few weeks. 'And precisely the right man for me. Seven years married and six of them a widow. I deserve a man in my life.'

'That's the Kara I know and love.'

Balancing the awkward crown on her head, Kara trod a careful path to the temple. At the entrance to the temple's grounds, she froze.

The temple overflowed with people, so many that they filled the courtyard. A great cheer and stamping of feet rose up when someone viewed her.

Kara fought the temptation to flee. She hadn't realised there were this many people in Raumerike, let alone in the capital. Suddenly, this wedding felt wrong, as though she was making the biggest mistake of her life. A marriage should be more than simple practicality—her mother's long-ago words welled up within her.

She firmed her mouth. Her biggest mistake had been marrying Ash in a haze of romantic dreams. This marriage promised to be different, based on mutual respect. No one was marrying under false pretences.

Towards the middle of the temple she saw Harald Haraldson, Ash's uncle, sitting like a spider in the middle of his web, and knew why this marriage had to be so public. His very being radiated hatred and smug arrogance. Only she and Rurik stood in the way of his inheriting all that her father-in-law had acquired. The Raumerike inheritance laws were quite clear—if a man died without an heir, the estate passed first to his mother, next to her husband and only then to the remaining relatives. And a jaarldom could only be confirmed when the warrior proved worthy.

He noticed her glance and his lips turned up into a humourless smile, the sort of smile a hunter gives before he brings down his hapless prey. A shiver went down her spine.

She'd fought so long and hard for Rurik's life when he was a baby that she wasn't about to stop now. And she wasn't about to be forced into a marriage where first Rurik's life and then her own would be forfeit. Valdar would protect them with his dying breath.

She'd endure this ceremony, knowing she'd be back in Jaarlshiem in a few days. She had promised Rurik that she'd bring him a new father.

The last few steps to where Valdar was standing were far easier than the first ones. Auda was right. He did look every inch the handsome warrior, a formidable opponent for any foe. In time she would welcome him in her bed. She could play her part in bedsport.

How hard could it be to pretend passion? Other people did. Ash had done it with her and she'd been fool enough not to notice.

Kara held out her hand and Valdar lightly grasped her fingers. The simple touch did much to calm her nerves.

The priest began to invoke the gods, calling on Freya, Odin and Var to witness the union.

This marriage would be a better marriage than her last one, she silently promised. She would be a good wife to a good man.

The priest asked if anyone knew of an objection why the gods would not look on this union with favour. He paused dramatically.

Wriggling her shoulders, Kara tried to remove the sudden sense of impending doom.

She nodded to the priest to hurry him up and get this ordeal over with. He cleared his throat and lifted his hand.

'I object! This woman is not free to marry! This ceremony must stop!' a voice thundered from the back of the temple.

The priest's hand halted. Kara forgot how to breathe. Ash! Ash's voice from beyond the grave?

Impossible! Ash was dead. Buried in a watery grave. Someone else had called out and it was a trick of the temple's walls. Sudden anger filled her. Who dared disrupt and dishonour this marriage? She would make them pay for it.

'Stop the ceremony now! Listen to my words. This woman is not free.'

Valdar gave her a questioning glance. Kara forced a tiny shrug as her head began to pound. A distraction, nothing more. She belonged to no man. But whoever had planned this knew her weak spot.

She placed a hand on her stomach. She had to stop hearing ghosts. This objection had no merit. False and unfounded. But logically it would have to be heard.

Giving in to her temper seldom solved anything. In fact, it often made things worse. Over the past few years, she'd learnt the value of appearing calm and collected even if her insides were churning.

A little delay now would save a lifetime of innuendo and false rumour. Clinging to that thought, she attempted to breathe.

'Make your objection known,' the priest intoned. 'Show your proof. This woman claims to be free.'

The crowds parted and the speaker came forward, walking with a distinct limp. His fine cloak swung about his body, highlighting the breadth of his shoulders and trim line of his waist. The deep blue colour set off his reddish-gold hair perfectly. There was something in the way he moved. Her stomach roiled as the scent of incense grew overpowering.

Kara shook her head, wished the crown was lighter and that the priest in the corner would stop waving his brazier about.

What her eyes saw was impossible. She dug her nails into her palm. Impossible.

The dead could not walk on this earth and Ash was dead. The ship had gone down without any survivors.

Ash's uncle had brought back the intricately carved sternpost from Ash's ship, charred from a fire, and laid it at her father-in-law's feet. The day was etched on her brain. Her father-in-law had made a dreadful noise and collapsed in a heap. She had had to nurse him back to health along with Rurik, who had been suffering from one of his dreadful colds. There hadn't been time to breathe, let alone grieve for the man whom she'd once made her whole world.

For a few days, both her father-in-law's and Rurik's lives had hung in the balance while Ash's uncle had strutted about the hall, issuing orders and proclaiming how the hall would be his. Finally she had ordered him out and he'd gone with bad grace, promising his vengeance.

Was this some ghastly dream and she'd wake up in her bed with Rurik slumbering close by? She knew she was awake from the growing pain in her head and the nausea in her belly.

A conjurer's trick? An apparition?

An insistent whisper went around the hall, growing in strength. Ash. Against all reason and expectation, it had to be. But utterly impossible.

It had to be a trick, a way of sowing dissent and preventing the marriage. Harald Haraldson had to be behind it. She refused to allow this pathetic outrage to happen. This time Harald Haraldson had overreached. He would regret it when she was finished with him, but first she needed to be married with a warrior who'd defend her land.

Kara shut her eyes tight and opened them again. The man stood in the centre of the hall, no more than a few feet away from her. Broad shouldered and red-gold hair. His clothes were finely cut and of Viken rather than Raumerike origin.

The man raised his arms. Kara attempted to peer through the heavy smoke and see his face. A number of emotions raced through her—fear, anger and a wild sense of hope—but mostly she felt as if she were watching the events unfold from far away.

'Hear me, good people, and listen well. Kara Olofdottar is my wife.' He turned to face the room. 'I dare any man to deny it. I have a prior claim over her and I will enforce my claim with my sword if necessary. I, Ash Hringson, claim Kara Olofdottar as my lawful wife!'

Chapter Two

The stranger's words bounced off the temple walls, echoing round and round. The entire hall ceased to breathe, waiting for her reaction. Kara knew she had to do something, make some sort of defiant gesture, but her entire being was paralysed with shock.

She stared at the man with his fine clothes and burnished red-gold hair, searching for a sign that the words were true, that he was indeed who he claimed to be, that it wasn't some sort of twisted trick from Harald Haraldson. Yet she knew it must be.

Anything else was utterly impossible. Ash had drowned. The entirety of Raumerike knew of the tragedy. The lament her father-in-law had commissioned about his only son's tragic end was sung every year on the anniversary of his death.

She glanced at Valdar under her lashes. The

big warrior stood stony-faced, his eyes trained on the priest's face. The knots in her stomach tightened. She had thought Valdar would understand immediately what was happening and leap to her defence. But, no, once again, she'd have to fight alone. Luckily she knew how to.

'You believe you have a prior claim to this woman?' the priest asked with heavy scepticism in his voice.

'I know I do,' the man replied evenly. 'Under Raumerike law, any claim must be investigated before a wedding proceeds further. Or does Raumerike law allow a woman two husbands these days?'

'It shall be investigated if the claim is made properly and with due reverence,' the priest countered. 'Approach and let your face be seen. The light is in my eyes. All men should look on your face as you make your claim.'

Valdar gave Kara's hand a squeeze, but moved away from her as if she had the plague. Silently she vowed that Harald Haraldson would suffer a slow and prolonged revenge for this shabby trick.

'Are you deaf? Let me see who you are,' the priest called when the man failed to move.

'Kara Olofdottar appears faint. I ask we go elsewhere and discuss this matter in private,' the man said. 'She fainted on our wedding day, you know. I caught her before she collapsed. The incense makes her head swim.'

Either this man was the consummate actor or… A small shiver of uncertainty combined with another flickering of wild exhilaration stabbed her, banishing her scepticism.

The more she heard the man speak, the more his voice rang of Ash. Kara clenched her fist. Logic, not unfounded speculation. She was becoming as fanciful as Rurik, who kept insisting that the sagas were real, rather than simply stories told about a fire to amuse. And she never fainted these days.

'It is the Raumerike way to conduct such matters in public,' the priest said.

'I merely thought to spare her the embarrassment,' he continued, seemingly unperturbed by the hundreds of eyes turned on him. 'My wife hates crowds. A husband knows these things.'

Kara gritted her teeth and clung to that small logical part of her which still functioned. The deception would be revealed soon enough. No one could carry it off for any length of time. All she had to do was to keep silent, wait for the inevitable mistake and allow others to take charge. She clamped her mouth shut.

'I must caution you,' the priest said. 'Kara Olofdottar's husband died many years ago on a sea voyage. This fact is well known in this land.'

'Ash Hringson. Son of Hring the Bold and Nauma,' the man stated in a firm voice. He thrust his hands forward and the cuffs of his tunic fell back, revealing his scarred wrists. On his right wrist he sported a purple birthmark in the shape of a coiled snake. 'I'm very much alive. Reports of my death were at best mistaken and at worst a shameful lie.'

A variety of emotions rippled through Kara—shock at his survival, bewilderment at the length of time it had taken to get news to her, a deep-seated anger that it had taken this humiliating scene to reveal the truth, but most of all a wild exhilaration that he was alive, that they'd have a second chance. Her son would have his proper father.

Her breath stopped. Accepting this man's claim of being Ash went beyond simply taking his word for it and her knowing it in her heart. Twelve members of Raumerike's Storting would have to declare for him and stake their honour on it. The penalty for attempting to deceive the Storting was either death or permanent banishment.

Kara clenched her fists and concentrated. In acknowledging this man to be Ash, she'd lose Valdar, the man who would be the perfect guardian for Rurik. He was going to be her saviour.

But it wouldn't be right. Not now. She had to speak up. She had to bring the dead back to life.

'Ash Hringson,' she proclaimed, crossing her arms. 'Where have you been? We thought you dead. Killed in a shipwreck off the Frankish coast over six years ago. A fine time you pick to appear.'

'Reports of my death were incorrect but, alas, the shipwreck was all too real. I would say my timing is impeccable.' Ash's ice-blue gaze raked her form, travelling from the top of her bridal crown to the soles of her slippers, as if he were mentally undressing her, stripping her of her bridal finery and leaving her naked in front of the crowd. 'I survived a fiery inferno on the sea and a Frankish prison. I have come to pay my debts. I have returned.'

'Have you indeed?'

'You look as lovely as my memory of you, Kara.' His lips curved upwards. 'I remember the garland of flowers you wore in your hair the first morning of our marriage while we took our vows again. The sunlight turned your head to pure gold and your skin to cream. Far more suited to you than your mother's bridal crown. I didn't like it on our wedding day and I like it even less now. It does nothing for your hair or your eyes.'

His rich voice flowed over her. Why did he have to remember the garland she'd fashioned and how she'd insisted they recite their vows again? But then Ash had always been good at remembering the little details which had no real meaning. It was part of his deadly charm.

She forced her mind away from any softening. Seven years! It had taken him seven years to return. Why so long if he thought her lovely?

'Can you be sure this man is Ash Hringson, Kara? Others might sport a snake birthmark.' Valdar put a heavy hand on her shoulder. 'Are you willing to risk your reputation by vouching for him in front of everyone?'

Kara thought about her young son and the nightly prayers that he made to the gods for a father. The man who had given her Rurik deserved her loyalty. Silently she bid goodbye to an easy and settled life with Valdar. The safe future she'd envisioned only this morning was an impossibility and that hurt. But she knew in her gut that her instinct was right. She owed it to the gullible girl that she had once been to fight for Ash. She shrugged off Valdar's restraining hand.

'I am certain, Valdar. This man is Ash Hringson. He can be no other. Reports of his death must have been false.'

Her words echoed around the chamber and she waited for others to agree with her. Ash's uncle rose to his feet.

'Can a woman vouch for a man's identity?' he

declared, banging his stick on the ground. 'The traditions of Raumerike allow for men to vouch for an identity, but a woman? It is unprecedented. Women and thralls are easily led and their judgement suspect. Raumerike law and tradition allows for twelve men, not a single woman, to vouch for a man's identity. I have not heard a single man speak in favour of this...this Viken!'

A low murmur travelled swiftly around the hall. Kara froze. Why had Harald Haraldson cast doubt on Ash's identity? Did he want his nephew dead?

'We are talking about my husband's life! Your beloved nephew!' Kara retorted before Harald Haraldson could garner any support. 'Would you have me deny my husband? What sort of troll wife would I be then?'

'I would have you declare the right man as your husband, Niece by marriage,' Harald Haraldson said, his smile turning to a gloating smirk as laughter rippled through the crowd.

Kara raised her clenched fist and knew whatever Harald Haraldson wanted, she wanted the opposite. 'This man is my husband. Reports of his death were wrong. Wrong, I tell you.'

'All we have is your word, Kara Olofdottar.' Ash's uncle pursed his thin lips. 'Ash Hringson tragically perished in the sea. We've all heard the saga his father commissioned. Can the dead return to life? Or is this man an impostor sent to prey on a vulnerable woman? We all know about the demons your mother battled.'

'My wits have never been questioned. Mistakes have happened before,' Kara stated in ringing tones as her stomach knotted. This was most definitely not how today was supposed to have gone.

'Indeed. I seek to save you from a grievous one.' Harald Haraldson spread out his gnarled hands. 'We must take our time and be sure. Investigate this claim slowly and carefully without womanly hysterics.'

Kara stiffened. Harald Haraldson would stall on the enquiry and in the meantime would press for the king to award him the lands which he considered rightfully his, but which really belonged to Ash and their son. He might even find a reason why Ash should be banished for ever or even killed.

She refused to hand Harald Haraldson an easy victory. Somehow, she had to figure out a way to fight for Ash and give him back his life. Later, she'd sort out the marriage and what that meant for her and Ash. She was doing this for their son.

'A woman knows her husband from a place deep within her soul. There is no need for a further investigation when one is as sure as I am,' she said when she knew she had her temper under control. 'You must know him, as well, unless you have gone blind and deaf, Uncle!'

Harald Haraldson only grunted.

'Kara Olofdottar is within her rights to speak on this matter,' the priest declared after an embarrassed silence where no one else spoke. 'Who could know a man better than his wife? Her words must hold weight.'

She turned towards the crowd, seeking a friendly face or two. 'Hear my words and mark them well, all of you. The man who stands before you is my husband. Lift the scales from your eyes. See that this man can be none other than Ash Hringson. How many horses have I saved through my skill? Or falcons' wings fixed? How many people have I sewn up? How many times in the last few years have I ensured that timber or wool was delivered on time? Have I ever failed to honour a single agreement?'

A few started to murmur in the crowd.

'This is Ash Hringson, the man who was once my husband,' Kara continued steadily, knowing everyone was finally listening to her, including Ash. Her voice wasn't going to vanish as it had when she was a girl and forced to speak in front of an audience. She was a grown woman with responsibilities now. 'I can see his birthmark and his voice sounds the same as I remember it, but more importantly something deep within me tells me that this is him. Why it took him such a length of time to return is a tale he alone can tell. Who will join me in recognising him and welcoming him back to Raumerike?'

She waited expectantly, but no one moved or cried out.

'What a thing to be recognised by one's own wife who is about to remarry, but no one else,' Ash said with his old dry humour to his voice.

The sound clawed at her heart and she had to look up at the ceiling. But still no one spoke. Most kept their eyes to the ground, though one or two stared defiantly at him.

'You were the one who wished this done today, Lady Kara,' Harald Haraldson said, rising to his feet again. 'Shall we end this deception? My lord king and good nobles, I have no idea why Kara Olofdottar entered into this deception with this Viken, but something must be done to halt her perfidious scheme before she endangers the entire country. What other dealings has she had with our old enemy? What mischief does she wish to unleash on this country?'

The colour drained from Ash's face, making his scars stand out as he recognised the gravity of his situation. Kara stared open-mouthed at Harald Haraldson. He had twisted the situation to suit his purpose. If she wasn't careful, Harald Haraldson would seek to gain control of Jaarlshiem, using this as a pretext to attack the estate and hold it under the pretence of the safety of the realm.

'My loyalty to Raumerike is without question,' she snapped. 'This is no act of Viken treachery.'

Harald Haraldson raised an eyebrow. 'All I asked for was a little delay. Suddenly you speak of loyalty and treachery. I vote to err on the side of caution and tradition.'

'Will no one else recognise this man as my husband?' Kara held out her hands to the crowd, trying to pick out faces. 'I trust my husband's uncle has his own reasons for wishing Ash to remain dead, but what about the rest of you? Why do you wish Ash Hringson dead?'

The silence was deafening. Kara's heart plummeted. What had she expected? For the entire Storting to stand up and declare for her, simply because she had asked? It wasn't how the world worked. She'd stopped believing in miracles when Rurik was born.

She wished the ground would open and swallow her. Maybe she should have erred on the side of caution, but it would have been wrong to deny her husband. Silently she fumed at how neatly she'd been trapped.

A man dressed in rough farming clothes stood up. 'Kara Olofdottar has vouched for him, I believe her. She cured my horse of lameness last spring and I know she always tells the truth. She never gives short measures with her grain.' He gave Ash's uncle a hard look. 'Unlike others I could mention.'

After he stood, ten other men stood up. All they needed was one more.

'I will vouch for him, as well. Kara Olofdottar must not be punished for speaking the truth,' Valdar thundered beside her. He, too, gave a significant look towards Ash's uncle before nodding at Ash. 'You have your twelve men, Hringson. You are alive again in the eyes of Raumerike.'

'The priest needs to decide,' Ash's uncle thundered. 'Is this a proper way to conduct affairs? Are we to be led by women in skirts?'

Kara put her hand over her mouth and waited for the decision.

'The gods have spoken. Kara Olofdottar has vouched that this man is indeed Ash Hringson, formerly declared dead, and twelve have agreed with her,' the priest intoned after staring at the altar for a lifetime. 'You are alive, Ash Hringson, according to Raumerike law. You may enjoy all the benefits of your former status.'

'And the marriage?' Ash's face appeared to be carved from stone. 'A woman, even a woman as beautiful as Kara Olofdottar, may not have two husbands. Do you accept my claim to her?'

The entire crowd laughed. A hot tide swept up Kara's face. Easy words—that was all they were. Ash didn't mean them, just as he had not meant the compliments he had given her seven years ago. Her father-in-law had demonstrated that fact when she'd fought for Rurik's life. Ash had always used charm and flattery to get what he wanted.

Ice-cold anger swept through her. She might have recognised Ash but it didn't mean she had forgiven him for what he'd done or how long it had taken him to return home. She would not revert to the starry-eyed naïve girl she had once been.

'The marriage between Valdar Nerison and Kara Olofdottar will not take place today,' the priest confirmed. 'Ash Hringson has returned to the land of the living.'

'This is not the end,' Harald Haraldson said, rising to his feet. 'I will ensure a proper investigation is held into where this man's allegiance truly lies. I refuse to harbour a Viken viper in our bosom. Our country's security should not be put at risk by this…this reckless woman.'

Without waiting for an answer, he stormed out of the hall. The room burst into pandemonium and a crowd of well-wishers swept Ash up, hoisting him on their shoulders and parading him about the room.

Kara stood at the altar, numb and shocked, unable to make any plans or even think straight as the noise surrounding Ash grew louder. Trust Ash to cause the most mischief and chaos that he could. He delighted in things like that.

They might be married, but it was not going to be the same sort of marriage that they'd once had. Her days of longing for approval and thinking he was her ultimate hero and saviour were over. No more. She had grown up. She required a good man by her side, helping her to farm the land and bring her son up, rather than one who went off to find glory. Someone steady and safe like Valdar, rather than someone who was only interested in their personal comfort or good fortune.

'Thank you, Valdar,' she said quietly, turning away from the spectacle Ash had created and looking directly at her former fiancé who had remained beside her. 'I appreciate what you just did. Despite Harald Haraldson's outburst, I know Ash will be a true Raumerike subject. He has only come back to claim what is his, not overthrow the king. He is no Viken viper.'

'Kara?' Valdar regarded her with an intent expression. 'Why didn't you tell me that there was a possibility that your husband might be alive? You should have trusted me with that knowledge, rather than allowing this to happen. Steps could have been taken.'

'Tell you what?' The crown pressed harder against her forehead and she struggled to control her anger at this latest injustice. Did he truly think she had arranged this near fiasco? That she wanted this? She had envisioned today ending very differently. 'You must know that I intended to be a good wife. I thought him dead, like everyone else. The dead simply do not come back to life. Or at least until today...'

'Your husband has returned. You recognised him without hesitation. Normally in these cases, there is an investigation. I thought maybe you had arranged in advance...'

'I'm as surprised as anyone to see him alive,' she snapped and instantly regretted her tone as Valdar looked very hurt and concerned. Whosever fault it was, it wasn't Valdar's. She sighed. 'I'm sorry, Valdar. I don't know what to say. Believe me.'

He squeezed her hand. 'I hope you are right, Kara, as you will be the one married to him. You'll have to share his fate if it is proven that he is a Viken spy or worse. This is the first time I've seen you act impulsively in the four years we've known each other.'

Kara closed her eyes. Valdar only knew the new Kara, not the one who had married Ash as quickly as she could in case he changed his mind.

'I can't marry you, Valdar.' Kara pressed her trembling hands together. 'I'm sorry. It appears I already have a husband. You deserve someone better.'

'Why would I want anyone else?' Valdar raised her hand to his lips.

'Find your own wife, Valdar Nerison! This one is taken!' Ash called from behind her.

'Please, Valdar. I hate scenes.'

Valdar dropped her hand and took a step backwards. 'At your command, my lady.'

The hurt in his eyes tore at Kara's heart. She'd only considered the marriage for Rurik's sake, but he seemed to have truly desired it. She hated that she'd wounded him.

Ash raised his arm and requested silence. The hall hushed instantly. 'I have been recognised and welcomed back. I assume a wedding feast will have been prepared. It should now become a welcome-home feast. I look forward to drinking toasts with each and every one of you. I bear none ill will or malice. But would it be too much to ask for time alone with my wife before someone else attempts to steal her from under my nose?'

The entire chamber laughed as Kara fumed. Ash had them in the palm of his hand, just as he always had. Hring had sworn his son had been born with a tongue which could charm the birds from trees, never mind the maidens into his bed.

The last thing she wanted was to be alone with Ash.

Before Kara could object, the priest nodded his assent and indicated that they should use his antechamber.

'We should go to the feast. People will want to greet you,' she said in desperation. 'Someone should be there to supervise.'

'Shall we go from here, wife?' Ash gave an elaborate bow, but his eyes remained colder than a glacier. 'The men will not miss us for the brief time it will take to exchange our private greetings. The food and drink will flow whether you are there or not.'

'Do you wish me to come with you?' Valdar asked in an undertone. He placed his hand on the hilt of his sword. 'I'm here if you need me, Kara. The priest will allow it if I ask. I want…I want to be your champion.'

Kara pressed her hand to her mouth. If she had ever had any doubts about Valdar, they vanished now. Not only had he been willing to recognise Ash, but he was also willing to fight for her. She truly had not deserved him. She wished that she felt something more than simple friendship for him. She wished she had been marrying him because she loved him, instead of to provide protection for her son.

'How touching, Valdar.' Ash's voice could freeze icicles. 'But my wife has no need of any champion except for me.'

'That is for the Lady Kara to decide.'

'I will be fine,' she whispered back. 'Fear is not something I have ever associated with Ash.'

Valdar bowed low. 'Remember, Kara, I wanted to marry you, not the jaarldom. There is always divorce.'

'I could never…' Her throat closed. How could she have mistaken his intentions so badly? Somehow it made everything worse. She had nearly repeated the same mistake as seven years ago, only in reverse. Did that make her as wicked as Ash had been? 'It depends on…'

Valdar nodded, understanding that she could never leave Rurik. In any divorce, the children stayed with the father. Ever since she had first felt Rurik move within her womb, she'd loved him unconditionally. She could not simply leave him with a father who was likely to leave on some adventure again, abandoning him. Equally she knew she could not stay with Ash as she once had, looking for the best in everything and instantly forgiving her hero anything.

'Shall we go?' Kara said with icy deliberateness. 'You have much to explain.'

Ash put his hand on the small of her back, pulling her close. His lips angled down. She turned her face. A tiny tremor went through her as they brushed her cheek. She stiffened, but his hand kept her close.

'As do you,' he murmured, giving Valdar a significant look. 'Wouldn't want anyone to think we weren't the happy reunited couple, would we?'

Kara clamped her mouth shut and knew his touch on her back was about possession rather than any real affection and that she might have made the biggest mistake of her life when she'd acknowledged him.

Chapter Three

'I owe you a life debt,' Ash said the instant he was alone with Kara in the priest's antechamber and before she had a chance to start shouting at him about how long he'd been gone.

With its collection of bowls, pitchers and stores of incense, the antechamber was more a storage room than a place of worship. A particularly ugly sculpture of Thor wresting Loki dominated one side of the room. Hardly the place he'd envisioned greeting his wife properly, but it would have to do. Kara needed to understand that he was aware of what she had done and that he appreciated it.

Kara tore off the bridal crown and placed it on the table with a heavy clunk. Her blonde hair hung about her shoulders like a cloud of gold. 'Of all the things to start with. No explanation or apology. You owe me nothing.'

Ash tensed. He had never seen Kara this angry or upset before. He'd expected her to be overjoyed that he had returned. And she was wrong—he owed her a huge debt.

The events in the temple could have easily gone the other way, endangering both their lives. He had never considered that his uncle would actively seek to deny his identity. His uncle had always encouraged him to chase adventure. Had he decided that the man who had returned was still not worthy of being called Hring Haraldson's son? Or was it some power game that he knew nothing about? All Ash knew was that his uncle was now his enemy and, therefore, his family's enemy, too.

'I always pay my debts, Kara,' he continued while she regarded him as if she wanted to wring his neck. He'd forgotten how beautiful she could be when aroused. 'And you gave me back my life.'

'How can I give back something you never lost?' Her voice dripped with sarcasm. 'Speaking the truth benefits everyone. Lies are always discovered. We did marry seven years ago. I'm pleased you finally remembered you had a waiting family in the midst of your adventuring.'

Ash struggled to control his temper. He'd always known he had a family. He'd endured the last six years of hell so he could return with his head held high and his honour intact…for his family. 'What was going on out there, Kara?'

'I was about to marry an honourable man. Generally that is what being a bride at a wedding means.' Her deep-blue eyes blazed defiantly. 'To the best of my knowledge, you died in a shipwreck, Ash.'

'I promised you I would return.'

'There are some promises people are unable to keep. I've learnt that lesson well, Ash.' She slammed her fists together. 'You must be aware how difficult it can be for a *widow* to survive.'

Ash rubbed the back of his neck. He supposed he deserved the rebuke. For as long as he could remember Kara had hung on his every word and adored him. When his father had ordered him to marry, Kara had been the natural choice. Safe. Comfortable. Always there and someone who believed in his dreams and him. He'd taken her for granted, just as he had all of his good fortune in those days. But when he'd been trapped in that dungeon with his men dying all about him, he'd known that he couldn't return to Raumerike ruined and broken. He'd sent a message.

He tried to think if the Kara he remembered would have spoken in front of a crowd. His main memories of her were her soft crooning voice as she tended one of the sick animals she had found. Or blushing crimson when he stole a kiss.

'Why did no one recognise me until you asked?' he asked to keep his mind off uncomfortable thoughts.

She tilted her chin upwards. 'If you wanted to be recognised without question, you should have returned sooner.'

'I ran into complications.' Ash waved a hand, dismissing the past seven years. The past was behind him. The less Kara knew of his struggles, the better. She only needed to know he'd returned a hero. She'd always loved a hero. 'Why were you prepared to marry Valdar Nerison? He is the wrong sort of man for you.'

She batted her impossibly long lashes and her lips quirked upwards, but anger and bitterness blazed in her eyes. 'How would you know what sort of man I require, Ash? Seven years, Ash, without word. Seven years is far too long.'

He silently counted to ten, rather than giving way to his temper. Did she really want the broken man he'd been after the dungeon? He could remember her last whispered words about making her proud and returning with gold in his purse. 'Where is my father? Why wasn't he there? Or doesn't he approve of the proposed union?'

Stifling silence invaded the small room. Her expression changed from fury to one of sorrow and pity in an instant. His mind reeled. Ash braced himself, hoping against hope that he guessed wrong.

'Your father collapsed when he learnt of your death. He never recovered the use of his limbs.'

'No! I sent a message back. I thought he understood what I needed to do.' Ash fell to his knees on the rushes. His entire body shook. One of the things that had driven him onwards was the thought that his father would finally have to admit that his son was worthy of being called a Raumerike warrior. His father would once again be able to hold up his head. All sense of shame would go. His father would realise the sort of man he'd become. And now he never would.

His father had always seemed as sturdy and steady as the oak which served as the family's guardian tree or *tuntreet*. His father had collapsed when he thought his only son had died and never recovered. Never recovered. Ash's mind shied from the word.

'Can you take me to see him?' he asked, hoping that his guess was wrong.

'There is more.'

'Don't spare me. I want to know everything.'

'You asked.'

Each new word rained a blow to Ash's heart. His father was dead, but more importantly Kara had spent the last few years caring for his bedridden father.

'He died last Jul-tide of a fever,' she said, finishing. 'I run Jaarlshiem the best I can, but the estate needs a master as well as a mistress. I refuse to lose my home, Ash, simply because I don't have a man.'

'I wish I'd known.' He closed his eyes and offered prayers for his father's shade to any god who happened to be listening. The sort of son his father wanted would have been there to sing the lament and pour some of the ash from the funeral pyre on the family's *tuntreet*.

There were so many things he had planned on telling his father. He'd looked forward to his father finally declaring his only son was worthy of being called the son of one of Raumerike's legendary warriors. 'I...I would have done things differently.'

'Undoing the past is an impossibility, Ash.'

Ash struggled to think. His father's demise gave an explanation as to why his Uncle Harald refused to recognise him and why Kara had planned to remarry. His uncle had always coveted Jaarlshiem and the title his father had won through the strength of his sword. The conferring of a jaarldom was far from straightforward if the heir was absent or not a strong enough warrior. It normally took a year or more. And Kara's fate would be tied to the land.

Ash clenched his fist and stared at the cold

hearth, aware of his many shortcomings. He'd simply never thought it possible for his father to die.

'I know you loved your father,' Kara said, breaking the silence. 'Your father certainly loved you. Weep, if you like. I cried when he breathed his last.'

He raised his face to hers. Tears might come later, but not now. He refused to cry in front of anyone. He remembered her finding him in tears once before when he had run away after his father had beaten him for some trivial offence. She'd wiped his eyes with the corner of her apron. The shedding of tears was an occupation for the youth he used to be, not the man he'd become.

'I sent word,' he said, turning back to face her when he knew he could trust his voice to remain steady. 'I did what was necessary for my honour. My father must have understood.'

She put a hand on her hip. 'Your honour? Since when does honour come before life? Before family?'

'For my father, always,' he said very slowly. There was no need to recount the beatings he'd suffered as a boy when he'd fallen short of his father's ideals or during the horrors he'd endured in his quest to restore his honour. The thought of returning home without that honour had been unthinkable and, not for the first time, he wished his life had taken a different path. 'I returned with enough wealth to pay all life debts and tributes I owe. I'm aware of what my father required from any son of his. He beat it into me as a boy.'

Kara slammed her fists together and her eyes blazed with fury. She looked like she had truly become one of the Valkyrie, rather than merely named after one.

'Your father thought you dead! Dead!' She stamped her foot. 'Instead of worrying about your precious honour, you should have returned. Your father wanted you here by his side, running the estate when he became too ill.'

'Hiding behind my father's shade, Kara? We both know how he used his fists. Be honest— you wanted me here, but you also wanted me to be a hero. You asked me to return one.'

She slammed her fists together again. 'I asked you to return.'

'I sent word when I escaped from the dungeon,' he explained, watching her intently for any signs of softening and understanding. For months he'd hoped for a word of reprieve, but nothing had arrived. 'The silence was deafening, but I knew what my father required. Return a hero or die. Pay my debts without his help.'

Kara dipped her head so that her loose hair fell over her face, hiding her expression. Ash watched a tiny heartbeat pulse in the hollow of her throat. Silently he prayed she'd understand what he'd gone through and would forgive him.

'The tribute was paid years ago, from the estate,' she said in a hollow voice. 'Shipwrecks happen because the gods wish it. He wanted his son.'

'My father wanted to preserve the honour of his dead son as he'd no use for the living one,' Ash corrected her with an impatient wave of his hand. Didn't she understand—it had to come from him, from what he'd earned, rather than from what he'd been given? 'My father should not have suffered for my mistakes. None should have suffered but me.'

'Are you that wealthy?' she asked lifting her head so her deep blue gaze met his. 'Four years to pay everyone. Jaarlshiem is one of the most productive farms in Raumerike.'

'Yes, I am. My last voyage became a raid on a church filled to the brim with gold and silver. My share provided the final amount and more.' He put his hand under her chin and lifted her face so he could gaze directly into her eyes. 'I came home, Kara. You will not want for anything. I know my duty now that my father is dead and I will do it. You are my wife.'

He bent his head, preparing to taste her lips and see if they were as sweet as he remembered. To kiss away her anger like he had done in the past.

Kara twisted out of his grip. Her gaze became fixed on the grinning statue of Loki, which dominated the priest's antechamber, rather than drowning in the deep blue pools of Ash's eyes. That god-like Ash had a silver tongue to charm people.

It would be so easy to give in and taste Ash's lips. Her entire being wanted to. But she knew kissing Ash would be a mistake. Her attraction to Ash was the hangover from a girlish fantasy. He couldn't just smile at her, touch her hand and make seven years disappear as if they were nothing. Her days of unabashed adoration and ready excuses had finished when her father-in-law had showed her the sort of man Ash truly was. He most definitely had not been the golden hero of her dreams who would magically appear to solve her problems.

Ash had thirsted after glory, putting it before everyone and everything, and he had found it. But how long until he needed to quench his thirst again? This time she had to consider Rurik as well as herself.

She'd grown up in the intervening years. A necessity. She had taken responsibility. She'd run the estate very successfully. She'd done all the practical things that Ash should have been doing, if he had put his quest for glory to one side. Now he expected her to melt in his arms as if nothing had happened, as if she was the same simple infatuated girl who always forgave him with a smile. Romantic words melted like dirty slush in the sunlight of practicality.

'This isn't the right time or place,' she said, fixing him with her eye as if he were the same age as Rurik and had done some mischief. 'We're in a temple. People expect to see us at this so-called welcoming feast.'

The excuse sounded weak to her ears. She lifted her chin and glared as if he were Rurik caught in some misdeed. He appeared amused rather than appropriately cowed.

'Kara, let go of your anger.' He put a gentle hand on her shoulder. The warmth invaded her body, melting the ice which had encased her soul for so long. 'What purpose does it serve? What matters is the future, our future. As long as the mead and ale flow, the feast will be deemed a success.'

'Keep away from me!' She took a step back from him. 'Your touch does nothing for me.'

Her body protested at the lie. A subtle brush of his hand and her internal flame sparked into a glow. For six years, she had considered it dead. Why did it have to be Ash and only Ash who did this to her? She wrapped her arms about her body, struggling not to lean in to him.

Slowly, he lowered his hands. She stumbled backwards.

'Careful. I don't want you to fall.'

She raised her chin. 'My balance is excellent. Thank you.'

Kara put her hand over the spot where his hand had been. Warmth pulsed through her. She concentrated on breathing steadily.

'A problem, wife?' he enquired softly. 'You used to beg for them—one, two, three. Have you forgotten so soon?'

Kara ground her teeth. Beg for his kisses! She'd behaved worse than she recalled. Or was he remembering another of his women? She had never begged. Asked, maybe. Hoped for, definitely. Did he take her for a simpleton?

'Your memory is faulty.'

He gave a triumphant male smile. 'Can you remember the kiss you begged for under the apple tree with the blossom falling all about you? I can. I asked you to marry me afterwards and you agreed.'

'Seven years, Ash Hringson,' Kara ground out, turning so she faced the Loki statue. He'd asked her to marry him because he'd wanted a ship to sail off and have adventures in, not because he wanted more of her innocent kisses.

She hated that she had once believed the lie of his unswerving devotion.

Twisting events to suit his purpose, a trait he shared with his son. She was finished with being an apologist for his actions, always searching for the good. 'You could have sent word of your progress, but chose not to. We're strangers now. Walking back into my life and expecting to take up where we left off is a mistake. It will not happen. I will not allow my heart or life to be trampled on.'

'You are my wife.' Ash's brows knit together as his hand fell to his side. 'It is natural for a husband to kiss his wife, particularly after a long absence. Especially after a long absence.'

Unbridled fury coursed through her veins. She spun round and managed to stop herself from shaking him by the narrowest of threads. 'Until I know for certain that I want this marriage to continue, I keep a separate bed.'

The words hung between them. The adoring girl she'd once been cringed. After she'd agreed to their marriage, whenever she protested about something, he'd kissed her until her senses had spun with desire. With so much at stake, she couldn't afford to return to that girl.

His face became ice-carved, emphasising the half-moon scar on his chin. Instead of the young man she remembered, a fierce warrior stood before her. Then, like the sun coming between the clouds on an autumn day, he smiled.

'Of course we shall stay married, Kara. You're simply a bit put out and not thinking clearly. I'm hardly to blame. The message went astray.'

A bit put out? Kara's jaw dropped. Ash made it seem like he had been gone for a few months and that she was overreacting. He should understand that seven years was an age and she needed time. They both did. Things had changed. She had changed. Going back to being the romantic dreamer she had been all those years ago was impossible. She had Rurik to protect.

Her stomach dropped. Rurik. He didn't know. She had to tell Ash about their son. She glanced about her at the statues and incense burners. But not here. Not now. He'd just heard about his father's death. She wasn't ready to explain the full story of Rurik's birth. It had to be done carefully.

She struggled with a calming breath. 'It is far more than a fit of pique over a small slight. I'm within my rights to divorce you. We haven't shared a bed for over five years. Consider my request for time as payment of your life debt to me if you must, but give me that time. Do not seek to seduce me.'

His eyes regarded her with a thoughtful expression.

'You're within your rights even without demanding payment for the life debt,' he said and held out his hands. An indulgent smile played on his lips. 'If it is what my beautiful wife wants, who am I to deny the request?'

The tension rushed out of her shoulders. He had agreed. She had time to find the right words and explain about Rurik and what she had done. She'd make him understand.

She tapped her finger against her lips. He had agreed, far too readily. Ash was up to something, but she knew all his tricks now. She would resist him.

'Thank you,' she said, inclining her head. 'Thank you for appreciating the difficulty we both face. We were friends once. I would like to remain friends.'

'I do appreciate the length of time, Kara. Believe me. But you seem to be nervous. There is never any need to be nervous around me. Ever. Your interests are mine. It is what husbands do.'

He took a step closer to her and ran a finger down the side of her face, sending a pulse of warmth radiating through her. Her body swayed towards him as the ache in her lips grew.

The door swung open and she jumped back. Her cheeks flamed. Silently she blessed whoever had opened that door and jerked her back to reality.

Valdar stepped into the room, filling the doorway with his steady bulk. Concern was clearly etched on his face. A slow tide of warmth washed up her face and she silently thanked the gods that he had arrived when he did.

'I wondered if there was some problem, Kara,' he said, bowing low. 'You were expected at the feast long ago. People are beginning to ask.'

'It has been a long time since I've seen my wife. People must wait their turn.' Ash laid a possessive hand on her shoulder. 'A husband's needs come first.'

'We are on our way,' Kara said, tearing her shoulder from Ash's unnerving touch. This was not about her, but putting his stamp on his possession for all to see. Men could be so obvious. She was far from a piece of furniture or an arm ring to be squabbled over. 'Ash needed to know about his father in private.'

Valdar inclined his head. 'Auda wondered if you needed help. I volunteered.'

Kara rubbed the back of her neck. She couldn't decide if she should hug Auda for sending Valdar or shout at her. She and Ash needed to get the boundaries of their relationship set, but Valdar was right—people expected them elsewhere.

Ash's eyes flicked from her to Valdar. He pursed his lips. 'I understand entirely.'

'Understand what?' Kara snapped

'Why you made the request.' He nodded towards where Valdar glowered. 'Obvious, Kara, very obvious. You have acquired a guard dog.'

Kara clamped her mouth shut. Valdar and what he did with the rest of his life was the least of her concerns, but right now any excuse would do. She forced a smile. 'There is nothing wrong with being obvious. Until you returned, I was Valdar's bride.'

Ash's eyes narrowed. A sudden pang went through her. She wished it was because he was jealous about the thought of her with someone else, not just because he was possessive and proud. If Ash had cared about her, he would have returned earlier. 'I see.'

'Do you indeed?' Valdar's hand went to his sword.

'I do.' Ash's went to his.

'The feast, Ash,' she said before a fight started. Before she could explain about Valdar, she had to explain about Rurik and there wasn't time to do it properly. Valdar was right. People expected to see Ash at the feast. 'A lot of time and effort went into making sure the feast would be memorable.'

'It will now be memorable for other reasons.' Valdar's hand remained on the hilt without moving.

'The right reasons,' Ash corrected glaring at Valdar and keeping his hand on his sword.

'Did Valdar say otherwise?' Kara asked, moving between the two warriors.

Neither commented. Each seemed to be poised, waiting for the other to make his move.

The nagging pain at the back of her eyes intensified. If she was not very careful, these two warriors would be at each other's throats. And the feast would be even more memorable. 'Thank you, Valdar, for heeding Auda's request and reminding me that the feast needs to begin. Ash, you will have to say a few words before everyone can eat unless you would rather someone else did.'

Ash's fingers relaxed. 'Whom do you suggest? My uncle? After all, he has been entirely welcoming.'

'Harald Haraldson sends his apologies.' Valdar lowered his hand, releasing the hilt. 'Today's events have overwhelmed him and he is far from young.'

Kara's heart sank. Ash's uncle was making a deliberate statement rather than taking to his bed in shock. He had not given up his quest for Jaarlshiem simply because Ash had returned.

'And the king?' she asked quietly. If the king had decided not to attend the feast, as well, it would send a very powerful message that his support lay with Ash's uncle in any investigation.

'He agreed with Auda and sent me. He does prefer an early night these days.'

Giddy relief poured through Kara. The king might not come out and declare it, but he would support Ash over Harald Haraldson in any investigation. Everything might be fine after all. Harald Haraldson was powerful enough to demand an enquiry, but Ash would achieve his birthright as long as he had the king's favour. Rurik's inheritance was secure. For the first time since Hring the Bold's funeral and Harald Haraldson's declaration, Kara felt she could stop looking over her shoulder—the king was with Ash.

'If he is the one asking, then we must go.' Kara clapped her hands together. 'One never keeps a king waiting.'

'We are not finished.'

'We can discuss things later.'

'I look forward to that with anticipation.'

After the feast, she'd explain about Rurik, Kara promised herself. Ash had to understand that she had a duty to their son. And she wanted to ensure he was properly brought up, not left to fend for himself with only a nurse for company as Ash had been. She remembered drying Ash's tears once after he'd been beaten and sent out into the forest again. Later Hring had boasted about Ash's rough-and-ready upbringing and his tales still made her blood run cold. That was not happening to Rurik.

Ash drew his arm through hers. He smiled down at her but his eyes were hard. 'We enter the feast together. Husband and wife.'

Kara wet her lips and tried to quell the nerves in her stomach. 'Together?'

Ash gave Valdar a significant look. 'You can hardly want people to think I had lost you…already.'

Chapter Four

The cheers and stomping of feet echoed in Ash's ears as he took his seat. His brief speech and toast in reply to the king's welcome had gone down well with the assembled crowd. Slightly different from the one he had planned on the ship.

It was the sort of speech they, in particular Kara, would want to hear rather than a precise recounting of events. Ash inwardly cringed at certain parts which made him out to be more of a hero. He'd been lucky. That was all. Nothing heroic. He had made it through alive even if at times he'd wanted to die, rather than continue on. But no one wanted to hear the truth.

'Your speech was well received.' Kara gave a polite smile as he sat down. 'It certainly seemed like you had an exciting time.'

'You missed two of my jokes. You never

missed them before,' he said. 'I put them in especially for you. I hoped you liked them.'

Kara raised an eyebrow. 'For me? I'm honoured that you thought much about me. My mind must have been on something else. I'm sorry.'

Ash tapped his finger against the drinking horn. Watching for someone? Valdar had not yet appeared in the hall, despite his ill-timed interruption in the antechamber.

'I just wanted you to know.'

'Impressing me should be the least of your considerations, Ash,' she said.

Ash took a thoughtful sip of his ale. She was wrong. Seven years ago, he had married her in order to demonstrate to his father that he was ready to shoulder responsibility and ready to be the captain of a ship. Kara had been the girl on the next estate who blushed every time he spoke to her and hung on his every word. She'd believed in his dreams of being a great warrior. He hated disappointing anyone. 'I wanted you to know.'

'I'll try harder the next time I hear the speech.'

Ash shuddered inwardly. The words had stuck in his throat, but people wanted to hear about heroes not failures. 'It won't be given again.'

'I was distracted. I apologise.'

The earlier glance between Kara and Valdar had been telling. She had welcomed the interruption in the antechamber, maybe even requested it beforehand. Valdar certainly was her devoted slave. How far had it gone? Kara was *his* wife. But did he truly have a right to her any more? All he knew was that he wanted her.

When he had seen her standing in front of the priest next to the blond hulk of a warrior, something had twisted inside his gut.

He remembered the man from his youth. They used to be rivals at games and swordplay. His father had always held Valdar up as the sort of son he'd wanted. Kara was *his* woman, not anyone else's, particularly not Valdar Nerison's. He would reclaim her. He would show her that he was worthy of being her hero. He could do it. He was more than a match for Valdar.

'You look very serious,' Kara said, frowning. 'The king's speech was more than gracious in the circumstances and your recital of your adventures is sure to have fired skalds' imaginations. You will get a saga out of this. You always wanted to be in a saga. Stop acting like it is Ragnarok because I didn't laugh at one of your jokes.'

Ash forced another swallow of the ale. Wasn't that what she wanted, as well—a hero for a husband? And what would happen when she discovered he was just a man, a flawed man? He pushed the thought away.

'Thinking. Things have changed since I last attended a feast in Sand. And I hadn't expected to notice the empty spaces and missing faces as much as I have.'

She toyed with a piece of bread, shredding it into ever smaller pieces. 'It must be hard to be the only one who returned from that *félag*.'

Ash gave a reluctant nod. The dead were always with him, but tonight more than ever. They knew he was no hero. They knew his words were an exaggeration at best, but he couldn't risk losing her by appearing less than a hero. 'You should know I'd have changed places with any of them if I could. They were good men, better men than me.'

'You knew them better than I.'

'That I did.' Ash gestured towards where the skald sat, tuning his lyre. 'When am I going to hear the lament my father commissioned about my death? Several have mentioned it. Or weren't you planning on that song at your wedding feast?'

Her cheeks flushed scarlet. 'I didn't think it appropriate for my wedding. He might know it. It was popular for a few years in Raumerike.'

'Ask him to play it.'

'Why?'

To know what my father thought about me. A man wants to know how he is remembered. Even if he is not worthy of that remembrance. Ash clamped back the words. If he wanted to regain Kara, she had to think he was a hero, the ideal husband for her. 'I thought it would be amusing.'

'Amusing.' Kara placed her cup down with a thump. 'That is what you think a lament should be—an amusement? Sometimes I wonder if I ever knew you, Ash Hringson.'

'What else? Amusement is far better than sorrow, but I will wait.' Ash clapped his hands. 'I wish to hear some Raumerike songs. It has been far too long. Please my ears, skald, and you will be well rewarded.'

Kara bore the feast for as long she could. She listened to the toasts and the songs. She made meaningless small talk with various people, but her sense of unease grew with every passing breath. She had to force her voice to be loud and firm, whereas Ash appeared not to be suffering any sort of fear or trepidation. He'd actually wanted to hear the lament his father had commissioned.

Silently she thanked the gods that the skald was one Valdar had hired so he hadn't committed the verses to memory. The last verses were about Ash's ghost imploring his infant son to grow up to be a brave warrior like him. There was never a dry eye at Jaarlshiem when the piece was sung. Instead the skald had sung drinking songs and songs of past Raumerike battles. Everyone had joined in and the ale had flowed.

The entire situation reminded her of the feasts before Ash had left when she'd faded into the background as he held everyone in the palm of his hand with his ready wit. He kept up a steady stream of banter and was willing to drink every toast.

Ash's shoulder nudged her after the third drinking song. When the fifth started, his hand brushed over hers as he reached for the trencher that they shared. A deliberate caress. She made a stabbing motion with her eating knife. He gave an unrepentant smile and reached for her hand again. This time, he brought it to his lips.

Kara straightened her back and stared directly ahead, ignoring the pulse of warmth. She was not a plum, ripe for the plucking and bedding, simply because Ash had deigned to return after seven years and desired a warm body.

She turned and saw Valdar staring at her and Ash. Heat stained her cheeks. Ash's gesture had been one of possession, rather than casual regard or desire.

She stood up.

Ash immediately stopped his conversation in mid-quip and caught her hand. 'A problem?'

'Time for me to retire,' she said, her throat tightening.

'Here, Valdar has finally arrived. He failed to follow directly. Odd, that.' He nodded towards where her former betrothed stood, gently swaying. His bridal finery was now rumpled and his jaw slack.

Kara turned her face away, trying to remember if she had ever seen Valdar drunk.

Ash put an arm about her shoulders. 'But if you are ready to go, who am I to deny you?'

She pulled away. 'That has nothing to do with anything. I have had a long day. Exhaustion hits the best of us.'

'And we are anticipating an even longer night!' one of Ash's former drinking companions called out from further down the table.

'You speak to my wife. Keep a civil tongue in your head.' Ash glowered at the man. 'Apologise.'

The man gulped. 'I apologise, my lady. The beer has made my tongue loose.'

Ash stood and put a possessive hand in the middle of her back. 'You're right, lady wife. The hour grows late. I accept your plea. Time we both retired.'

'Please don't feel you must,' Kara said in a hurried undertone. 'I can see myself home. Your many admirers are here, wanting to speak with you and hear about your adventures. The celebrations are poised to continue until the cock crows in the morning.'

His eyes became hooded. 'Why should I want to be parted from you, my loyal wife?'

She moved and his hand fell away. The tiny touch burned its way up her arm. Ash was up to his old tricks—saying things and allowing her to interpret them in a specific fashion when he meant entirely the opposite thing. 'Teasing fails to become you. I'm not in the mood and I am serious. People expect the full story. You only gave the briefest hint of your adventures. Do you wish for people to feel cheated?'

He reached down and rubbed the side of his leg. 'The feast grows wearisome for me as well as you. The telling of tales means reliving my experiences. The words are stuck in my throat. Tomorrow when I have found better words, I will tell them. Today has unfolded in a different fashion than I had thought it would.'

Kara noticed the tired circles under his eyes and the faint pinching around his mouth. It reminded her of when Rurik protested at having a nap, but was about to fall asleep on his feet. She was being hard on Ash. She had been so caught up in her own discomfort that she hadn't seen the toll the day's events had taken on him. 'Today was a different day than either of us planned. In the morning…'

'The morning will look after itself. Right now, let me look after you.'

Her breath caught in her throat. Once she had longed to hear those words from Ash, but now she knew they were meaningless phrases. The only person Ash looked after was himself. 'No need. I am capable.'

'Every need. You are my wife.' He cleared his throat and stared straight at Valdar. Valdar glowered back. 'I must leave you all. My lady wife begs for bed.'

His voice echoed about the hall.

There was a great stamping of feet and a fresh round of laughter. 'A kiss! A kiss! A kiss! We want a kiss!'

Kara froze. Not here. Ash was just proving a point to Valdar.

His eyes turned speculative, then he shook his head.

'I do my wooing in private. Haven't you seen enough for one day? Find your own women.' He glared directly at Valdar. 'This one is taken.'

He ushered her out of the hall into the cool night air, putting his hand firmly on the small of her back. The shouts and ribald jests followed them into the dark night. A large yellow moon hung in the sky, giving a real glow to the street. The sounds of the feast filtered out.

'Thank you.'

'For what? For not kissing you?' He rubbed the back of his thumb along her mouth, making it ache. 'I told the truth, Kara. I've no need to kiss you in public. I'm willing to wait, knowing what the prize is.'

Easy words. She had made the mistake before of believing such things. It was deeds which counted, not words. Deeds lasted. Words faded as soon as they were uttered.

'For leaving with me. My father...' Kara's throat closed as she thought of the humiliations her father had piled on her mother when he'd returned from his voyages and how her mother had retreated into her own private world.

'Your father was a difficult man, plagued with his own demons,' Ash said.

'Anyway, I'm grateful.'

'Feasts are a chore at the best of times. This one was far harder than most, but it is over...for both of us.'

'You used to love them. You spent days practising your jokes and quips on me.'

'I'd forgotten that. Hopefully I didn't bore you.'

Her mouth went dry. 'I enjoyed hearing them.

Sometimes…sometimes I think about them even now.'

His eyes became huge pools of midnight blue in the moonlight. 'Other things became more important. And my long-ago words were the babblings of an unwise youth.'

She forced her face to turn away from him. In another heartbeat she'd melt into his arms and that was wrong. 'I can find my own way home.'

'You're my wife. Allow me this. Allow me to keep you safe.'

The stones in the road swam in front of her eyes. She blinked rapidly. The only person who could keep her safe was her. 'I've no objection.'

They walked in silence to the door of the small house she used when she was in Sand. The night held the chilly promise of winter. In the sky, a large harvest moon hung, illuminating the silent town in silver.

It seemed such a short time ago that she'd left the house to marry Valdar and now she was returning with a different husband, one she had once mistakenly thought knew her intimately, but now was a total stranger.

Kara gave him a quick glance. Would he want to stay? Would he expect it? The house was his by right. She could hardly refuse him entrance, but she could refuse him her bed. It was too

much to tell him about Rurik tonight. No one
had said anything at the feast despite her worries.

His set face gave nothing away.

'Here we say goodnight.' She held out her
hand as they stopped beside the door.

'Kara...' He reached for her, tilting her chin
upwards. 'Is that how you say goodnight? When
did an ice giant touch your heart?'

In the pale moonlight, his face had become
like Loki's—beguiling, but treacherous. It would
be easy to melt into his arms and give her mouth
up to his touch, but also it would be the worst
thing she could do. She had finished believing
he was what she wanted. She no longer had need
of heroes. She needed a steady man. To bring up
Rurik properly.

Rurik.

Her mouth went dry. She needed to tell him.
Before anyone else did. She had kept trying to
find the correct way on the journey home, but
her mind had been devoid of ideas. It had to be
done right.

'That would be unwise, Ash.'

His hand fell to his side. 'Why?'

'Much remains unsettled. We need to finish
our discussion. I won't be forced or seduced.
Ash, I know your tricks. You say things you
think people want to hear. I remember enough
about your old stories to know things were far

more difficult and less pleasurable than you made out in tonight's speech. Some day, when you're ready to tell me what truly happened, then maybe we can begin again.'

She watched him silently and willed him to tell her the truth of why he'd been gone so long. After that, she'd confess about their son. It was hard knowing the right time and way to say it. How did you tell a man that he had a six-year-old son?

'I wasn't planning on asking to stay unless you requested it. We go at your pace, Kara. I've never forced a woman. I've no plans to change that habit, particularly not with my wife.' His hand caught a strand of her hair and wound it about his finger. 'Are you afraid of admitting that truth? You desired me as much as I desired you. And I still desire you. We could have beautiful children, Kara. You always wanted children.'

A cold prickle ran down her spine. It was the opening she'd waited for. She had to tell him the truth before she gave into cowardice. Ash had to hear about Rurik from her, rather than learning from someone else. She silently prayed that she would not have to tell him the full story. Not tonight.

'Ash, listen to me.' The words came out in a rush as she tore her hair from his grasp. 'Everything between us changed six years ago when I gave birth to your son.'

His mouth dropped open. In the pale moonlight, the laughter drained from his face. He looked as if someone had hit him over the head with a sword. He shook his head as if to clear it and all the while watching her with a stunned, uncomprehending face.

Her stomach roiled. She had said the words far too bluntly. She should have eased her way in.

'I have a child?' The words were barely above a whisper. Shocked and utterly unlike his usual voice. 'A son from you?'

'Yes, we have a son—Rurik.'

A son. He had a son. His son. The words pounded into Ash's brain.

The overwhelming tiredness fell away. He was a father. He scarcely knew what to think or say. He was utterly unprepared for it.

He had never even thought of the possibility. Never allowed his mind to consider such a thing as a child of his own. Kara had had his child. All sorts of conflicting emotions coursed through him—elation at having a child and the horror at knowing how unworthy he was, as well as a sense of responsibility and the bitterness of regret.

His son had grown up without him—cut his first tooth, taken his first step and ridden his first horse without Ash being there to see it. He had always sworn that he'd never do that to a child, behave like his father had done. But he had. He'd been even worse. His father had at least welcomed him into the world before departing for four years of adventuring. Ash had never seen his boy. Never even considered his existence.

Was ignorance an excuse? Not for the first time, Ash wanted to turn back the sands of time.

He ran a hand through his hair and tried to keep his emotions under control. He glanced up at twinkling stars in the night sky and blinked the tears away. He was a father. It changed everything and nothing. One more mistake for his shade to carry. He should have known deep within his soul and he hadn't. What sort of man did that make him?

'What is his name?' he asked, through the lump in his throat. 'Did you say Rurik?'

'Rurik, Rurik Ashson. Once you said you wanted your first-born to be named Rurik.'

Rurik, his mother's father's name. The memory came rushing back. He had been standing on a rock above the lake, proclaiming what he'd do after he conquered the world and sired a batch of sons.

How had she remembered that? He didn't deserve that sort of consideration, but he was grateful for it. More than grateful.

'You did well. My first choice,' he said and knew his words were inadequate. Anger surged through him. She'd known. She'd carried the knowledge with her through the morning and afternoon. All through the feast. But she'd kept the most important piece of news from him. It felt good to be angry. Anything was better than the all-consuming regret. 'Why wait until now to tell me? Why not tell me at the temple?'

'Ash...' She held out her hand.

Ash ignored it. With a hurt expression, she slowly lowered it. Ash hardened his heart and forced the guilt back down his throat. Every other man at the feast had known, but not him. Had she wanted to humiliate him?

'It should have been the first thing you said to me,' he ground out. 'Before you spoke of my father's death. You risked making me the laughing stock of Raumerike. Or maybe that was your intention. A way to get back at me for something not of my making? I thought you better than that.'

'I was interrupted before I had a chance...' Kara pressed her hands to her eyes, hating the guilt that swept over her. She'd made a mistake. He was absolutely right. She should have said something. She hated that she'd been a coward about her son whom she loved with every fibre of her being. 'You'd just learnt your father had died. Losing a father and gaining a son in the next breath is far too much for any man to bear.'

'You're sure he is mine?' Ash gripped her shoulders, his face intent.

Kara's entire body went cold. He had to believe her. She hardly wanted to confess that Ash was her only lover, not after learning about the parade of women who'd graced his bed before her and more than likely since. He was not the type to endure an empty bed for seven years. She had her pride.

'Rurik is your son as well as mine.' She lifted her chin. 'Once you see him, you will know. He has your eyes, Ash, and your nose. Your father used to proclaim how like his father Rurik was and how I ought to be careful or he'd be steering ships on to the rocks.'

The tension eased in his shoulders. His hands fell to his sides.

'I wouldn't wish my nose on anyone,' he mumbled, hanging his head.

'I've always liked your nose.'

'When was he born?' he asked in a gentler tone.

Kara wound a strand of hair about her finger and tried not to think back to that fateful day. Ash needed the bare minimum. Later, maybe, she'd tell him the full tale. 'He was a Jul-tide baby. The day of his birth was icy.'

Ash expelled a breath. Five months after he'd departed. Two months after he was supposed to have returned.

He'd been in the dungeon then, waiting for help which never would come. Nothing he could have done. The thought failed to ease his sense of guilt. She must have known before he'd left. Had she kept the news from him?

'I want to see him. Immediately! Take me to him.'

Kara opened the door, her shoulders quivered like a nervous horse, scenting battle. 'Shall we discuss this inside, rather than on the street for all to hear?'

Ash entered the dimly lit room. He would never have recognised it. Instead of the gloomy tapestries of battles which had frightened him as a little boy, the walls were hung with the most fantastical beasts. The weaving loom was set before the small hearth rather than being banished to the back room. The house which he remembered as a cold and austere place had a definite air of warmth. Things had changed for the better here, but he dreaded to think about Jaarlshiem. The farm had suffered when his mother had looked after it.

'Is he here?' he asked as Kara stood quietly just inside the doorway. 'I want to see him. Now. Wake him up! His father is home!'

'He is at Jaarlshiem with Gudrun, your old nurse. She is Rurik's nurse now.'

'At Jaarlshiem, rather than Sand for your wedding. Interesting.' Ash tilted his head to one side and tried to quell the prickle of anxiety. Kara had left their son with his old nurse, rather than bringing him to celebrate the wedding. 'Are you ashamed of him?'

Her fists slammed together. 'Never! I could never be ashamed of Rurik. How dare you suggest such a thing!'

'Did your Valdar request it?' He balanced on the balls of his feet, ready to storm out and challenge Valdar. Silently he thanked the gods he'd arrived back in time to prevent anything from happening to his son. Kara would have to see that she needed to stay with him for Rurik's sake.

'Valdar and Rurik are friends. They enjoy spending time together.' Her lashes slid over her eyes, hiding her expression. 'It was one of the deciding factors in why I consented to the marriage. Valdar is very good with Rurik. He seems to steady him.'

Disappointment struck Ash's heart. Of course Valdar would be. 'But he was the one against it,' he tried.

'Valdar would have been happy to have Rurik at the wedding. I decided it was for the best for him to remain at Jaarlshiem.'

Ash clung on to his temper. Barely. Kara was keeping something from him. There was a reason she had kept their son from Sand and the wedding. Did she fear his uncle? Bile rose in his throat.

'Is he a halfwit?' he asked, preparing for the worst.

Her shoulders relaxed slightly and the first genuine smile crossed her face, utterly transforming it. If he had thought her beautiful before, now she was dazzling. The pride she had in their son was clear. 'He has more wits than men twice his age. He notices everything, Ash. Always asking questions. His mischief rivals yours, but Gudrun's eyes are sharp as ever.'

'He'll come to no harm now that I've returned,' Ash declared, making a silent vow. His son wouldn't be brought up to fear in the way he had been.

The smile faded as quickly as it had come. 'That puts my mind to rest no end.'

'I look after my own, Kara.' A prickle went down his back. How great was his sin? 'Did you know you were pregnant when I went?' he asked with a sudden uncomfortable thought. Had Kara kept the pregnancy from him, knowing how much he wanted to go on this adventure? He could remember the way her eyes had lit up when he told her about the ship and the proposed timing of the voyage. There had been no shadows. If anything, she'd encouraged him to go and prove that he was a great warrior.

Ash shifted uncomfortably. The boy he had been would never have questioned her closely. He had accepted her word because it had made it easier to chase his dreams.

'Would that have stopped you?'

Ash closed his eyes. The boy he once was had been desperate to prove himself a great warrior like his father. He had wanted the adventure. He had assumed he'd be back for Jul-tide. He'd never considered failure. Every new obstacle he faced he'd always conquered.

Now he knew how important children were. Serving at the Viken court, he had seen warriors brought to their knees by the birth of their children. He had seen the grief his best friend Ottar went through when his wife died and then a few weeks later, the baby girl had breathed her last. Ottar had eased his pain in drink and fighting. He'd died in the street after he'd picked an argument with the wrong warrior, a berserker named Bjorn. It was his death that had redoubled Ash's efforts to get home and make something of his life.

The truth was he had never considered that Kara might be pregnant. Not then. Not later. It had been easier not to think about such things as his past life when he had been in the dungeon or later serving as a mercenary for the Vikens. Kara had belonged to a part of his life that he hadn't dared think about when he'd had nothing. And he knew it was one more failing to add to his list.

The past was impossible to change. He could change the future and he had a son, the very talisman of a future, a son whose face he'd never seen. He wanted to see his boy's face.

'What would you have done if you had known?' she asked softly.

'I would have come back sooner,' he said, when he trusted his voice.

Scorn poured into her eyes. 'And the possibility never occurred to you in the long years you were away?'

'I tried to focus on the task at hand, rather than speculating about home. Home was closed to me until I could erase the shame.' He held out his hands and hoped for a softening of her heart. 'How was I to know?'

Kara gave a queer smile. 'You did make sure you did your duty before you left, Ash.'

He watched the heartbeat in the hollow of her throat. His duty? Maybe he hadn't been ready to wed and his father had pushed him into it, but he clearly remembered the sweetness of Kara's body and the way she had willingly given herself to him. He had liked her and looked forward to returning to her. He'd never met another woman whom he would have married. 'I remember our time together with great fondness.'

'Fondness? I always have found that a very weak word.'

Ash winced. 'My tongue has never been eloquent, Kara, You know that.'

She crossed her arms, which only served to highlight the curve in her breasts. 'You do yourself few favours trying to claim that. What I want to know is will you recognise Rurik as your son? Will you be a father to him?'

'He is my son. Has he been accepted into the family?'

Her eyes slid away from him. 'Yes…yes, he has.'

It came to him like a clap of Thor's thunder— how he could win her back. He could protect her and their son.

He'd no rights to her, no matter what the law said, after what she had gone through. But it didn't stop him from desiring the woman she'd become and wanting to protect her and their son.

He needed to do something for her, something to atone for his neglect. His mind raced. He had to hope that she had only chosen Valdar because of the threat his uncle posed. He could protect her and show her that he was in truth the hero she longed him to be all those years ago.

Maybe, he would become a better man for doing it, the sort of man Kara deserved—steady, dependable and there in a crisis. And if she saw through his act, saw who he truly was and hated him for it, he'd go once she was safe. And she wouldn't have to marry simply to save his son's life. She would have freedom, something she had not had before. He felt better now that he had a plan.

'Who accepted him into the family?' he asked in a voice he barely recognised. 'Who played my part in front of the *tuntreet?*'

Chapter Five

'Your father accepted him.' Kara hated the way the words stuck in her throat.

It wasn't a lie, but not precisely the truth either. Hring the Bold had eventually accepted Rurik. And she was not going to explain about Hring's threat to expose Rurik when he was born too soon and was as weak as a kitten. Some day. After Ash had met Rurik. Or maybe after Rurik had grown to honourable manhood. She glanced up at Ash's fire-lit face, trying to see the gentle youth she'd once worshipped.

'He made the appropriate sacrifices in front of the *tuntreet,* pouring the water on the tree's roots in the correct manner,' she said into the silence. 'You would have been proud.'

He bowed his head. 'I'm pleased my father played the part well.'

There was no need to tell Ash how long after

Rurik's birth the sacrifice had happened. Or how Hring had tried to starve her into submission. All he needed to know was that Rurik was accepted into the family. It was the best way.

Kara picked up a disused spinning whorl, tightening her fist around it until her knuckles shone white. She hated how guilt welled up in her throat, as if she were doing something wrong.

Saving Rurik's life had become paramount ever since he'd been born in the ice storm, ever since she'd woken on the floor of the stable with the stallion standing over her, pawing the ground and the blood staining the straw. She should never have gone there. It had been her fault and she could never undo the sense of guilt, but she had ensured that Rurik lived despite her mistake.

'You know what your father was like for ceremony,' she said when she trusted her voice. 'He liked things to be done precisely and with all due reverence.'

He nodded. 'My father had exacting standards. He always said that unless a baby was strong, it was kinder to everyone that there be a quick death, rather than a lingering one.'

Barbaric standards. Kara bit back the retort. She truly had no idea how Ash felt about exposure. For Hring, it had been all about ensuring that only the strong survived, that weaklings didn't take up food and resources. For her, Rurik was part of her flesh and blood. Fighting with her last breath for his survival was natural. She had done everything to ensure his survival, arguing that when Ash returned, Ash should have the final say over whether or not his child was strong enough to survive. After trying to starve her into submission and demonstrating to her the truth of the marriage, Hring had reluctantly agreed.

The morning after they had learnt of Ash's death, Hring had finally formally accepted her son as his heir—her price for nursing him.

As soon as he could stand, Hring had made the signs and mumbled the words as Kara poured the wine over the *tuntreet*'s roots. The ceremony had been far from the ringing endorsement she'd hoped for, but it hadn't mattered. Her son had a name and a future.

Before he'd died last winter, Rurik and his grandfather had become good friends. In his last days, Hring had even apologised to Kara with tears in his eyes. He'd named Rurik as his heir once again. But Harald Haraldson had mentioned the oddity of the ceremony at the funeral and she had known what he intended.

Kara wrapped her arms about her waist, trying to keep from shivering. Nothing was going to happen to Rurik. She'd won the fight for his life. He would be a good lord who looked after his people and his family; he wouldn't abandon them in pursuit of glory.

'Rurik is a healthy six-year-old,' Kara said carefully. Rurik was healthy, even if he did have a weak chest and an inclination to get colds which lasted all winter.

'When can I see him?'

'When we go back to Jaarlshiem.' Kara forced her voice to be steady. 'I've no wish to expose him to court life until he is ready.'

'Why not? I can remember coming to Sand with my father when I was about Rurik's age. It opened a whole new world for me.'

'Sand seems to be constantly suffering from one illness or another.'

'Yet you risk it.'

'He is safest in Jaarlshiem. He remains there.'

'Safest?' Ash's face showed his incredulity. 'Accidents and illness can happen anywhere.'

'If you wish to see him, go to Jaarlshiem.'

'I intend to. If you wish to join me on the journey, you may or if you wish to stay with your lover, you may do so.'

'I have no lover.' Kara bit out every word, shocked that he could even think that!

A wide triumphant smile crossed his face. 'Good to know.'

She gripped the spinning whorl tighter so she

wouldn't give in to the temptation to throw it at him. 'I was about to become Valdar's bride. You must know the difference between a bride and a mistress.'

'What a pity I spoilt the party,' he commented drily. 'I apologise, but I do have a prior claim. What is mine stays mine. Let this Valdar find his own bride…and his own son.'

'Rurik is my son, as well.'

'Rurik will become the sort of man any man would be proud to call a son, rather than clinging to your skirts.'

Kara concentrated on the spinning whorl, weighing it in her hand. She'd battled Hring about Rurik's training. She'd battle Ash, as well. She needed a man she could count on to train Rurik properly, rather than abandon him to the fates or push him too far too soon. 'We've an agreement, Ash. You are going to give me time.'

He slammed his fists together. 'Made under false pretences. You should have told me of my son before you asked. Why didn't you, Kara? What did you fear I'd do?'

Kara kept her head up and concentrated on a spot behind his shoulder. The man standing before her was a stranger, a warrior with no gentleness in him. The caring boy-hero who had once rescued her from a fall into the freezing waters while skating was no longer…if he'd ever existed anywhere but her imagination. 'I've told you now.'

His jaw hardened. 'What did you think I'd do to you?'

'Does the agreement stand?' she whispered when she trusted her voice. 'Please, Ash. You owe me a life debt.'

The silence stretched between them. Kara pressed her hands together and concentrated on the dying embers in the hearth. He had to agree.

'Made under false pretences and a bad bargain, but I gave my word,' Ash said. Each word seemed to drive another nail into their relationship. 'You have your time to decide about our marriage. But my son is my blood. I won't give away my blood, not even to you.'

'You know nothing about him.'

'I want to learn. I will learn everything.' He slammed his fists together. 'I leave in the morning for Jaarlshiem. Everything else will wait. I will claim my blood.'

Kara stared at him, not bothering to hide her astonishment. He wanted to meet Rurik and learn about him. What would he think of their son? Her child with his skinny long legs and lopsided smile? His inability to throw a stick? Or run very fast? She bit her lip. She wanted Ash to love him and be proud of him, not see him as a weakling who should have been exposed at birth as Harald Haraldson had proclaimed at the funeral.

'You plan to leave in the morning? But surely the king and his council…' Her voice trailed away at his incredulous look.

'The king will understand. A man wants to see his son for the first time. Some things override politics.'

'And the enquiry?'

'Will have to be delayed.' He put a hand on her shoulder. 'My uncle has no power in this matter. He seeks to bluster and muddy the waters. The king knows whose son I am and the debt he owed my father.'

'And if the king disagrees?'

'Then he is unworthy to be called king.' He turned on his heel. 'I leave in the morning after I have pledged my loyalty to an honourable man. I know the way back to Jaarlshiem. I could walk it in my sleep.'

'And me?' Kara put her hand on her hip. She would be there when he met Rurik to make sure he saw Rurik's potential, rather than his shortcomings.

'Your choice, but if you come, you come alone.' He looked at her, slowly travelling from the top of her head to the bottom of her gown. 'Valdar is unwelcome. I meet my son without interference.'

Kara swallowed hard. She had not even considered asking Valdar to accompany her. Too many complications. She'd inadvertently hurt him and she refused to use him. 'I doubt he'd want to come. He has duties at court. They come before everything.'

Ash stepped forward. His hand caught a strand of her hair and ran it between his fingers before gently tugging. She took a step towards him. 'You underestimate your charms. You always did.'

'Our memories differ.' Her voice sounded far too breathless. Her entire body tingled with awareness of him. She swallowed hard and tried again. 'I mean, I've a good idea of my charms. My face and figure are not my fortune. My fortune lies in the trees and land I brought with me as my dowry.'

'Pardon me if I disagree with you.'

He lowered his mouth to hers and brushed her lips. The feather-light touch pulsed warmth through her. It asked, rather than demanded. For one brief instant her body melted against him, felt the hard planes of his muscles.

His hands instantly fell away, letting her go.

'You see. Still the same, Kara. You delight in provocation.'

She stumbled backwards, hitting the table. Her body thrummed but Ash couldn't know that.

She had to play it cool and collected. She put out a hand and steadied herself. Lifted her chin. 'A kiss changes nothing, Ash.'

'You are wrong, Kara. It changes everything.' He caught her chin between his forefinger and thumb. Her breath caught in her throat. Was he going to kiss her again? More thoroughly?

'Unhand me.'

He released her instantly. She rubbed her aching lips, silently cursing her body's attraction to him. She could do this. She could withstand his charm until she decided if he was the right sort of man for her. This time she would listen to her head, rather than allowing passion and romance to overcome her sensibility.

'I've no wish for Rurik to meet you without me being present.' She pointed to the door. 'If you leave without me, I will catch you up before the sun fades from the horizon.'

He lifted his brow. 'How swift is your horse?'

At his incredulous expression she rolled her eyes. 'Swift enough. You know I can ride. Valdar and I planned to return to Jaarlshiem after the feast. He wanted to make sure everything was in readiness for the winter.'

'How romantic. Your honeymoon spent on the estate. Were you going to count your trees? Or the amount of grain you harvested?'

'It was what we both wanted.' Kara longed

to beat her fists against his chest. She refused to think about the little hut where she had spent her wedding night with Ash and the way he had suckled honey mead from her fingers. 'Valdar is practical like that.'

'I'll keep it in mind.' He touched her cheek. 'Until the morning. Pleasant dreams. Be ready when I call or be prepared to test your assertion that your horse is swift.'

He closed the door with a distinct click. Kara shook her fist at it. Pleasant dreams indeed! The wretch probably hoped she was going to dream of him. Not likely. Dreams of that nature were for the girl she'd been once, not the woman she'd become.

Ash stared at the shuttered and silent house where his wife was. Since leaving Kara, he hadn't slept, but had used his excess energy to ensure his scheme would work. It was amazing what a determined man and a handful of gold could accomplish.

His breath plumed in the mid-morning air. One step at a time. Careful planning saved time later. But from what he could learn, Kara was in more danger now that he'd returned. His uncle appeared more determined than ever to gain control of Jaarlshiem. His uncle would have to make the next move, but Ash was determined it would be on his own terms.

He would keep his promise and protect Kara and their child, this time. With each scrap of information he received, he knew he was not worthy of her, but he wanted her in a way he'd wanted no other woman. Having so carelessly discarded her, he had to win her again.

If he couldn't win her before he'd finished with his uncle, he'd set her free. But this time, she'd be free to marry whomever she wished, rather than being forced to marry for the good of the estate or her son.

'Let this final game begin, Uncle,' he said in a low voice and raised his hand. 'This time, I will win as I know what it is like to lose.'

Heavy pounding woke Kara from her uneasy sleep. Her eyes flew open. Early morning sunlight streamed into the house. One of the house servants had relit the fire.

She had slept far too long. When she'd first gone to bed, sleep had evaded her and then it had overpowered her.

'Kara! If you don't open this door, I will break it down! The sun has been up for hours.'

Ash! Making good his threat! What a time to oversleep! Kara hastily grabbed a blanket and threw it about her shoulders while signalling to one of the servants to open the door. As she did so, the door crashed open.

Ash stood in the doorway. His short cloak emphasised his trim waist and the broadness of his shoulders. The fur cap set off his hair. His lips twisted to an ironic smile. 'Are you coming or not?'

Kara gaped at him, aware of how his hair softly curled under his cap and how few clothes she had on. She tightened the blanket about her shoulders. 'You never start early.'

'I've changed. And it is hardly early.'

Kara retreated to her bedchamber, reached for her travelling clothes and slipped the apron dress over her head. She stabbed her finger with one of the brooches, dropped it and watched it roll away. She softly swore.

'Problem?'

'My hair is a tangle,' she called out and she picked the brooch up. 'Do I have time to fix that?'

'How like a woman.' He coughed. 'A few moments, but then I will go. You may catch me if you like.'

'A threat?' Kara concentrated on undoing her braid. 'I react badly to threats.'

'Threats have no meaning. Actions do. My father taught me that. Either you come with me when I go or you make your own way back to Jaarlshiem.'

She bit back a retort and concentrated on plaiting her hair and twisting it up as her hands trembled with anger. Thankfully she didn't like the over-complex plaits that were so popular at court.

'Do you always enter a house like that?' she asked as she re-entered the main room. 'Knocking the front door down? A Viken custom, I presume.'

'My house. My door. I dislike having it barred against me.' He bowed low to the servant and put a gold piece on the table. 'To pay for the door. Are the servants capable of looking after this house?'

Kara rolled her eyes. As if she'd have untrustworthy servants! 'There would not be the need to fix the door, if you had waited.'

Ash tapped his finger against his lips. 'Valdar failed to arrive at court this morning. Along with my uncle. Both were conspicuous by their absence.'

Kara wet her lips and deliberately ignored the Valdar remark. 'You've seen the king?'

'First thing. The king is sympathetic with my plight and gave me leave to see my son. I wanted to inform Valdar, as well, in case he felt the need to say goodbye.'

'Valdar wouldn't expect me to say goodbye,' Kara retorted. 'He'll approve in any case. He likes Rurik. And he has never been in allegiance with your uncle, if that is what you are implying.'

Ash's face hardened. 'Yes, you did say what an excellent person he is.'

A tiny flutter developed in the pit of Kara's stomach. Ash was jealous. She quashed it as wishful thinking. Ash didn't care about her. He did want to meet Rurik and that was all she asked.

Ignoring Ash's glower, Kara issued a few final instructions to the servants, including delivering a message to Valdar of her leaving. The youngest kitchen maid volunteered to run over to Valdar's house straight away. Kara shook her head and told her that it could wait until after she'd gone.

'Have you finished?' Ash slapped his gloves against his wrist. 'Or do you need to instruct the maids on how to spin wool?'

'The servants need to know what to do. I take my responsibilities seriously, but all is sorted now.' Kara walked past him and out into the street.

She stopped in surprise. Rather than two or three men as an escort, a host of twenty men sat on horses, with their weapons clearly displayed as if they expected trouble. One held her horse, saddled. The back of her neck prickled. Despite his earlier assurance, Ash expected trouble.

Various townspeople gathered, staring open-mouthed at the number of outriders.

'No cart?' she asked, frowning.

'As you can ride a horse, a cart is unnecessary. If you need one for your dignity, you'll have to employ your own escort. I intend to travel swiftly.'

'I've ridden to Jaarlshiem before. Bring my horse here and I'll mount.' Kara sent a silent prayer up thanking various goddesses that her skirt was full enough to allow her to ride a horse without displaying her limbs. But even if they had showed, she'd have refused the cart. Silently she vowed that she would be there when Ash met Rurik. She wanted to make sure Ash didn't reject Rurik once he saw him. It would absolutely devastate Rurik. Hring's vicious remarks about how she was lucky that Ash had died as he'd never have accepted the boy resounded in her brain.

She mounted swiftly.

'Kara!' Valdar strode down the street with about fifteen friends. Their hands hovered above their undrawn swords, ready for battle. As they neared her horse, they spread out, taking up the street's entire width. The message was abundantly clear—if Ash wanted to go to Jaarlshiem, he'd have to pass through them.

Kara struggled to control her horse, which had reared up at the noise. Men! She hated violent posturing, ever since her father used to pick fights just to prove he was the stronger. One day he hadn't been and he'd died of the infected wound.

'Valdar.' Kara inclined her head when she had her horse under control. 'I return to Jaarlshiem. What brings you here?'

'Willingly?'

'You will let us pass, Valdar the Unwed!' Ash manoeuvred his horse so that it pawed the ground directly in front of Valdar.

'Not until I hear from the Lady Kara. Do you go willingly, my lady?'

'Of course she does! Do you see any chains?' Ash swung down from his horse. In unison, his men followed suit.

Two armies facing each other. One wrong word and blood would spill. Kara's head thumped. In an odd way she was certain both enjoyed the confrontation, but it ended here.

'I go willingly to Jaarlshiem. Ash Hringson speaks the truth. As you know, I am more than capable of speaking for myself.' She gave Valdar a hard look and then Ash, who looked unapologetic. 'Allow us to pass. Next time, Ash, allow me to answer questions directed towards me.'

Valdar raised his hand and his men cleared a

path. 'If that is what you truly desire, my lady, it will be done without question. I…that is, we… aim to serve you.'

She pulled the cloak tighter about her shoulders and wished that she had deserved the loyalty. 'It is.'

The warrior's face fell. 'And you need no assistance. Send word, any time, if you need me.'

'I trust my husband will see to my safety, if not my comfort. He has more than enough men. Perhaps it is because he is used to travelling in Viken rather than in Raumerike. The roads are far quieter here.'

Kara glanced at Ash, who stood jaw set and hands clenched. Her heart hammered. She spoke the truth. In his own way, Ash had always looked after her…when he had been here.

Valdar nodded, accepting her words. 'Hringson, will I be welcome at Jaarlshiem?'

'I've no quarrel with you, Valdar. Never did,' Ash proclaimed. 'I've no quarrel with any man. I simply claim what is lawfully mine. The king understands. You would know this if you had been at court this morning.'

'I will take your word for it. I had other matters to attend to.' Valdar's cheek flushed slightly and Kara wondered where he'd been. He never missed court when he was in Sand.

Kara made a little clicking noise in the back

of her throat. Her horse started forward. 'Shall we go before anything else happens?'

'Are you expecting more trouble, my lady?' Ash made no attempt to mount his horse.

'You always have to make a scene, Ash,' she said. 'There was no cause to do that. And there is no reason except simple extravagance to have this many men accompanying us. You would think we were riding off to battle, rather than returning to Jaarlshiem to see our son.'

A muscle jumped in his jaw. 'Hardly extravagant. Prudent. What is mine stays mine. I trust Valdar the Steady and everyone else understands that now.'

Kara's mouth went dry. 'Does that include people?'

'I look after my own.'

Kara straightened her back and dug her heels into her horse's flank. 'Then I was never yours. Seven years, Ash, seven long years.'

Chapter Six

❧

*K*ara had never belonged to him.

Kara's words resounded in Ash's head with every step his horse took. Once he had thought she was his without question. Kara had always been there with her ready smile and hero worship. He'd failed to appreciate her and her potential.

This trip was about more than meeting his son. It was about protecting Kara, even though he was certain she'd claim that she didn't need protection. With each encounter, her steely strength and clear head impressed him more.

Kara might have thought Valdar the right man for her, but he was not. Ash knew this in his heart. All he wanted was a chance to prove that he could be the sort of husband she'd longed for all those years ago—brave, steady in battle and valiant—a true hero.

He wrenched his mind away from his circling thoughts and concentrated on the road ahead.

The twilight drenched the road to Jaarlshiem in shadow. The air bore a distinct chill of winter as a bone-chilling drizzle began to fall.

'Were you listening and watching, Uncle? Did you understand my message was meant for you, as well?' Ash muttered under his breath. 'When are you going to make your move? On this journey or against my ship as it moves slowly up the river towards Jaarlshiem? Or are you a spider, willing to sit and wait for me to make a mistake? I no longer make them. You have now become the hunted.'

He glanced back. Kara's head nodded. She jerked awake, making her horse start, but then her eyes began to flutter again.

'I'm fine,' she muttered. 'Keep going.'

'Did I say anything?'

He glanced about them to judge where they were and smiled. Tension flowed out of his shoulders. The gods were with him today. His younger self would never have noticed her exhaustion.

The gods favoured those who noticed small details. He'd learnt that lesson in the mud of his first victory, six months after he had escaped the dungeon. It should have been a defeat, but he'd noticed the Franks had not bothered to defend their western flank and had forded a river. After that, he had started to win other men's respect. The lesson had stayed with him ever since.

'We stop for the night.' Ash pulled his horse up as the rain intensified. 'A woodcutter's hut sits in the clearing up ahead. I used it years ago. Shelter on a night like this. No one will dare refuse us. I carry the king's rune, promising safe passage.'

At his words, Kara scrubbed her eyes with the back of her hand. 'I'm prepared to go on. All night should see us to Jaarlshiem's boundary.'

'You have regained your tongue, my lady. That is news worth celebrating!'

'When the occasion calls for it.' Her look flung daggers at him.

He shifted uncomfortably in his saddle. Maybe his earlier choice of words had been lacking in subtlety, but he wanted Valdar to take a message to his uncle.

If Kara had remained, there was every chance she'd be taken hostage and he couldn't allow that.

'Do you have a problem, Kara? I'm not prepared to play guessing games.'

'I'm no man's possession. Shall we get that clear? You need not make any concession for me either.'

He opted for a smile. 'We were able to leave Sand without being molested.'

'Why should anyone want to stop you? Is there something you are keeping from me?'

A single drop of rain ran down her cheek, shimmering in the half-light like a tear and highlighting the circles under her eyes. 'When did you last sleep properly?'

'I could ask you the same thing! It takes time to organise a journey like this.'

'Not as much time as you might think. I'm used to getting by with little sleep. When you've sold your service, you have to be prepared to reach the battle on time.'

'Are you going to battle? I thought you were going home.'

'Have you ever travelled all night?' he asked rather than answering her question. Going home for him was a matter of facing his demons, but she didn't want to know about his suffering. Kara wanted an invincible hero. 'You seem more than half-asleep.'

Kara reached up and pulled her cloak's hood more firmly over her head. 'My horse and I can go many miles yet.'

'You and your horse can, but I require rest. This place is good ground for a battle. I've learnt to always camp where you are sure of the ground,' he said, pulling his horse to a halt. 'Good ground about this hut.'

'Who is going to attack here in Raumerike?'

'I want to be prepared in case of the unexpected,' he said lightly. Maybe he was wrong and Kara was right. His uncle might use the law instead, but he doubted it. Maybe he had lived far too long with war and he'd seen the look in his uncle's eye before his uncle had stormed out of the temple. 'Tonight mainly I want my rest. I hope I get it.'

'Perhaps if we had started later, you wouldn't be so tired.'

'Tomorrow I meet my son. I want to do that fully alive rather than half-dead.'

She pushed her hood back and he caught a glimpse of her expressive eyes. 'You truly want to stop? You aren't simply being kind because you think me weak?'

'Why would I ever consider you weak?'

'You used to get impatient when I couldn't keep up. Even on our wedding night, you kept going when I begged you to stop.'

'I was younger then.' He instinctively rubbed the knot in his leg. The hours of riding had caused it to seize up. 'When you are older, you learn the value of respecting your body. I've learnt the value of conserving my energy until the battle begins.'

'You plan to do battle with our son?'

'Hardly…unless he wishes to do battle with

me. Sons have a habit of doing that with their fathers.'

Ash waited for an answering smile. Her eyes drooped further and her hands went slack on the reins.

'You never fought your father,' she murmured, her head nodding. 'Rurik dreams of being a warrior. Your father encouraged it.'

Ash slid off his horse. His father. He knew all about that sort of encouragement. And his father had always said that he wasn't ready to fight, that he'd never make a true warrior.

'Down you come. Stop protesting. When did you last have a proper sleep?'

He put his hands about her slender waist and lifted her down. She weighed less than he imagined, but there was an inner strength in her back.

'I know how to dismount.' She gave a half-hearted push against his chest. 'You try planning a wedding which gets interrupted as well as running a large estate. Hardly any time to breathe, let alone sleep.'

He gave in to temptation and held her for another heartbeat, drinking in the soft floral scent.

Something stirred deep within his memory. No other woman he'd ever encountered smelled like Kara. It had been one of the biggest mistakes he'd ever made, leaving her in the way he had. He had to hope he wasn't making another one coming back and turning her life upside down. But now he was here, he had to try.

'Were you always this independent?' he murmured against her hair, making a new memory. 'In my mind, you always agreed to my suggestions, no matter how outlandish.'

'I learnt the value of independence and using my mind.' She wriggled and he set her on her feet. 'It means the only person you have to blame is yourself.'

'The only thing you do tonight is sleep. Orders. In there. Sleep with no one to disturb you. Know you are safe.'

She shook her head. 'There is a lot to be done before I sleep. The men will need food for a start. Someone will need to make certain the horses are secure and fed. The fire will have to be started. Food cooked.'

'My men look after their own needs. It is understood.' He straightened her hood. 'You will do no one any favours if you try to keep awake. It is when accidents happen, Kara. The last thing we need is you getting injured. You look half-dead.'

She made an annoyed noise. 'You know how to make a woman feel special.'

Ash regarded her soft hair and creamy skin. She looked exhausted, but utterly delectable. It was all he could do to keep from gathering her into his arms again and kissing her thoroughly. Patience, rather than force. He had to prove himself to her. 'I was under the impression that you preferred the unvarnished truth these days. Shall I pay compliments instead?'

'The truth is preferable to compliments which you've paid to a hundred other women.'

Ash ignored the 'hundred other women' remark. He couldn't remember any other women. He certainly had not had one while he'd been away. It had been easier to keep his focus that way. 'I'll remember that, but you mustn't complain if the truth is not to your liking.'

She tilted her head to one side. 'Are you certain your men know how to make a proper camp? Some of them appear quite desperate.'

Ash cast a practised eye over his men—a diverse bunch of men and not pretty to look at, but they were good men to have in a fight. 'Warriors, pledged to me. If they didn't know their business, I wouldn't have them.'

'But so many of them.'

'Safety in numbers.' Over the years, he'd learnt that there was value in numbers. On his way to Sand, he'd laid careful plans—make his peace with his king and his father before going to the east and finding new trade routes. The money he planned to make there would have paid for another estate as he refused to live under the same roof as his father. But now with the problem with his uncle, he was glad of his men. They'd keep Kara and Rurik safe, should anything happen to him.

He had charged his best oarsmen and a handful of his men with the task of bringing the boat upriver. Right now, he wanted to see how his uncle would respond to the division. Would he chase after him or go after the ship?

The departure from Sand had gone far too smoothly. Ash distrusted smooth. His uncle would show his hand. Soon.

'Viken warriors?' She put her hand over her mouth. 'Does the king approve?'

'Men without a country, but with strong sword arms and a keen will to fight. I know what it feels like to be without a country and we've fought together in the past.'

He waited for her to understand why he refused to leave these men behind and why he needed them now. But the last thing he wanted was to give Kara an excuse to leave him or bar him from Jaarlshiem. He would claim his son and he would keep his inheritance. And he would show Kara that he was the sort of hero whom she'd dreamt about.

'Sell-swords.' Her lip curled about the word. 'And you think our son will be safe with them?'

'You say sell-sword like it is a dirty word. It

is best to be honest about why you are fighting for a particular side. Coin is a wonderful motivator. Far better than glory.'

He looked over her shoulder at the darkened hut. Its door gaped open, but there was no one inside. All was silent. He forced his shoulders to relax. The ambush would not come from the hut.

'Can you trust a sell-sword?'

'I was a sell-sword until very recently,' he said bluntly. 'I find such men to be pragmatic. The ones who pretend to fight for lofty ideals and principles or simply for the joy of killing are the ones you need to be wary of. Men who fight for money know what fills an empty belly. They also know when to stop. I'll have no berserkers under my command. You can't control them. I learnt it to my cost.'

The sleep fled from Kara. She looked at each of the men with new eyes. They were harder and more desperate than she had first considered. They fairly bristled with menace and scars. And Ash? Did he remain a hardened sell-sword? Or did the gentle boy she remembered lurk under everything? How would he react when he met Rurik? Rurik needed kindness and a steady hand rather than blows and harsh words.

Her hands curled into fists. One used hardened sell-swords to raid and to conquer. Earlier she'd overheard several of them complaining that they missed the sea and couldn't wait to get back to their ship. Proof if she needed it that Ash intended to go raiding again, rather than staying to farm.

She knew the heartbreak that came from loving a man who just went. Ash had broken her heart once. She refused to allow him the chance to do it a second time. She wanted a man who would share the burden of running the estate, rather than adding to that burden.

'Loyalty which lasts as long as the gold in your pocket,' she whispered. 'That is what hiring a sell-sword buys—temporary loyalty.'

'Nobody truly buys a warrior. Ultimately a warrior fights because he wants to fight for a particular leader. My men trust me because I'm tried in battle, pay an honest wage and pick my fights.'

'And some don't.'

'It rarely happens twice.' Ash's face hardened to a furious stone mask. 'Cheats and cowards tend to end their days with a knife in their back if they're lucky. Slow torture if they aren't. I can't abide such men. Death is far too good for them.'

A cold prickle crept down Kara's back. Ash had encountered someone like that. Had he been the one to plunge in the knife and buy his freedom that way? Did she want to know how many people he'd killed? Her mother used to say that

the reason why her father had changed was that
a man lost a little of himself with each man he
slew. Kara wasn't sure if it was true, but the Ash
who stood before her was very different from the
boy who had left. Had he become empty in the
same way her father had been in his final years?

'Have you fought many battles?' she asked,
putting the thought from her mind.

'Enough to know that, given the choice, I
never want to fight another one. I only fight
when forced to these days. Luckily my reputation is such that few dare cross me.' He made
a bow. 'My days of fighting for someone else
have vanished.'

'What do you want?' she whispered, fingering her throat.

'My needs are simple tonight—a warm fire
and food in my belly. Tomorrow will take care
of itself.'

'Where did you fight your battles?' Kara
asked carefully. 'Did you kill many men?'

'Twenty-one major battles, my lady, your lord
has fought,' one of Ash's men called out. 'The
little skirmishes are not worth the sweat it takes
to fight them. But they reckon your man has over
thirty victories to his credit. It is what they whispered when I signed with him. They reckon he
is luckier than most.'

'And who told you that?'

'Your husband, just after he killed the robber who tried to lift my purse.'

Kara's heart beat faster. 'It doesn't surprise me. Ash always did enjoy playing the hero.'

'Not just playing, my lady. He's the genuine article. The sea water flows in his veins. The way he can handle a ship and time his raids—nothing short of perfection. He lives for the battle.'

'Thank you, Saxi.' Ash gave a bow, but his features had hardened to an impenetrable mask which reminded her of Hring in one of his tempers. 'It is good to know my men think highly of me.'

'You are like your father.'

'I'm his son.'

Kara put her hand on his sleeve. 'And were you a hero? Did you turn the tide of battle every time as you always claimed you would?'

His blue eyes assessed her. 'A young man's claims are not worth the spit it takes to say them. Odin harvests the bravest from the battle. I returned. It should tell you much.'

Somewhere in the woods an owl hooted, swiftly followed by another. All about her, the men instantly became alert, fingering their weapons. Kara narrowed her gaze. A natural reaction of mercenaries, or was there something else?

'The tawny owls call to their mates,' she commented, seeking to defuse the tension. 'A true sound of autumn, hardly a call to battle.'

Ash gestured towards the hut with an impatient hand. 'Do you walk in or do I carry you?'

'And your men? Where will they sleep? The hut appears scarce big enough for all of us.'

'They are used to the cold ground. We have no enemies here. And the rain has cleared. There is no need for them to sleep in the hut. You needn't worry. Guards will be posted.'

The men agreed with Ash.

'There haven't been any bandit attacks recently. The king keeps a good peace.'

'Did I say I was worried about such a thing?' Ash retorted. 'It is always important to take precautions. Now sleep so this journey does not take several days longer than it should. We stop every time you fall off your horse.'

At Ash's indulgent expression, the back of her neck prickled. Did he have alternative plans? *What is mine stays mine.* Did he mean her? Seduction with his men camped around the hut? Was he going to ensure they stayed married?

Traitorous warmth curled deep within her as she remembered what it was like to lie in Ash's arms and feel his mouth on hers. She banished it. Making love with Ash would cause more problems than it would solve. She wasn't going to lose her heart again. She was not going to become that gullible girl who believed heroes really did exist.

Instantly she was awake, cursing herself for not insisting on her own men or at the very least a woman companion.

'And you, where will you sleep?' she asked, narrowing her eyes, searching for a loophole in Ash's intentions.

'With my men. I prefer to sleep outside these days.' A dimple flashed in his cheek. 'Unless you have a better idea… I await the invitation, my lady. If you feel so inclined, you must speak and save us both a cold and lonely night.'

'I sleep alone.'

'Some other time, then.' He rubbed a hand across his chin. 'I gave you my word. It should be enough.'

A hot tide flowed up Kara's face. He had known what she was thinking. She hurriedly straightened her pinafore dress. 'You used to enjoy your creature comforts. It surprises me that you give them up so readily.'

'A roof over my head, a full belly and a half-way decent cloak.' His lips curved up. 'Yes, they are luxuries rather than necessities. I've done without them in the past and survived. Tonight will be no different unless someone takes pity on me.'

Kara put a hand on her hip. This teasing Ash

she could handle. The other Ash when he was being kind or spoke about his experiences as a sell-sword, that Ash was a stranger. 'You seek to mock me when I was only curious why you were so willing to give up basic comfort. I deserve better than that.'

He tapped a finger against his mouth before smiling. 'Curious. A start, I suppose.'

Kara blinked. 'A start?'

'You have to care about something to be curious about it.' He clasped his hand to his chest. 'A tiny crumb of comfort from my lady as I lie on the cold ground.'

Her heart flipped to be called his lady. She hardened it as a memory clanged from years ago. 'I know that trick from years ago. I am my own lady.'

'Alone until you say differently.' He sketched a bow and his eyes twinkled in the dusk. 'I will be here when you wake, even if you should wake at noon.'

Kara tilted her head to one side. 'And this morning's little demonstration? The need to leave like the Valkyries were at our heels? What was that about? Showing Valdar you had claimed me?'

'I like to know who my enemies are and how they will strike.'

'Do you know them?'

'Now I do.'

Kara walked with as much dignity as she could muster to the hut. Inside her something ached. The new Ash was every bit as dangerous to her heart as the old one had been.

Ash struck a spark and lit a reed, holding it above his head. The light threw shadows over the nearly bare hut.

'The roof appears solid enough to keep the damp off for the night. And no large animal appears to be making this its home.' He gestured towards an old pile of leaves. 'I regret I can't do better for a bed, but it is better than falling asleep in the saddle and getting hurt.'

'You needn't make any concession for me.'

He laughed. 'You're beautiful when you are angry. So fiery and full of passion. But I like my women rested.'

'Stop trying to change the subject.' Kara concentrated on the makeshift bedding. 'I don't belong to you. I never have. We might be married, but I am no slave to do your bidding.'

He came over to her and laid his hand on her shoulder. 'I can only apologise for the boy I used to be. I should have waited until the spring to leave. I was wrong and I paid a high price.'

Something melted inside Kara. His eyes in the dim light had become pools she could drown in. She wanted to lean her head against his shoulder and draw strength. There were far too many reasons why that would be a bad idea.

Memories assaulted Kara's brain. Thousands of images of Ash being kind that she had deliberately forgotten. She shook her brain to rid it of them. What was in the past had to stay there.

She curled her fist. She refused to go back to being the girl who expected her hero to solve all her problems. She didn't require a hero. She required someone who would pull his weight. 'All that is in the past.'

'That is the trouble. Lie to yourself if you must, but don't expect me to believe it. I can always tell when you are lying, Kara.'

She thought about how she had waved him goodbye. 'Not always.'

'I came back, Kara. And I intend to show you that I can be the right sort of husband for you.'

Summoning all of her failing energy, she turned her head. 'The sooner I sleep, the sooner we leave this place.'

His hands let her go. She stumbled away from him towards where he'd piled the leaves up. It wasn't much, but it would be far more comfortable than sleeping on the bare floor.

The little gesture showed Kara he had changed. The old Ash would have expected her to do that. Something tugged at her heart. Maybe

Hring had exaggerated Ash's faults. Maybe she had been mistaken.

'Bravado serves no one.' He cleared his throat. 'And if I think we are going too fast, we slow down. Do you understand?'

'I'm hardly some fragile glass bead. I can take a faster pace. I want to see my son. Rurik is the light of my life.'

'Tell me if you feel the need for a break. My talents fail to include mind reading, more's the pity. Our son will want his mother to return home safely. We both know what it is like to lose mothers through accidents.'

'I'll remember that.' She screwed her eyes up. She'd forgotten how Ash's mother had died—returning to Jaarlshiem. A wave of sheer exhaustion hit her. 'I want to sleep, Ash. You were right to stop. I'm sorry if I seemed ungrateful earlier. I hate to admit any weakness.'

'Progress of a sort—you see sense in my actions.' He started to go towards the door, then halted. 'Shall I bring you some supper in? Or do you wish to sup with my men? It won't be fancy, but it will be filling.'

She shook her head quickly. The thought of food made her feel queasy. Sharing an intimate supper with Ash was folly in the extreme. Her defences were down. It would be easy to give in to that little voice in the back of her brain which kept whispering that she wanted to be held and Ash was the man to do it. She needed to keep Ash at arm's length tonight if she wanted to retain an ounce of self-respect. She wanted a man who would be more than a memory. She wanted someone with whom she could share her life.

All she really wanted to do right now was sleep, a deep dreamless sleep so she'd wake refreshed and they could reach Jaarlshiem tomorrow without her slowing them down. Once there, it would be much easier to keep a distance between her and Ash. The last thing she wanted was for her body to overrule her brain.

'I need sleep more than food. I'll eat before we leave in the morning, I promise.'

He nodded, accepting her word. 'Pleasant dreams.'

'I rarely dream.'

His lips brushed her forehead. 'A man can hope.' With that he left the hut.

Kara pressed her hands together. Being angry with Ash had been easy when she thought him dead. And when he returned yesterday, she had clung on to her anger easily. But when he was like this, she found the unwanted memories crowding in of Ash's kindness or Ash behaving in a way that made her breath stop.

Once he'd been her idol, but he had taken advantage of her, using her as a way to follow his dreams. Her heart had shattered into a thousand shards when Hring had recounted his betrayal. She could still hear the women's laughter as they told her one by one the things Ash had done or said to them. All the while Hring had looked on, triumphantly expecting her to give up her son. She'd held Rurik tightly in her arms, vowing to remember every last word and never to be fooled again.

She had listened to her heart once. She had to listen to her head now.

'I gave up all my dreams of you years ago.'

His lips came closer, teasing her senses to wakefulness, even though she knew instinctively it had to be a dream. His tongue tip circled and touched her eyes, lips and throat.

She was far too warm and comfortable. His tantalising scent filled her nostrils, making her feel secure and safe. For far too long she'd been on her own and struggling.

He ran his hand down her back, pulling her closer so that their bodies collided before he rained kisses down on her mouth, her eyes and skin.

Sweet kisses, mind-numbing kisses, kisses which caused her body to ignite and burn. Wet and hot. She looped her arms about his neck and returned his kisses, opening her mouth and allowing him to drink from her and she supped from him.

His lips trailed their way to her earlobe. Suckled and tugged. With each new onslaught, the ache in her body grew higher. His hand slipped lower, teasing her, rubbing her breasts, cupping them and pulling at her nipples.

'Have you been waiting for me?' His voice rasped in her ear. 'Have you missed me? Are you ready for me?'

She drew her arm tighter about his neck and her body arched towards him, aching and ready. She wanted this. She wanted this joining.

'Never leave me, Ash,' she whispered against his lips. 'Stay. Stay with me this time. Promise me.'

But he was already fading into nothingness. Gone when she needed him the most. Leaving her empty and aching.

Chapter Seven

Kara woke with a start. Her body throbbed from her dream. Sweat drenched her skin. The dream had been so vivid and real, one which she had not had in a long time. Years ago, she used to have erotic dreams about Ash, but all that had stopped after she gave birth to Rurik, after Hring had explained the truth about why Ash had married her and how little he really thought of her.

Yes, she was attracted to him, but attraction wasn't enough. Not this time. She'd grown up and knew there was more to a marriage than a meeting of bodies at night.

Seven years ago she had found every excuse for his behaviour, believing he did care for her and his words were more than pretty phrases. After Rurik's birth, Hring had paraded Ash's discarded women in front of her. Each had confirmed Hring's words. In the end she had felt dirty and used in a way she'd never considered before.

Her idol had turned out to be base metal rather than gold. And she'd sworn no man would ever have that sort of power over her again.

Kara hugged her knees to her chest. Hring's sole purpose had been to punish her for defying him over Rurik. He had raged that Ash never cared about children or people and that he would never accept a weakling as a son.

Having met Ash again and seeing how much he wanted to meet Rurik, she had to wonder if Hring had twisted things. It would not be the first time. Deeds, not words.

Ash had left before and he would leave again. She should never forget that. What was it that his man had said—sea water ran in his veins? How long until the sea and the lure of raiding called him again? That was real, not whispers on the wind.

She could not count on Ash to be there when she needed him, for anything. She learnt from her mistakes.

She turned her head and saw that someone had placed a piece of hard bread and cheese beside her head. Whoever it was had also put an additional cloak over her. She moved her arm and a rich spicy scent enveloped her.

Ash. Who else? A lump formed in her throat at the thoughtful gesture.

After taking several mouthfuls of food, she wrapped the additional cloak tighter about her and tried to get her body to relax. The faint scent of expensive spice tickled her nostrils and she worried about the dream returning. Or, worse still, starting to believe the little gestures meant something more.

The hut remained cloaked in darkness. She stared up into the blackness and started to make lists of all the things which she'd have to do once they reached Jaarlshiem. Mundane practical things like seeing to the wool carding, making sure the apples were properly stored and the livestock had enough food for winter. Tedious tasks, but ones which made the estate prosper.

If she kept her mind on the real practical things, she wouldn't start believing in fantasy again.

Once they had returned to Jaarlshiem, it would be easier. She would be in familiar surroundings. Rurik would be there to distract her if she found herself at a loose end. There was rarely time to breathe, let alone dream.

She straightened her clothes and strode over to the door, pushing it open. The drizzle of yesterday evening had given way to a clear autumn sky. The last few stars hung in the rapidly greying sky. Her breath plumed in the very early morning light.

The sell-swords slept in the cold half-light. Indistinguishable lumps. The campsite was at peace. No one had even bothered to post a guard, despite Ash's earlier words. Kara rolled her eyes.

A movement made her turn and she saw Ash returning, obviously having been for a swim. Droplets of water fell from his hair, turning his tunic translucent. Kara shook her head, trying to get the last remnants of her dream from her brain.

He hurried over to her. Up close, he was even more intoxicating. A single drop of water hung in the hollow of his throat. Her fingers itched to capture it.

'If I had known you were awake, I would have asked you to join me.'

'To join you?'

'In the lake. Bathing. All is quiet. I've taken the last guard duty of the night along with Saxi.'

'Saxi?'

'One of my men. He is resting now that I've returned. The early hours always trouble me. But I remembered the lake over the crest of the hill and went swimming.'

Ash's words painted pictures in her brain of them in the lake, playing and splashing. She rapidly averted her gaze and concentrated instead on a twisted pine tree.

When she felt her heart calm, she risked a glance at him. In the dim light, she saw his eyes twinkled with mischief. He knew what pictures were in her head!

'It is…not the right time of day for that,' she stammered, pressing her hands against her gown.

'A pity.' He tilted his head, sending a soft spray of water over his shoulders and chest. 'Let's hope the next time I ask, it is the right time of day.'

It was never going to be the right time of day, Kara silently vowed. To go swimming with him would mean giving up her hard-won independence as she knew precisely how it would end. The memory of when he had taught her to swim invaded her brain.

Kara put her hand on her throat as the silence grew between them. She couldn't stand here tongue-tied, thinking about touching Ash.

'I had the food you left. Unnecessary, but welcome,' she blurted out.

'Good. I can't have you feeling faint or weak. You will slow everyone else down. You need to think about others.'

'I will get your cloak.' Kara swallowed her quick retort. Fighting solved nothing. 'You must have been freezing without it. There was no need to do that. I was quite comfortable with what I had. Remember for the next time.'

His eyes instantly hardened. 'I have other cloaks. No hardship. Without rest, you are a liability. I'd do the same for any of my men if they were exhausted.'

'Of course. I hadn't thought.' Kara shifted from foot to foot, feeling like a young girl again. She had once again rushed to the conclusion that Ash had done something for her benefit when it had been nothing of the kind. She ruthlessly squashed the feeling. She'd done nothing to be ashamed of except perhaps to be ungracious. How many times had she told Rurik off for doing the same? 'Thank you all the same. I appreciated it.'

'The water was wonderfully refreshing.' He gestured towards the lake and it was clear the subject was closed. 'There will be time if you would like to bathe before we depart for Jaarlshiem. It will refresh you. I promise not to peek…much.'

'No!' She put out a hand and slowly lowered it. Ash's expression showed her quick refusal amused him.

'I will be fine. I am fine,' she said, pleating her dress through her fingers. 'Perfectly refreshed after my night's sleep…and the food.'

'Indeed. I thought you might have had a disturbed night, which is why you are up so early.'

'You are up early, as well,' she countered, balling her fists. 'Stop this false concern.'

'There is nothing false about it.'

'I will be able to keep up today. Will you?'

'My ability to stay in the saddle has never been in doubt.'

'You have been away for seven years so I must take your word for it,' she said with crushing dignity.

A smile played in the corner of his mouth. 'Put me to the test. But why won't you swim?'

'I'm anxious to get home and see my son. My saddle needs checking. I hardly want to be accused of holding everything up as I was yesterday morning. Swimming will have to wait until I have time to spare.'

He dipped his head. 'You used to enjoy swimming. Every chance you had once I taught you, you went swimming. I remembered that about you when I was in the lake. Funny how simple things come flooding back once the key to memory is found. What happened to that fearless girl?'

Kara curled a fist. He only remembered now. What he meant was that he had not thought about her while he was gone. She kept back the words asking him how many times he had swum in a lake over the last few years. 'I grew up.'

'And forgot what fun you used to have. Does my son swim?'

Kara hesitated. Swimming had to wait until Rurik was older. She'd argued with Hring about it on the day he died. She dreaded to think how much she'd worry when Rurik finally did learn to swim. 'He is only six. Far too young.'

Ash made an irritated noise. 'My father made sure I could swim before then. Too many men drown for the lack of knowledge.' His face became carved from stone. 'Far too many men. But not me. I swam when the fire rained on the sea.'

'Your ability to swim saved your life?'

'We had to swim ashore when the ship went down.' His eyes looked straight through her. 'Lightning struck the mast and the entire ship blazed within a matter of heartbeats. Those who could not swim, died. I used to wonder if they were the lucky ones.'

'Why?'

'They didn't have to endure a fiery furnace and then the ice-cold hell of a Frankish dungeon.'

Kara clasped her hands together so she wouldn't gather him into her arms. He looked so much like Rurik when he said that. She had never realised how much they were alike. 'You must never consider that. You are alive and breathing.'

'I would still change places with them in a heartbeat. They deserved better.'

'You can't decide any man's fate but your own,' she said and hoped it helped.

'Rurik will start his lessons in survival as soon as we arrive in Jaarlshiem.'

'But...but...'

'I insist. It is my right as his father.'

Kara bowed her head. She knew Ash was right—Rurik should learn, but not yet. His last cold had been fierce and had lasted for months. 'There is plenty of time for it. Winter is coming on. The lake will be far too cold at this time of year. Ice will completely cover the lake in a few weeks' time.'

'I will teach him, Kara.' Ash gave a sudden heart-melting smile. 'And to ice skate...unless he already knows. Skating on the lake at Jultide is magical.'

'He will like that.' Kara knew she spoke the truth. Rurik loved anything that smacked of danger. He had asked last winter several times about skating on the bone skates. She had put him off, promising some time this winter. 'The ice must be thick enough. I won't have him skating on thin ice. Even walking on the ice is forbidden. I know how easy it is to fall through.'

'Of course you do. Very wise.'

'Thank you.'

'And my son obeys you?'

'I'm his mother. Of course he does as I ask.' Kara wrinkled her nose, considering. Rurik might be naughty on occasion, but he hadn't ever done anything truly dangerous, not in the way Ash had. And she had Gudrun to thank for keeping an eye on him and informing her if he misbehaved. She hated that Rurik accused Gudrun of being a spy or worse, but it was necessary, particularly after Hring died.

'What does he know how to do?'

'He knows lots of things,' Kara answered quickly. She had put a number of things off, telling herself that Valdar would teach Rurik and then he'd know how to do things properly, but it didn't mean she kept him tied to her skirts. 'Last winter was particularly troubling for me. Your father was ill... I wanted to be there when he learnt to skate. I scarcely had time to breathe. Rurik understood. He kept away from the lake.'

She winced. Except for that one incident, but luckily the dogs had found her before he had gone towards the thin ice.

Ash hung his head. 'I would say sorry, but words won't ease anything.'

'No, they won't. Ever.'

'He can learn this winter. There will be no

need for excuses.' He titled his head to one side. 'Do you still skate? You used to take terrible chances when you were little. I had to rescue you once. Your mother wrapped us both in blankets after you fell through the ice.'

Kara's cheeks flamed. Trust Ash to mention something she had done to try to get her father's attention. She had gone out farther than she should have. And her father had been too busy with his latest mistress to notice. Ash's jumping in and rescuing her had sealed her adoration of him.

'Far too much to do. Estates need careful management. If I took time off to skate, vital things would be left undone. But I know enough about the dangers of thin ice.'

He put his hand on her shoulder. 'Everyone deserves time to play. I am back now. You will be able to skate again and I will make sure no one gets into trouble.'

For how long? How long until the quiet comforts of home paled beside the possible glories of war? She choked the words back with difficulty. 'How kind, but will you even be here?'

'Winter is coming. I'm not about to leave an unsettled estate. When the spring comes, then we will see. You can't ask for more than that.'

Kara concentrated on breathing. In and out. What had she expected—Ash to declare that his travelling days were over because he had kissed her? Those delusions belonged in the past. He would go again. Late spring, if he could be bothered to stay for the planting. Early spring, if treasure and adventure still interested him. She had to make sure he didn't take Rurik's heart with him. Or hers, whispered a little voice. She silenced it.

'You can have your father's chamber. It is only right and fitting. I will move my things to Rurik's bedchamber. We shared it before your father died.'

His eyes became shadowed. 'You are determined to keep to the letter of our agreement.'

She pushed a strand of hair behind her ear. 'Nothing has happened to alter it.'

'I intend to honour the agreement.' He put a hand on her shoulder. 'You may have my father's chamber. I've no wish to occupy it. Too many memories of being dragged there by my ear in trouble for one thing or another. My old cupboard bed will be sufficient if it still exists. If not, I will find a spot to rest. Sometimes I find it difficult to sleep in an enclosed place.'

'It does.'

'It will do for now. Remember, Kara. I'm here. I want to make this marriage work.'

Kara's stomach clenched. How many times had she wanted him to be there and he wasn't?

How many times had she looked up at the painted ceiling and imagined his arms about her? 'I will let you know when I intend to take you up on the invitation.'

He gave a sudden bark of laughter, rich and flowing over like honey.

'What is so funny about that?' she asked, trying to sound fierce.

His smile transformed his face, reminding her of the old Ash. Younger and more carefree. Her breath caught as she realised that she had missed that smile more than she wanted to admit. 'You said when, not if. Progress. Little by little.'

'If, I meant if.' She rolled her eyes at her stupidity. Ash always twisted words to suit his purpose. 'I dislike being teased. Always.'

He sobered instantly and the carefree Ash vanished from his face.

'Be honest, Kara—' his hooded look penetrated deep into the hidden spaces of her soul '—there were times you enjoyed teasing very much. Surely you haven't forgotten the kissing games we used play?'

'I…I…' She knew precisely what he meant. During their short marriage, he had used to tease her body into pleasure, leaving her trembling on the brink. She was surprised that Ash remembered. She squashed the thought. He had not been enthralled enough to return quickly.

She glanced over her shoulder. 'Your men are stirring. Morning comes. We need to go.'

'You're far prettier when your cheeks have colour.' He cupped his fingers around her cheek. His breath fanned hers. 'Has your guard dog Valdar ever dared to tease you?'

'That is a personal question!' she said, turning her face away. She should have known. It was not about her, but fighting over her like a bone. She should lie or at least she should imply a greater intimacy, but she knew it was impossible. Valdar could not be a shield between them. It wasn't fair to use him in that way.

'Has he?' he demanded, capturing her chin. His mouth loomed above hers.

Her heart pounded in her ears. Say the wrong thing and he'd kiss her. A punishing kiss. What was worse was that a great part of her wanted to melt into it and see if it was like the kisses in her dream.

'He treats me with respect,' she said finally, turning her face from temptation. 'Valdar helped me immeasurably after your father died. But he is honourable. He wanted to wait for our wedding night.'

The tension went out of Ash's stance. He let her go. Kara stumbled backwards.

'You do not know how glad that makes my heart to learn what I always suspected—Valdar

Nerison failed to capitalise on his opportunities. If he had, we would be having a very different conversation.'

Kara pressed her hand to her temple. He'd deliberately misunderstood. 'Valdar was being honourable. He waited because...because I asked him to.'

Ash held out his hands. 'Hush. It's in the past. Know what I did, I did in order to return here with my head held high. I want to be the sort of husband you wanted and not a failure.'

'Do you know the sort of husband I require?'

'I like to think I do. I aim to be that man.' He put his hand on her shoulder. 'We are going to meet our son. To be a family together. Properly. I came home in part because I wanted a family.'

When she was a girl, she had thought she wanted a hero for a husband, but it wasn't what she really wanted. Kara's stomach turned over. She wanted to have a man to share the burden of running Jaarlshiem with, rather than being forced to be the sole person making soul-altering decisions. She wanted a husband who would welcome his children into the world and who would be there when trouble struck. She wanted someone who would be her life's partner, not her master.

Clanging in the back of her mind, she knew

all the things Ash had said before about his dreams and what he wanted to accomplish in his life. They had been dreams of glory and travel, not harvests and hearths. What if she started to count on him and he decided to go off adventuring again?

'Kara?' He gave her a questioning glance. 'Did you hear me? Your eyes have a faraway look. We are going to our home. I want to see what you have done to it.'

'I look forward to showing you, but now I need to see to getting my horse ready for the journey. The saddle kept slipping yesterday.'

'You suffered in silence? Speak and it can be fixed, but I have to know what the problem is.'

'You are impossible. That is the problem.'

Ash watched Kara stalk off. Her dress swished, revealing the shape of her ankles and the delicious curve of her bottom. He felt his body respond to the sight.

The years had enhanced her. The gods favoured him finally. Or perhaps they were playing one of their many tricks like the time three years ago when he'd thought he had enough money, only to be cheated.

He pinched the bridge of his nose. He had refused to look back and remember his old pleasures because it was soul-destroying and pointless to long for things which he couldn't have.

Memories assaulted him of how her skin flushed after they made love and how pleasant it had been to wake up with that bottom snuggled tight into him.

He shook his head and attempted to get his body under control.

It amazed him that simply being near to her did this to him. He wanted to learn all about her and the things she'd accomplished. Every time he encountered her, he wanted her more rather than less.

Women had not affected him in all the time he'd been gone. He had always supposed that it was because regaining his honour was far more important than a quick tumble. But it was more than that. And the fact scared him far more than facing any horde of warriors or the sea in full fury.

He hadn't allowed himself to think about her properly for years, but now that he was here, he wondered how he'd ever forgotten her. He had to hope that he could be the hero of her dreams. He certainly wanted to be.

'What made you so reluctant to take a risk?' he whispered. 'Who did this to you? And how can I get the trusting woman I married back? Can you accept me as I am or do I have to prove myself?'

* * *

Kara sat bolt upright in her saddle, willing the road to grow shorter and take less time. The closer they got to Jaarlshiem, the slower time seemed to go.

Always when she had been away she searched for the changes. Something was always different. This time there was no need to search. She knew—the man who rode beside her brought change.

She had left Jaarlshiem thinking she would be the bride of one man and had returned home with a different husband.

As Jaarlshiem and her reunion with Rurik came ever closer she had to seriously consider how she was going to break the news to him that his father had not died before he was born, but was alive. That his new father would not be Valdar, the man he nightly prayed to be his father, but instead his real father. Would it be better if she could convince Ash to wait and to gain Rurik's trust first? Rurik could be shy, particularly with strangers. She wanted the meeting to go well, rather than be strained.

'You're miles away,' Ash said, catching the reins.

Her horse stumbled and she managed to keep from falling by grabbing on to the saddle for dear life.

'What are you doing?' Indignation rose in her throat. Ash had no business grabbing the reins. He had nearly caused a bad accident.

'You allowed your horse to wander off the path. You were headed straight for the bog. It would have impeded our progress. Those bogs are notoriously tricky. Until my father had this road built, we lost men and horses every year, particularly in the autumn. When I was ten, my father made me find my way out. I was covered in stinking mud and shaking with cold by the time I reached home.'

'Your father was cruel.'

'But effective. I never boasted about my ability to navigate again. It helped me survive after I'd escaped.' He shrugged. 'I've no idea what you think about your horse's life, but I value it and yours.'

Kara saw where Ash pointed. A shiver went down her back. She hadn't even realised that they were that close to the bog.

'I was thinking about home and what waited for us,' she admitted, keeping her gaze straight ahead of her. 'There are so many things to be done once we arrive. I keep getting this feeling that something is wrong. Something has happened… It is always this way when I am away from Jaarlshiem. I can't wait to be back, but I worry that something terrible has happened.'

'You worry about our son.'

'Yes,' Kara admitted reluctantly. 'He is in my thoughts constantly. He's a little boy, Ash. It is a mother's job to worry. I want him to grow up happy and well.'

'What are you going to tell him, about me and my return?' He handed her back the reins. 'I assume you will want to be the one to tell him.'

Kara concentrated on her horse's twitching ears. He was giving her a choice. She thought he would blurt it out the instant he encountered Rurik. Ash had never been one to be tactful or realise that another's feelings mattered. 'You are giving me the opportunity to tell him? You are not simply going to leap down from your horse and demand to see your son?'

'How old is the boy? Six? The last thing I want is a scene in front of the *tuntreet*. I can remember what it was like to meet my father for the first time.'

'Can you? Hring never told that tale,' Kara said, surprised. Funny, it was the sort of tale Hring liked to tell—a warrior returning home.

'He had left just after my birth and didn't return until I was five. After my mother died.' He tilted his head to one side. 'Is my son timid? I hid behind my aunt's skirts when I first beheld my father and refused to greet him properly. It went badly.'

Kara bit her lip. Rurik was far too reckless for his own good. Far too impetuous. He liked to boast that nothing frightened him, but she knew the truth. She'd seen his white face and trembling hands. 'Not timid, but he adores Valdar and has talked of being his son for months. He takes disappointments hard.'

'I want him told, Kara. Before the sun goes down.'

Kara concentrated on her horse's twitching ears. 'You are going to allow me to do this in my own time.'

'As long as you do it when we arrive, you may use your own words.'

'That is far from the same thing.'

'Consider it a favour that I allow you that.' He gave a crooked smile which made her heart thump. 'To stop you from riding your horse into another bog.'

'You are not making this easy for me. I think it wise that we wait for a few days,' Kara said, making her mind up. 'Give him time to get used to you before you start demanding he love you.'

'He is my son. I have spent far too many years away from him.'

Ash spurred his horse on around the last bend before Jaarlshiem.

With every mile they had covered, Kara had

grown quieter and more remote. For a few heart-beats this morning when he had first spied her, he had thought he'd broken through her reserve, but she had retreated again into that impenetrable shell. And now she wanted to keep the truth from their son. Was he ever going to do enough?

'Ash! Stop! You are going too fast. It isn't a race.'

Ash turned slightly in his saddle. 'I take it the hall is in the same place.'

'It hasn't burnt down. You said I could tell Rurik. If you go before me...'

Ash stroked his chin. What was Kara concerned about? From everything she had said, it appeared she kept the boy tightly on the lead strings. It was the wrong approach. He knew when he had been forbidden things, he'd acted out, often times getting into more danger than he should have been in.

'We go together. Arrive together. I want to be there when you tell Rurik.'

Her cheek coloured. 'Yes, of course, if you don't trust me.'

'Caution remains my watchword.'

They rounded the bend and the gabled long house with all of its outbuildings stood before him. The road through the bog might be in disrepair, but the farm certainly wasn't. A prosperous air hung about the place.

The *tuntreet* with its leaves in autumnal splendour stood in front of the double doors. Even the air felt different, softer. Ash's heart clenched.

How many times had he dreamt of this? Riding in to reclaim his heritage. To see his father's eyes light up with the knowledge that his son had returned the sort of warrior a man could be proud of? And even now, he couldn't be sure he was. All he knew was that he had returned home.

It was harder riding the final few miles to Jaarlshiem than it had been when he first learnt of his father's death in Sand. Everywhere he looked, he saw ghosts and reminders of his former self, lurking and waiting for him to make a mistake.

'Ash, your father would be overjoyed that you have returned.'

'Are my feelings that obvious?' he enquired in a tone that normally had his men running for cover, rather than continuing with the subject.

Kara's hands tightened on her reins. 'They have always been to me. I'm your wife. I learnt to notice things years ago. Otherwise…'

A wave of guilt swept over Ash. Kara noticed things about him, but she didn't expect him to notice anything about her. There were times when he wanted to shake his younger self for his arrogant selfish behaviour.

'I hope you will allow me the chance to learn

things about you. I do want to learn. Everything. I already have immense admiration for you. There are not many women who could have ridden as hard as you have.'

Her red lips curved up into a sad smile. It was all Ash could do to keep from stopping their horses, hauling her into his arms and kissing her senseless. And that would be a mistake. She reminded him of his falcon, the one who had not trusted him after the broken wing. It had been Kara who had showed him how to tame the bird and regain its trust.

Patience where he had wanted everything at once.

He had had to relearn the lesson of the falcon several times, but it had served him over the past few years. All things came to the man who was patient and who noticed the little details.

'You mean you have forgotten.' Sadness and resignation laced her voice.

'I want to learn about the you of today, rather than trying to force you to be the young woman you once were.' Ash's nerves coiled. He had to get these words right. He had to undo the mistake of yesterday's careless words. He had to hope that the woman she now was would see the sort of man he wanted to be and approve. Faced with the *tuntreet,* he knew he'd never be the sort of warrior his father demanded.

'Do you?'

'You are infinitely more complex and I want to uncover all your secrets.'

He waited for her answering smile. 'I have no secrets. I never did.'

'Women always have secrets. Denying them simply makes me more determined to uncover them with you.' He turned in the saddle and looked directly into her deep blue eyes. Silently he wished he could do something to make her see that he was capable of being a hero. 'I do remember, Kara. You could always make your horse go faster. You have a way with animals, but I could climb higher than you and reach the birds' nests more swiftly. A point which used to irritate you to no end.'

'You're being impossible.'

Ash stilled and the teasing remark died on his lips.

He strained forward to see better. There was a movement on top of the left gable. His blood ran cold. The gods still had the strangest way of granting his wishes. Not a raven or even a cat, but a person. A child, clinging to the gable, who attempted to move, but slipped and started to dangle dangerously. And he knew being a hero didn't matter. Rescuing the unknown child did.

He spurred his horse, signalling to his men to follow.

'Is there something wrong, Ash?' Kara called after him.

'Look!'

'Help me!' A child's voice floated towards them. 'Someone please help me. Gudrun! Anyone!'

Kara's anguished scream rang out. 'Oh, gods! It's Rurik! And he is going to fall!'

Ash urged his horse forward. 'Not if I have anything to do with it.'

Chapter Eight

Rurik dangled from the top gable, hanging on with two hands with his little legs kicking out and his face screwed up in concentration. Beneath her two favourite elkhounds, Dain and Durin, circled, whining and howling, adding their cries to the sense of unease. Kara watched frozen in horror, unable to help. She was too far away and climbing up to the roof without a ladder was a tricky proposition, particularly in a dress. A wave of helplessness washed over her.

'Somebody do something. Please.'

Ash rode up to the house, vaulted from his horse and began to climb the longhouse wall with sure steps, favouring the right more than the left, the higher he went. 'Everything will be fine. Just keep talking to him. I will get there.'

Kara bit her knuckle. Ash walked with a limp. Was it paining him to climb? And once he reached Rurik, would he be strong enough to carry him down? Surely he was strong enough to rescue their son. He had to be. She didn't want to lose either one of them.

She tried to think of another plan, something that had a greater chance of success.

Gudrun rushed out of the longhouse, swiftly followed by several servants, flapping about like crows rather than doing anything productive. The two dogs went down, covering their eyes with their paws as if afraid to watch.

'Gudrun!' Kara called. 'What is going on here?'

The elderly woman glanced up at where Rurik dangled and immediately started to wail that it wasn't her fault, that it was all Virvir's doing. Kara readily believed that. Gudrun's great-nephew had led Rurik astray before. Too many times for her liking. If there was the slightest bit of mischief, Virvir was sure to be involved. But the boy was an orphan of eight. She simply didn't have the heart to banish him, but this time, he had gone too far, enticing the younger Rurik up to the top of the roof.

'Hang on, Rurik,' she called, giving Gudrun a hard glance. 'Mor is here. We will get you down!'

The words were somehow inadequate, but better than nothing.

Rurik kicked out his legs. 'Mor! Mor! Please help me.'

'Hang on.' Kara watched Ash steadily make his way up to the roof. He had done it before, many times. 'A...a friend of mine is coming for you. He is climbing the far wall now.'

The word 'father' struck in her throat. The last thing she wanted was for Rurik to become distracted and forget to hang on.

'A good friend!' she called out. 'He has climbed many times. He'll get you down. Hold on!'

'Valdar?' The note of hopefulness in Rurik's voice was painful to hear.

Ash turned his head and gave her a strange look. Kara clenched her teeth. Ash had to understand Rurik's safety was paramount.

Gudrun pulled Kara's sleeve.

'Is that who I think it is?' she asked in a loud whisper. 'There is only one man I can think of who could climb like that.'

Kara gave a brief nod. The elderly woman's eyes went round as plates.

'I always used to wonder how he climbed up on the roof,' the woman muttered. 'But he'll be too late.'

'A very good friend is coming to get you. Hang on!' Kara called again, ignoring Gudrun's mutterings. 'He will get you down. Trust him.'

'Want Valdar!' Rurik kicked out again, trying to swing his legs up to the gable, but they were too short.

'This man is a friend. You will like him.'

When they were both safe, she'd make the proper introductions. To everyone.

Right now, Ash seemed to be taking far too long climbing up. She knew he had climbed up to the gable in the past. Many times, normally to cause mischief. She could remember being utterly terrified and refusing to follow, but he had gone ahead. His father had beaten him for his bravado when he'd come down, but Ash had never cried or flinched. Kara had brought over ointment for his wounds the next day. He had taken it, but he had also made a point of climbing up the wall again and carving his rune on the topmost gable, simply to show he could.

'Mor! I didn't mean to, Mor! Don't be angry. Help me!'

Angry? She was terrified and she wanted to murder Rurik for doing something that was utterly forbidden, but she would never beat him like Ash's father had beaten Ash. Virvir might have suggested it, but he didn't have to follow like some devoted thrall. But mostly she wanted him to be unhurt and she couldn't see how this was going to end happily, even with Ash here.

'Keep still. You will be rescued, but you must

stay absolutely still. Conserve your strength. Hang on tight to the gable. You can do that. For me?'

'Mor, my arms are getting tired.'

'You must hang on! For me. Do it for your mother!'

Ash's men arrived and clustered around the base of the gable.

'Your cloak, give them your cloak, Kara,' Ash called down. He had reached the roof ridge and was inching along towards where Rurik clung. His face was contorted with concentration and pain. Clearly the climb had taken its toll.

'My cloak?'

'For a net…in case… Yours is large enough.'

Then she saw what he was saying. If the men held the cloak beneath Rurik, they could potentially break any fall. Her fingers fumbled on the string. She gave an impatient tug and the cloak came off. She threw it down.

'Thank you, my lady,' one of the more scarred sell-swords said, catching it with an easy grace. 'Your son will be fine. Ash knows what he is doing. Now you go in. Let us do our job.'

Kara slid off the horse and planted her feet firmly in the ground. Gudrun put an arm about her, but she shrugged it off. 'I stay here. I'll keep out of the way and won't interfere. Just catch him if he falls.'

'We intend to, ma'am. We intend to.'

Silently she prayed to any god who might be listening that her child would be spared. And that nothing would happen to Ash either. She had only recently had him return to her life. It wouldn't be fair to lose him so quickly, but when was life ever fair or just?

She wanted to curl up in a ball and hide her face, but that was impossible. She had to watch. Both of them. Ash inching along, moving ever closer, and Rurik desperately clinging on.

How had this happened? How had he been allowed to run free with Virvir when she had given strict instructions that the pair were to be separated? And that Rurik was to be watched at all times.

She'd trusted Gudrun to look after him properly and this had happened. She should have guessed that this could happen, but taking him to Sand would have caused more trouble.

Time enough for answers later. And she'd get them. Virvir would have to be punished. And Rurik would have to learn the consequences of following the older boy's lead.

Ash reached Rurik. His fingers closed around one of Rurik's wrists at the same instant the boy let go. For a heartbreaking moment her son dangled, then Ash pulled him up the roof to safety of a sort.

Kara remembered to breathe again. Her son was safe. She brushed away a single tear. Her limbs trembled and she wanted to sink to the ground. Ash had reached Rurik in time.

Now to get them both down. She could hear the low murmur of his voice, but not what he actually said.

Then she saw Ash pointing to her and Rurik giving her an enthusiastic wave.

Kara ground her teeth. Ash should be getting Rurik down, rather than encouraging wilful behaviour.

'Come down now! The pair of you!'

Ash cupped his hand to his ear. 'What was that? I can't hear you properly. The view is lovely up here. Thank you for asking.'

She heard Rurik's laugh ring out and ground her teeth. Typical Ash, playing to the crowd. Everything had to be made into a joke.

Surely Ash understood the job was only half-done. Rurik needed to be coaxed down. Not until his little feet were on the ground and she'd been able to wrap her arms about him would she believe that he was truly safe.

'On the ground now!'

'Impossible,' Ash retorted.

'But...but...you climbed up there,' Kara said in dismay. 'Surely you can carry Rurik back the way you came.'

'We climb down once you arrange for a ladder to be placed somewhere where we can actually get to it.' Ash indicated where he wanted the ladder put. 'It would be foolhardy in the extreme to take Rurik back along the ridge of the roof. He is far too tired. My leg aches too much to be trusted.'

'I'm not tired, Mor. I can do anything.' Kara heard the tell-tale whine in Rurik's voice.

'A ladder is on its way,' Kara said, ignoring Rurik's continued protest.

Kara motioned to two of the farmhands, who ran to get a ladder from one of the outhouses. The ladder was rapidly placed against the gable end, precisely where Ash had indicated.

It was a good four feet short, but there were some clear handholds. It should be a simple enough matter to get down to the ladder and then descend.

'Be careful, the pair of you,' Kara whispered.

As she watched, Ash had Rurik loop his arms about Ash's neck and hook his legs about his body. Then he slowly began his painstaking way down to the ladder. Every breath seemed to take an age. He reached the ladder and Kara expected Rurik to scrabble down, but his arms remained firmly locked about Ash's neck.

The tension ran out of Kara's shoulders. Ash

was being sensible. He was not enticing Rurik to do more and more dangerous things.

Suddenly they were down. Rurik let go. Ash sank to the ground, rubbing his bad leg, his face contorted in pain.

Rurik with his blond hair flying came running across the yard to her, seemingly oblivious to the danger he had just been in. 'Mor! You're home! I thought you would be coming and I wanted to see. Only I couldn't see very well and Virvir dared me. Only he took away the ladder once he got down as the men needed it. He said that only babies couldn't climb down. I am not a baby!'

Kara struggled to keep her temper. Shaking or beating Virvir wasn't going to do anyone any good. But he would be gone from here before the day was out. She gave Gudrun a significant look. The elderly woman had the grace to pale.

Gudrun pulled Virvir by the ear. The overly plump boy gave a shriek. 'I will deal with it, ma'am. It won't happen again. But you know how your son is. Always into mischief. Just like his father.'

'We will have words later, Gudrun.'

The woman dragged Virvir, protesting loudly his innocence.

Kara knelt down and looked directly into Rurik's eyes. Even though she knew he disliked being touched in public, claiming that he was far too big for such things, she couldn't help running her hand down his thin shoulders, checking to make sure her son was fine. Rurik made a face and tried to shrug her off.

'I promised I'd come back,' she whispered against his hair. 'Climbing to the gable would not make me come any quicker.'

Rurik struggled. She reluctantly forced her hand to her side. Only six and he was already growing away from her, chafing at the apron strings.

'You promised me Valdar! Where is my new father?' Rurik peered around the yard. His little face showed increasing signs of anxiety and dismay. 'Virvir said I was lying and no warrior like Valdar Nerison would want to be my father. That was why you refused to take me to Sand. You were…you were ashamed to have a boy like me. But I said that was a lie! A lie! But I want Valdar!'

'Good for you!' Kara declared. She should have banished Virvir months ago when this friendship first started to develop. 'You had to stay at home to look after the estate while I was gone. It had nothing to do with my being ashamed of you! How could anyone ever think such a thing!'

'Listen to your mother, Rurik,' Ash said, coming up behind Rurik and placing his hand on Rurik's shoulder. 'I know how proud of you she is. She rode until she nearly dropped with exhaustion to reach you and explain the news.'

Although he was upright and moving now, his eyes still bore the shadow of pain. Seeing him tower above their son, Kara was struck at how much alike they looked. They had the same nose and chin as well as the same basic body shape. No one could mistake Rurik for being anyone but Ash's son.

'Mor won't understand why I had to climb,' Rurik protested. 'Virvir dared me. I'm not a baby Mor's boy.'

'I told you she would be far from happy about you being up there. There are good reasons why gable climbing is expressly forbidden. Warriors take their punishments like warriors.'

'Yes, sir, you did.' Rurik stuck his little chest out. 'Mor, I'll take my punishment like a warrior. Like he says warriors do.'

Kara's heart sank. Punishment like a warrior. She knew what that meant. She'd fought Hring for years. Now she had to had fight Ash, as well? Just when she thought her son was safe.

'But why is Valdar not here?' A tiny tear trickled down Rurik's face. 'What did I do wrong? Did he leave like my father did…because…because of me?'

Kara glanced at Ash. He had been true to his

word. He had saved her son and had not said who he was. She also had failed to realise about Rurik's worries and private fears.

'You've done nothing wrong except climb where you know it is forbidden. And how could your father have left because of you when I didn't even know I was carrying you?'

Rurik's mouth formed an O.

She took a deep breath. She had to tell him now. Rurik's little adventure might be unwelcome, but it provided the best possible introduction to Ash. Ash had been right. Rurik needed to know as soon as possible who his true father was. He had to understand that Ash wasn't ashamed of him.

'Valdar is not going to be your father, Rurik,' she said gently, kneeling down and preparing to draw him into her arms again.

Rurik's face crumpled, but he pulled away from her. He probably would have run, but Ash had hold of his shoulder. 'Then I won't have a father like always. Virvir is right. No warrior wants to be my father. Ever.'

'No, Virvir is utterly wrong. You have a father. Your real father returned. Just as you said he would when you were a tiny boy. He came back and he is very excited to meet you.' Kara stood up and kept her eyes trained on Ash. Ash did not release his grip of Rurik's shoulder. 'Did the man who rescued you tell you his name?'

A frown developed between Rurik's brows. 'He...he said he was a friend of yours and Valdar's. If I did everything he said, I'd see both of you soon. My mother and my father.'

Kara put a hand over her eyes. She had misjudged Ash. He kept his word. The temptation to tell Rurik up there, when he could not have been sure that they would make it down, must have been immense, but he was allowing her to explain. 'He is certainly a friend, a true friend, but the man who rescued you is your real father.'

Rurik's bottom lip stuck out. 'My father is dead. Stop funning, Mor. I am not a baby. Far-far told me never to forget that. My father died in a shipwreck and he is never coming back. I need to be a braver warrior than my father.'

Ash stood frozen. Kara wished that Hring was there so she could wring his neck. Here she thought he had been filling her son's ears with tales of adventure to pass the time, but he had been setting Rurik an impossible task. And he still held the power to hurt Ash after his death.

'No, sweetheart. Your grandfather was very wrong. We all were. We all thought he was dead, but we were wrong. Your father is alive and a great warrior. See all the men who follow him.'

Over Rurik's head, she looked at Ash. He mouthed 'thank you.'

'Did my father leave because he was ashamed of me?' Rurik asked the ground.

'I am very glad to meet you,' Ash said.

'Don't you want to greet him? Properly?' Kara asked gently when Rurik refused to lift his head. 'What is wrong, Rurik? Your father just saved your life.'

'Did he leave because of me?' he whispered.

'Who on earth would have told you that?' Kara asked completely perplexed.

'Virvir.'

'Who is Virvir? Where is this know-nothing? You have mentioned him several times and I want to see the measure of him!' Ash exploded. 'You should listen to your mother. She knows better than most that I had no idea about you until I returned to this country.'

Rurik cringed slightly at the strength of his voice.

Ash shifted uncomfortably and wished he'd controlled his temper.

The last thing he wanted was for his son to be frightened of him. He could clearly remember how dreadful it had been to meet his own father. He'd been so excited that he'd wet his trousers and his father had been utterly disgusted. Despite his aunt's soothing words, the memory of his father's fearsome look had haunted him for years, drove him to try things far too soon.

The ache in his left leg reached a fever pitch and he bent down, rubbing it, all the while keeping his gaze on Rurik. The leg had never properly healed since the shipwreck, but the pain in his leg did not compare to the pain in his heart. His son. His son had done something very dangerous and, had he not arrived when he did, the outcome could have been unthinkable. And his son thought that he'd left because of him! The thought beggared belief.

'You spoke about him up on the roof, Rurik, and now I learn he has been speaking lies,' Ash said in as gentle a manner as he could manage.

'Virvir is my best friend for ever,' Rurik said, puffing out his chest. 'He knows everything. Everything. Where to find the best birds' eggs, how to ride a horse bareback and how to lift a sword. He runs faster than the wind and he can ice-skate on the thinnest ice. He isn't a baby like me.'

With a great effort, Ash pushed his temper away. Virvir would be dealt with later. Right now, he wanted to make a proper start with his son. He wanted to clasp the boy to his chest and drink in the fresh clean scent of his skin. It had been a magical but utterly frightening experience rescuing his son. Being able to hold his hand for the first time with the certain knowledge that if he failed to get it right, they would both perish.

'He doesn't know everything because I am your father. I know why I left.' Ash regarded his son's blue eyes, which reminded him so much of Ash's late mother. 'I would never have gone if I had known that I had a son, particularly a son who can climb like you do. You are the sort of boy any warrior can be proud of.'

Rurik dipped his head and drew a line in the dirt with his foot. 'What I did was dangerous. But Virvir called me a baby and a liar. I had to show him.'

'You're neither. You must know that!' Kara said sharply. 'Why did you have to prove it to him?'

Ash gave her a warning look. Didn't she understand about little boys? He had done a number of equally dangerous things on a dare. And it was no good talking about how horrible this boy was, Rurik had to be shown the truth. Rurik needed other heroes.

'Because I did.' Rurik's bottom lip trembled. 'Because I never get to do anything! I'll never become a warrior if I never test my skill. Far-far made me promise to always test my skills.'

Ash glanced over to where Kara stood, looking completely shocked and drained. It was sheer strength of will that was keeping her upright.

He wanted to pick her up and carry her to the bed they used to share and then watch over her until she recovered. He checked his movement. It would be wrong for so many reasons.

From what she had said earlier, he doubted Kara liked Rurik to do much of anything, particularly anything that held a hint of danger.

He had constantly rebelled against the strictures Gudrun had put on him. Kara knew that. She and her mother had bound up his wounds after his mishaps enough times.

Why would Rurik be any different?

The boy needed to be taught how to do things properly. When his father had returned, Ash had finally been allowed to learn things, but Ash intended to be a different sort of father. For Hring, it had all been about being the best warrior and ensuring his son excelled. Ash wanted his son to have the skills to survive should the worst happen.

What Rurik did when he was grown up was up to Rurik, but he would have the skills necessary to make an informed choice. Kara would have to give way on this matter. A boy's training was a father's responsibility.

'I'm sure your mother means you need to learn the proper time and place to climb. A warrior needs to learn to obey those he serves. And at the moment you serve your mother.'

Rurik's mouth became an O as he digested the piece of information. 'But she says I'm too young. Always when I ask, she says this. And Gudrun, too. Nobody lets me do anything.'

Ash struggled to keep a straight face. Gudrun he could have predicted, but Kara had always seemed eager for an adventure, or agreeing that he should take a risk. It pained him that she had changed so much. 'Things will change now that I have returned.'

Rurik's eyes shone. 'Truly?'

'You're only six,' Kara said with a no-nonsense tone in her voice. When had Kara developed that tone? 'How many times do I have to tell you, Rurik—wait until you get older. The time will come.'

'I want the time now.'

'Now that I have returned,' Ash said, giving Kara a significant look, 'I will make sure you learn how to do all the things a warrior needs to know. Like my father taught me.'

He ignored Kara's swift intake of breath. He was willing to give her time to decide about their marriage, but he absolutely refused to compromise on their son.

'You knew Far-far? We scattered his ashes at the base of the *tuntreet*. I was very big and brave then.'

Ash did not trust his voice for several heartbeats. Big and brave, because he hadn't been there. He had missed out on so many things. Some from necessity, but some from his stubbornness. He could not replace the sands of time, but he could try to be there in the future, for the important events. He swallowed hard and waited until the lump in his throat cleared. 'He was my father. It is good to know you stood in so well for me. I will visit the *tuntreet* later and you can show me precisely where you poured the ash, if you remember.'

'I remember.'

He ruffled Rurik's blond hair. 'Good boy.'

He swore the boy grew several inches in front of him.

'Ash Hringson, you have returned,' Gudrun said, coming forward, destroying the moment. She'd always had that knack of butting in.

Ash gave a curt nod to Gudrun. 'Good day to you, Gudrun. It is good to know you were looking after my son with the same zeal you used to look after me.'

Gudrun flushed, but she dropped to a low curtsy, hiding her features. 'Your lordship…are you real?'

Silently he swore the woman and this Virvir, whom Rurik appeared to idolise, would be gone before nightfall. Changes would have to be made. 'I had better be or otherwise a ghost rescued my child.'

Two bright spots appeared on Gudrun's cheeks. 'Of course. My great-nephew had just come to fetch help before you arrived. The young lord had climbed when he shouldn't have and my great-nephew realised the danger. He would have been rescued, but it was good that you arrived when you did.'

Ash schooled his features. Trust Gudrun to tell the tale her way. She always did.

'Your great-nephew's name wouldn't happen to be Virvir?'

'That is right, your lordship. He is a strong boy. My sister's son's child. You remember my sister? She used to give you cake.' Gudrun motioned to a sturdy-looking boy with pig-like eyes. Ash knew the type—a bully and a coward, always willing to lead others astray. He had encountered enough of them on his travels. 'A bright strapping lad he is, too. Not an ounce of trouble in his body. A real credit to your old aunt. He came straight away when he saw Rurik was in trouble.'

Virvir beamed. Ash ground his teeth and retained a narrow lead on his temper.

'Indeed.'

'Virvir, see, I made it down and I do have a father,' Rurik called out.

'I'm sure he never doubted it, your lordship.' Gudrun dropped another curtsy, but not before she gave Virvir a cuff on the ear. 'If you don't mind me asking, where have you been, your lordship? These past seven years?'

'He has been in Viken, Gudrun,' Kara said with an edge to her voice. 'Ash has returned a hero. He was involved in the raid on Lindisfarne which has been on everyone's lips lately. He will tell the tale where everyone can hear so there can be no mistakes or embroidering. I think you had best take Virvir to the kitchen where he can do his job.'

Ash struggled not to smile. Kara obviously had dealings with Gudrun's trade in gossip.

'Does your uncle know you are home, my lord?' Gudrun asked, stopping in mid-waddle. 'He will be overjoyed to see you. I can remember how close you once were.'

Close once. Had he been as naïve as Rurik with his hero-worship? He could recall Kara berating him for it. He should have listened, but with a young man's arrogance he'd seized the opportunity to prove his worth with both hands.

Ash inclined his head. 'My uncle was there when I made my presence known…at the wedding, which was cancelled for obvious reasons.'

'Mor, you are not marrying Valdar?' Rurik's voice sounded shrill. 'Why?'

Ash kept his body still and waited. Kara was fully capable of not telling him what she was thinking, but he doubted she would lie to their son. Her cheeks flushed.

'How can I be when I am married to your father?' Kara's eyes pinned him to the spot.

Their son seemed to accept the statement at face value, but a cold prickle ran down Ash's back.

An answer, but not the emphatic one he desired. Another scrap of comfort, but he wanted more, particularly now that they were back in Jaarlshiem. He would show her that he was the right sort of husband for her and that she should give him a second chance. The key to her was through Rurik. He felt certain of that.

'I want to have a look around the estate,' he said to prevent the urge to pick Kara up and take her somewhere and seduce her into agreeing. Patience. 'Perhaps you would care to show me, Rurik, as you have been looking after things in my absence.'

Rurik flushed. 'It is Mor. Mor runs everything.'

Of course, Kara would. Who else? It was obvious from the state of the outbuildings that the estate prospered. 'I am sure your mother will allow you to show me. She will have things she wishes to do or she may come with us.'

He waited for Kara to say that she wanted to join them. Absently he rubbed the knot in his left leg. The climb had done more damage than he'd thought it would. It had never been right since that fight with the Ranerike three years previously. Ivar the Scarred had done his best to set the bone, but he was no healer. If he asked Kara to look at it, she might start questioning why he hadn't come home then. The longer he was back here, the more the guilt rose in his throat. Ash attempted to push it away. He could not change the past. The less said, the soonest mended.

'What do you think, Kara? Is Rurik capable of showing me around the estate? Or he is too young?'

Kara's face was a study in self-control, utterly expressionless except for the firming of her mouth. Her stubborn expression, her mother had called it. Ash smiled. He could remember things.

'It is good of you to ask Rurik,' she said stiffly. 'There are things I must attend to.'

'A bath?' he enquired softly. 'You mentioned it earlier.'

She rolled her eyes. 'Please grant me a little intelligence. I've a list of things that has to be done before I can consider looking after my own needs.'

'Or maybe you are waiting for me to join you in the bath?'

'Go!' She pointed, but her cheeks flamed bright red and she made no attempt to contradict him. The thought made him absurdly happy. 'Rurik, make sure you show your father everything, but no more climbing.'

Rurik promised and they started off. Ash came down far too heavily on his left foot on the third step as he adjusted his stride to keep pace with Rurik. He winced at the bone-jarring pain.

'Wait! What have you done to your leg, Ash?'

'An old injury. It will pass.' He forced a smile. 'One would almost think you cared, Kara.'

She tapped her foot on the ground. 'It doesn't look old to me.'

'I strained it a bit during the climb. We rode a great deal without stopping. My muscles always seize up. The walk ought to ease it. Movement seems to help. Always.'

'This has happened before?'

'Enough times. I injured the leg many years ago. It is when I sit in one position for a long time that it locks and aches, Loki take it.'

'Have you seen a healer about it?'

'What can a healer do?'

Her brows puckered delightfully. 'There are things…'

'Maybe my favourite healer wasn't around.' He leant forward. 'You can have a look later.'

'You are being impossible, Ash. But I will hold you to it. I want to see that leg.'

Ash absently rubbed it. 'Some time. Not now.'

She cocked her head towards Rurik. 'Your son wants to show you Jaarlshiem.'

'You don't mind?'

'He has waited a long time to meet you. Now go. I have other things to do.' Her full lips curved upwards. 'And I do promise to rest, once I have satisfied myself that everything is how it should be.'

'I expect you to rest whether everything is to your satisfaction or not.'

Ash shook his head. He had done something right for a change. He was going to figure out a way to get Kara back into his bed and into the marriage. It would be like he had never left. It would be as he had planned back in Viken—his wife and his family waiting for him. He could have everything.

'Come, Far.' Rurik slipped his hand into Ash's. 'You need to see what Mor and I have done to your estate.'

Ash's fingers tightened around the slender hand. Far. He had never expected to be called that ever. Not truly. Silently he vowed to be more worthy of that name than his father had been. He would ensure Rurik grew up with the proper guidance, rather than being continually challenged to prove his worth.

He looked over to where Kara stood discussing something with one of her women. A gentle breeze caused a strand of hair to work itself free. With her slender fingers, she captured it and put it firmly back into place. The very picture of the perfect mother and homemaker.

He owed her so much. She had made his estate prosper, but more importantly she'd given him a son. Words were inadequate. He knew that she only had to ask and he'd do his best to get anything for her.

Anything.

Ash checked his words, swallowing them. Rash statements had led to his current predicament. The one thing she was likely to ask for was the only thing he refused to do—allow her to go. This time he would take his time.

It came to him. This was not about getting her into his bed as he'd thought back in Sand, but having her in his life. He wanted her as his wife and the mother of his children, not some mythical person, but Kara. He wanted to share his life with her. And it scared him more than when he had lain amongst the corpses. To allow someone to have that sort of power over him.

Why was it that he only appreciated things when he had lost them?

Patience. It had served him well when he'd looked to regain his honour. He had to wait when every instinct in his body told him to act. He couldn't. His entire future was at stake and he knew he wanted this far more than anything else.

'Help me to make the right choice, Kara,' he whispered. 'Before either of us does something irrevocable.'

Chapter Nine

The shouting alerted Kara that something dreadful was wrong. She had just finished inspecting the kitchens and was about to go to the bath house. Anything to avoid checking up on Ash and Rurik. She owed him that much for saving her boy. What could go wrong with a simple tour? But now she could hear his voice shouting across the yard.

She picked up her skirts and ran to the graveyard where she was certain the noise had come from. Rurik stood alone outside the family crypt, weeping.

Kara wrapped her arms about her son. 'Is something wrong? Where is Ash? Where is your father?'

'My father...' Rurik gave a convulsive shudder and broke into fresh sobs. 'I only wanted to show him where his gravestone was and he started shouting at me. Make him go away. I don't want him here. Far-far said that he was always disappointed in him and that I had to be a better warrior because of it.'

'When did he say that?'

Rurik scrubbed his eyes with the back of his hand. 'Once when we were out here.'

'Did you say something to your father?'

'He didn't want to see the gravestone Far-far had carved for him! Then he shouted at me because I told him he had to.'

'Go and see Thora. I was just in the kitchen and she might have a treat for you.' Kara motioned towards the kitchen. She had to hope that Ash hadn't heard Rurik's words. She knew how much Ash wanted his father to be proud of him.

Rurik's eyes grew big and the crying instantly stopped. 'I like treats.'

He raced off. Kara heaved a sigh as no one else appeared. What she had to say to Ash would be said in private. But she renewed her determination that she would keep Rurik safe.

She went into the graveyard and saw Ash, sitting on the ground with his head in his hands.

'Ash? Why did you shout at Rurik?'

Ash lifted his head. 'The boy wanted me to go into the graveyard. He said my father would be ashamed of me. I told him that I couldn't care less what my father thought.'

'Rurik hates being shouted at.'

'I wasn't shouting at him precisely, but I don't want to see my gravestone. Not today. And I don't care what my father would have wanted! Or how he feels about me! Why break the habit of a lifetime?'

Kara put her hand on her hip. This had all the signs of a disaster. Rurik and his grandfather used to love going to visit Ash's gravestone. Rurik had probably been very excited to show his father and then Ash had ruined it. 'This could have been avoided.'

'How?'

'You yelled at Rurik because you were far too stubborn to let me look at your leg earlier. What sort of man shouts at a six-year-old because of what a dead man might think?'

'He needs to accept that men shout or otherwise he will be no good on the battlefield.'

'Will you allow me to see the leg? Now?' Kara knelt beside him. 'If you had done so earlier, maybe you wouldn't have such pain. Rurik has been through enough today without this. You were his new hero. You destroyed him.'

'Forget it, Kara!' Ash made a cutting motion. 'Obviously there is nothing I can do which is right in your eyes, so just forget it. What is the point of explaining? And I told you before I know how to deal with my injury. I've learnt how. It wasn't the pain in my leg. I don't know if I can do this.'

'Why did you bother to come back, Ash? Why won't you accept any help?'

'Just go!'

'I will go, but maybe you should think about why you came back at all.'

Ash dropped his head on his knees, rather than watch her walk away. The sheer pain in his leg was excruciating, but it was nothing compared to the searing pain in his heart. And there was nothing anyone, not even a skilled healer like Kara, could do to ease that pain.

He had frightened his son. Rather than being a hero, he had behaved like the snivelling weakling his father always used to say he was. And he knew he couldn't play at being a hero any more. He couldn't be the man he wanted to be for Kara and that hurt worse than the pain in his leg.

Ash pressed his hands to his eyes. He might not be able to be the sort of man his father wanted him to be or even the hero of Kara's girlish dreams, but he could be a father to Rurik. He could be the sort of father he'd wanted as a child, the proper sort who taught his child skills, rather than shouting at them. And he wasn't prepared to walk away from Kara. Not yet, not until he'd tasted her lips.

'Go? I have just begun to fight, Kara, but this

time, I am fighting for you on my terms, not my father's.' Ash wiped his hands on his trousers. 'And the place to start is looking at my grave.'

Coward, she was being the worst sort of coward. Avoiding Ash. Finding little jobs to do so that she wouldn't have to confront him about his behaviour at the graveyard.

She wanted him to like it, but was certain he'd object to various things, when it shouldn't matter. His opinion should make no difference. She refused to go back to being the girl whose entire well-being hinged on whether or not Ash smiled. She was proud of her accomplishments and she wanted him to think her a good mother, but after Rurik's little escapade, he must think her awful.

Kara pressed her hands against the low table where the wool skeins were spread, ready for her inspection, and willed the doubts to be gone.

Her women had been busy while she was away. She couldn't fault them, especially Gudrun. She could always tell Gudrun's skeins because of the way she wrapped the thread. No one else managed that little twist at the end. Gudrun had done all that she'd said. Kara was impressed by how much she had managed to do. Unfortunately Gudrun's efficiency meant that, after she'd finished the inspection, she would have run out of excuses. She would have to return to the hall and face Ash.

'What would you do? Would you go to the stables and see if the horses were bedded in properly or go to the great hall?' she asked Dain, who gave a soft woof in response.

'My thoughts exactly. The stables next and then the great hall.' Kara bent down and stroked his silky fur. It helped to be back amongst her animals. They never judged her. It was so much easier than dealing with people. Over the past few years with Hring's illness, she had not been able to escape as often as she might have liked, but she jealously guarded the time she had with her animals, allowing them to have free run of the house.

What could she say to Ash after he had saved Rurik, and then frightened the boy with his shouting over nothing? She'd lost her temper, but it didn't change things. Ash was going to be precisely the wrong sort of father for Rurik.

'Here I find you.' Ash's low voice flowed over her. 'I never thought wool would take precedence over guests.'

Kara dropped one of the skeins and sent several spinning whorls flying. Dain gave a sharp bark and disappeared out of the room. She hurriedly bent down to pick everything up, concentrating on that, rather than on Ash's solid figure in the doorway.

'Hardly guests. This is your home, where you grew up. Were you expecting a ceremony?'

'My welcome was eventful enough, but I wanted to know why you have gone into hiding. I wanted to let you know I looked at my grave and my father's. Thank you for the runes on both stones.'

'I thought you might want some time alone.'

'It was harder than I thought to go to that graveyard.'

Kara resisted the urge to smooth the creases from his forehead. His father's death was hard for him. For her, she'd seen the relief in Hring's eyes when he had died after years of struggle. Ash only remembered his father in good health.

'Your father would have appreciated it.'

'Rurik said—'

She put her hand up. 'Hush, Rurik is a child. Your father did appreciate you. It was why Rurik wanted to show you the gravestone.'

'I wish I believed that.' He captured one of the whorls and dropped it on the table. 'At the *tuntreet,* I felt more at peace than at the graveyard. But even after you had gone, it took me an age to work up the courage to look at the runes. I'm glad I did. The words were simple, but my father did put the stone up. And the pain in my leg has eased. I know what to do with it. It knots up sometimes.'

Close up, Kara saw the water droplets clinging to his hair. His clean masculine scent teased her nostrils, replacing the stench of wool and dye. She was absurdly glad that she had changed into a deep-blue gown, with a lighter blue for the apron dress over the top. Something to bring out her eyes and make her skin look less sallow. She tried to squash the feeling. Looking for Ash's approval was the way towards madness. She knew what had happened before. She couldn't risk her heart being broken again. It had taken far too long to heal last time.

Ash needed to show that he was here to stay and shoulder responsibility.

'I had it put up. It seemed the right thing to do. Hring agreed when he regained some measure of speech,' she said into the silence.

Ash nodded. 'Thank you, then. You have done more than I thought possible. Without you this estate wouldn't exist.'

'The welcome feast is well in hand for tomorrow night.' She placed the skein on the table with a trembling hand. He did appreciate what she had done. 'There will be plenty to eat and a skald to sing. He knows the latest sagas, or so Thora assures me.'

He raised his brow, acknowledging the change of subject. 'You didn't wait to bathe with me.'

She hated the way the words brought old memories to the surface. Of Ash and her sharing a bath and then cooling off in the lake. She wrenched her mind from that memory, replaced it with the memory of Hring's revelation about Ash's intentions and his other women. Her breathing steadied.

'The opportunity presented itself and so I took it. You wouldn't believe how much has to be done. Goodness knows when I will be finished tonight. It is always the same whenever I'm away.'

She picked up a skein and pretended to count, waiting for him to make his excuses and leave.

'You haven't even asked me what I think of your stewardship.' He captured the skein from her nerveless fingers. 'I thought you'd be curious.'

'There were a lot of people who wanted to speak with you and welcome you. I knew you would find me when you had the time to spare.' The excuse sounded feeble to Kara's ears, but it was the best she had.

'You excelled. Rurik said that it was all you, not Valdar. And I am inclined to agree. I owe you a debt I can never repay.'

Kara pretended to straighten the pleats of her apron dress. 'Thank you, thank you very much.'

'We need to discuss Rurik's training. It is a way I can help take the burden off you. What skills does he have?'

'His training doesn't have to begin right away.' Kara concentrated on the wool, trying not to think about Ash's broken arm or the other injuries he had suffered during his training. 'Allow him time to get used to you. At the graveyard, he said—'

'His training begins in the morning. You have kept him as a baby for far too long.'

Kara stared at Ash, open mouthed. After turning her son into a quivering jumble of nerves, he wanted her to entrust the same child to him. 'And you know how to train a young boy?'

'I was one.'

She knew his father's methods and what they had done to Ash. The trials Hring had put Ash through made her blood run cold. Like being left alone in the woods at night, being forced to fight with an injured arm and being beaten for failing to win. No son of hers would face that sort of trial. Ever. It would utterly destroy Rurik and his fragile confidence. He wasn't that strong.

Somehow Ash had to be made to understand why Rurik had to be kept safe, instead of filling his head with nonsense about things he'd teach him and expecting him to excel. Rurik would start to love him and then he'd be let down. Badly.

A little voice warned her that she was doing Ash an injustice. Just because he'd done it to her, he might be different with their son. She silenced it. She wanted to be logical and calm, rather than making decisions based on emotion. Ash training Rurik would be wrong. She knew that in her bones. There was far too much potential for hurt—physically and emotionally—for Rurik.

'I wouldn't want to presume on your time. You need to get your men settled before you start thinking about training. We can discuss it when you have time to spare.'

'When I have time to spare?' A hurt expression flitted across Ash's face. He picked up the whorl and tossed it in the air, expertly catching it several times before placing it down again. 'Was I truly that selfish when we first married? You should have kissed me until I noticed.'

'You were always busy. Things needed doing. You were preparing for the trip of a lifetime.' Even seven years later, the excuse still sprang readily to her lips. She ducked her head, hating her lapse.

She had made so many excuses for his behaviour when, in truth, he simply had not cared. She had not been important to him. It had taken her a long time to accept that fact, but eventually she had no choice.

'Preparation is fine, but it is the sea which decides how your passage is. Neglecting her moods can lead to disaster.'

'You weren't to know.'

'It sounds like you are too ready to excuse my younger self.' He tilted his head to one side. 'I was very selfish and spoilt and utterly unfair to you. But know this, Kara—the one good thing I did was to marry you. A man could not ask for a better custodian of this estate and our son in his absence. I want you to continue to look after the estate like you did for my father. I haven't done much farming for the last few years.'

Kara dipped her head. Custodian. The word slammed into her. Ash didn't want the responsibility. 'I want someone who will help run the estate. It is one of the reasons I was marrying Valdar.'

Ash stood silently for a long time, digesting Kara's words. Each word was another nail in his heart. He'd made many mistakes, but the one good thing he had done was to marry her. His tour around the estate convinced him of that. He had thought she'd be pleased that he wanted her to continue. He could farm. The responsibility of an estate didn't frighten him. He'd always known that he'd have to.

He'd never understand women. And he knew he couldn't stay if she didn't want him. But he refused to tell her that.

'I will take it under consideration.' He tilted his head to one side, trying to assess her mood. 'I can remember being very glad that first night on the ship that you had made it easy for me. There was no need to feel guilty.'

'And would you have done?' she whispered. 'Would you have stayed if I had revealed my fears about being here alone without a friendly face?'

He sighed and ran his hand through his hair, fighting against the urge to take her in his arms and kiss the doubts away. With hindsight, he could see that he'd worried about her being left with his father to cope. Not that he should have as she'd obviously coped admirably. She didn't need him. The realisation hurt. He wanted to be needed.

'No way to answer that,' he said slowly, trying to explain without giving her more cause to hate him. He simply had not even seen the possibility of failure until too late. 'I do regret not having been here for so many things, Kara, but that is in the past. From here on, I plan to do right by you and our son. I want our son to grow up to be a credit to the both of us, rather than just to you. He will be trained properly, Kara.'

'I will try to remember that,' she said, picking up another skein of wool and not meeting his eyes.

'Do.' He moved closer to her, took the skein from her nerveless fingers and laid it down on the table. 'Stop using tasks to avoid talking to me. Tell me what worries you and how I can ease those worries. I want to do my duty.'

'I'm…' Kara's heart thumped so loudly, she thought Ash must hear it. Every nerve screamed. She wanted his words to be true with every fibre of her being. She wanted to believe him. For Ash, words always came easily. She needed more than simple lip service. She pressed her hands to her eyes and regained control of her body.

'You're what?' His voice held a husky rasp.

'I want you to have time to get accustomed to the changes before we discuss Rurik's training,' Kara mumbled, pressing her hands against the table to steady her body.

If he took her in his arms, she knew she'd melt and give in to his kiss. Too much remained unsettled between them. It was how they used to solve arguments—Ash kissing her, using her attraction to him against her. Sometimes she had even provoked arguments simply for the aftermath. A mad and dangerous thing to do. Her mother had done that with her father and she'd seen the consequences.

'How long were you gone this time?' he asked, not moving towards her.

'A week.' Kara looped a strand of hair about her ear, feeling on more solid ground. Her heart would survive if she kept her focus on practical things. 'You would be amazed how much can change in a week. And how much can remain undone if the servants think you are not concerned. This estate nearly fell apart when Hring took to his bed.'

'More changes in seven years. I had no right to expect the estate to be in any shape. It is a pleasant surprise.'

'I hope you like the changes, in particular the new outbuildings for the animals.'

'I knew that must have been your doing. You always wanted to make sure the animals were well looked after. My father was only interested in the glory and prestige that an estate could bring.'

She forced a seemingly unconcerned shrug, but her heart sang. He approved of the outbuildings. 'When your father was alive, I used to seek his permission, but towards the end, it became easier to make decisions myself and, of course, for the last few months there has been no one to ask.'

His eyes narrowed. 'Not even Valdar?'

'Valdar never lived here. I was the one who

had to take responsibility. But he approved of the new stabling for the horses. I looked after his prized mare earlier this year when she was in foal.'

'What Valdar thinks has no bearing on this estate or in this marriage.' Ash's fists banged together. 'It was long past time to get new stables. Our son confided in me about the stables and how he hopes for a horse when he is bigger. He also wants a dog of his own, one to sleep on his bed. I gather the two elkhounds sleep at the foot of your bed. He is definitely his mother's son with his love of animals.'

She picked at the wool, untwisting a bit and retwisting it. 'When he is old enough, he may have a dog, but I won't have any animal neglected. He is six and he forgets things.'

'Maybe at Jul or possibly in the spring. He'll be ready for full responsibility of an animal then.'

A glow filled her. He liked what she had done and he liked Rurik. He even made it sound like he would be staying. And he'd agreed without hesitation to her suggestion that they wait for Rurik to grow a bit before expecting him to look after a dog. 'We will discuss it then and see if he is ready. I won't have an animal suffer simply to prove a point.'

'He will be ready.' He gave a half-smile. 'You should have seen the way his eyes shone.'

'Rurik likes to talk. Your father used to say that he was related to a mockingbird. I hope he didn't bore you.'

'Rurik could never bother me. A real credit to you, but you protect him too much.'

'I do not!' She narrowed her eyes. 'How would you know? You only met him today. You missed six years of his life.'

He flinched and she knew her barb had hit its mark.

'You were always like that about any animal you care about.' He gathered her hands between his. 'There is something I want from you. Let me train Rurik. Let me show you that I can get it right when my father got it so badly wrong.'

Her heart thumped in her ears. He liked Rurik. She ought to confess about Rurik's birth before it was too late. The words refused to come. 'I did tell him, Ash. I acknowledged you as his father. What you did was magnificent. You are a real hero in Rurik's eyes. I suspect we shall have to listen to the tale of his rescue many times over. But we need to wait.'

'You are always asking me to wait, Kara.'

With every breath she took, the room seemed to be getting smaller and she was more and more aware of him. This was far from ideal. She wanted to make a pragmatic and logical choice, not one based on desire and a few kisses.

She sighed. 'I refuse to have pointless arguments with you about the past like we just had. This is precisely why I asked for time to make up my mind. The past looms too great between us, Ash. We should recognise that and move on.'

'What if I am not ready to move on?' He reached out and grabbed her shoulders.

His mouth loomed large over her. Her heart thumped unsteadily.

His lips descended for a kiss which invaded her senses. It called to something deep within her soul. She wanted to melt against him. She wanted to deepen the kiss and return it with vigour.

A warning bell resounded in the back of her mind. Giving into the kiss would be the worst thing in the world for her. It would signal that she was prepared to return to the old ways and she wasn't. Logic had to prevail, not desire.

He rubbed the back of his thumb across her hyper-sensitive mouth. 'Give me a second chance, sweet Kara. Let me prove myself to you with Rurik. You will see. We are good together. We can be a family.'

With the last ounce of self-control, she broke free and wiped her hand across her mouth. 'You think you can kiss me into doing what you want?

Into forgetting what went before? Into agree-ing that you should do precisely what you want? You do me a grave disservice. You promised you wouldn't force me.'

'Force? There were two of us in that kiss, Kara. You wanted it.'

She clenched her fist, hating that her mouth ached for more. 'It hasn't worked.'

He regarded her from under hooded eyes. 'It worked in the past. Once. Stopping your mouth so you wouldn't talk me out of going.'

'Things changed, Ash. I refuse to be manip-ulated in this fashion. The kiss did nothing for me except make me more determine to resist.'

She crossed her arms over her aching breasts and prayed he wouldn't hear the lie in her voice.

He gave her a speculative glance. 'It was ei-ther kiss you or shake you to make you see sense as you refuse to listen. I chose the more plea-surable option. A pity you didn't see it in that fashion.'

He spun on his foot and left the room.

Kara slammed her fist down hard on the table, making the skeins jump. Three fell on the floor. She knelt down and picked them up. Both the elkhounds Dain and Durin came into the room and nosed her face, wagging their tails furiously. Kara dug her fingers into their soft fur.

A well of misery opened up within her. Ash

hadn't even been back a day. Already he questioned her judgement over Rurik. He was the one who had frightened Rurik, behaving worse than Hring in a bad temper.

She hated that she might have to fight the battles all over again. And then, just when she'd begun to count on him, he'd leave, thinking she was a good custodian. She thought he might have sought her out because he wanted to kiss her, but, no, it was to order her about.

Kara pressed her hand to her forehead. Less than a day and she was already questioning her schemes to keep Rurik safe. It had to stop. She had to get back to her old certainties and the place to start was with Rurik.

Chapter Ten

'Mor! You came to say goodnight and you brought the dogs.' Rurik sat up in his bed. His blond hair fell in wisps across his face. Kara's heart lurched. Seeing him earlier with Ash showed her how much the pair looked alike. Her blood ran cold at what could have happened if Ash hadn't acted decisively.

'Don't I always when I am home?' she said, struggling not to scoop him up and hug him to her chest. These days, Rurik seemed to resent any physical contact, struggling to get away from her hugs or submitting with bad grace.

He held out his hand to the dogs. They immediately came over and he fed them a treat, oblivious to her inner turmoil. 'Watch! I've been training them while you were gone.'

'Very good.'

Rurik was obviously so proud of the way both

dogs sat for him and waited for the possibility of another treat. 'Then I can have my own dog? To sleep at the end of my bed?'

'We will see,' Kara replied carefully. Ash was right. Rurik did need the responsibility of owning a dog and training one. In the new year, rather than at Jul-tide as Ash suggested. In the new year, he'd be that much older and ready to look after a dog. 'Both Dain and Durin love saying goodnight to you. How could I deprive them of their treat?'

Rurik flushed. 'Gudrun said you might not because I had been so naughty. I didn't mean to be naughty. I just wanted to…be the first one to see my new father. I knew he would come today, despite what Virvir said. And I'm not a baby!'

'Who called you a baby?' Kara grew indignant on her son's behalf. 'Your father in the graveyard?'

'It…it doesn't matter.'

'I want to know!'

'It was Virvir in the kitchen when he saw my tears. Gudrun agreed with him.'

Gudrun! Kara pressed her lips together and concentrated on arranging the blankets and sheets so they were tucked about Rurik's shoulders. She would have words with the woman again. She was not about to have her son belittled like Hring had done with Ash. She thought she had stopped it years ago.

'I know what you wanted to do and climbing is expressly forbidden. I wouldn't want anything to happen to my boy. And you didn't ruin anything. I just want to keep you safe.'

'You are not angry with me. Far said you wouldn't be, but then he started shouting and I became frightened. I acted like a baby.'

'Gudrun was wrong.' She smoothed Rurik's fair hair from his forehead. 'His leg pained him because he saved you.'

Rurik wrinkled his nose. 'I thought he might be scared. It can't be easy to see your own grave. Do warriors get scared?'

Kara bit her lip. Out of the mouth of her child. She might love this house, but it could not have been easy for him coming back, wondering what his father would have thought. 'You know, I think you are right. He was scared. Everyone gets scared.'

Rurik's eyes widened. 'I thought so. But his leg hurts him, too. I could see that. He didn't want me to know, but his lips were white with pain.'

'You notice little details, Rurik. That is really good. It will help you when you become a warrior. Your father told me that one.'

'Will my father be proud of me?'

Kara pulled up the blanket so it was tight about her son. 'You are his son. All fathers are proud of their sons.'

Rurik gave a large yawn. 'Far-far wasn't. He told me once.'

'Your grandfather sometimes said things he didn't mean.' Kara wished she could have shaken Hring. 'He had the saga written about your father. You know the one which said he was a great hero.'

'Oh, I forgot.'

A tiny pain developed in her eyes. She had been hiding important things from Ash. If he understood why she worried about Rurik, maybe then he'd see why Rurik's training had to wait. And why Rurik needed to be trained differently from how he was.

Kara screwed up her eyes. She had to tell Ash the truth about Rurik's birth. Tonight before she lost her nerve. She had to stop being afraid about what Ash might think about the way she had saved Rurik's life. Having met Rurik, Ash would understand why she had acted the way she did. The time had come to explain about their son and why he needed to be kept safe. And she'd bring him some salve for his leg as a peace offering.

'Mor, is everything all right? You look upset.' Rurik put a hand on her shoulder. 'Far is going to stay. He won't be ashamed of me and go? Because of what I did? How I cried when he shouted? Gudrun said he might unless I was super-good and brave.'

'Gudrun should never have said that.' Kara struggled to contain her anger at Gudrun. Maybe it was time the elderly woman retired. 'She is completely wrong. Your father is very proud of you and the way you handled yourself on the roof. You did what he asked and did not panic. You kept hold until you were rescued. Not many boys your age would have done that.'

Kara knew the words were true. Ash was proud of Rurik. Whatever happened between them, he would not be leaving because of his son.

'But will he stay? For ever? Or will he go again to seek out fresh lands? Sometimes warriors take their families with them. Valdar said that he might, if he were my father. Will my real father? Will he teach me?'

'I hope he will stay.' Kara kissed Rurik and moved the wooden horse he always slept with to the side of his pillow. Going with Ash? The thought was tempting, but how could she leave this even if he asked? 'Sleep. I have to see your father about something.'

'About my getting a dog?' Rurik snuggled down. 'He already promised. I am going to get a dog of my very own to train as soon as he can arrange it. He knows how to make you do things.'

'Did he say that indeed?'

'Before I was a silly baby and got frightened. Warriors never mind a bit of shouting.'

Kara forced the ire back down her throat. Ash should have consulted her before making promises to her son. Or demanding that he behave in a specific fashion. 'You are willing to try again?'

'Mor, he is my father. I want him to be proud of me.'

Kara discovered Ash in her father-in-law's old chamber, her chamber. They had agreed—this was to be her space. Renewed indignation flooded through her. He seemed to be awfully free with his promises and presumptions. He hadn't truly changed. He just said whatever was easiest and bound to get him the result he wanted.

Now he was engaged in playing a game of tafl with one of his men in the room he'd declared was for her private use. She prayed that Skaldi and the other goddesses would give her strength. She had to be logical and cool, rather than provoke another fight. Her few fights with Ash used to end with them in bed and now the bed piled high with furs loomed far too near.

A tiny voice deep within her asked if she wanted to be kissed, properly...

Kara tore her gaze away from it. When she slept tonight, she would sleep alone.

She cleared her throat and held the small bowl of salve in front of her. 'Pardon me for interrupting.'

Ash made a swift gesture to the other man. The man jumped up, made his excuses and left.

'You aren't interrupting. Your chamber, not mine,' Ash said, leaning back with his hands laced behind his head. The torchlight showed the faint golden stubble on his chin. 'I thought you would return here eventually and I wanted to be prepared. It does neither of us any good to be angry with each other. We need to work together. Rurik belongs to the both of us, whatever happens.'

Kara struggled to keep her temper. Working together for Ash had always meant her following his lead and doing what he wanted. No longer. 'Indeed.'

'I've no real love of this room, even with the change of tapestries. Far too many memories of waiting alone for my father to appear and punish me for some misdemeanour whether real or imagined. Njal the Squint wanted to go over the training rota for the next few days and stayed to play a game of tafl at my request.' Ash screwed up his face 'We've unfinished business, you and I. I want it completed tonight.'

'Unfinished business!' Kara took a steadying breath and concentrated on the tafl board. She needed to keep her focus, rather than be distracted about Ash's childhood memories, particularly after Rurik's earlier insight. 'What unfinished business?'

'We had not reached an agreement about what needs to be done about Rurik and his supervision. My son will be properly supervised. I insist on that. Things need to change. I have trained men, Kara. It was one of my duties in Viken for the last two years.'

'He has survived for six years with me.'

'He isn't being properly supervised.' Ash banged his fist on the table, making the pieces jump. 'Today's events made that perfectly clear. Gudrun is far too old and mean. She seeks to curry favour with whoever is the most powerful. She used to lock me in a cellar. But it is more than that. Rurik needs to learn the skills to survive as a warrior. He has a position in the world.'

'Are you saying that I am a bad mother? Overprotective? Making him weak?' Kara prepared for battle, tightening her grip on the little bowl of salve she carried. All her good intentions about involving Ash in Rurik's upbringing were forgotten as she remembered the words she had had with Hring over the past three winters. She refused to cede control simply because Ash happened to return. She had coped perfectly well. Today was an aberration, rather than the normal state of affairs. Surely he had to realise that. 'How dare you make a judgement of that sort based on the little time you have spent with your son! What happened today was a dreadful accident. It could have been much worse, but thankfully Rurik is fine. I am a good mother!'

'If you are a good mother, then you will want the proper supervision of our son.' Ash's smile turned triumphant. 'You will want him trained properly so that he is not a danger to himself and others.' He stood up. 'It must happen, Kara, he can't stay tied to your apron strings. He is growing up. Do you want a son who is not respected and can't hang on to this estate when you are gone? It is about what is best for Rurik, rather than what is best for your nerves.'

Kara struggled to control her temper. Less than a day home and Ash had already decided she was over-protective. She wanted to throw the bowl of salve at his head.

'That goes without saying. And I have done everything in my power to make sure that Rurik is kept safe while you have been off travelling the world. It was one of the reasons I had been about to marry Valdar, to provide Rurik with a good father who would train him properly.'

'You're not marrying Valdar. He is the wrong sort of man for you.'

'If you are going to be like that, leave.' Kara pointed to the door. 'This is my room, not yours. Remember that in the future. I refuse to discuss my relationship with Valdar. Ever.'

His eyes flashed dangerously and his hands clenched. Kara waited. A fluttering started in her stomach. A large part of her wanted him to kiss her again. Then, with a deliberate effort, he slowly unclenched his fists.

'You misunderstand me because you want a fight. Because you remain angry with me for not returning sooner. I was an irresponsible fool when we married with no real appreciation of the important things. And I have grown up and I have returned, hopefully a wiser man. I do take my responsibilities seriously and know that good things are earned, not given by right. But I also know I am damaged. I can never be the man I once tried to be,' he said in a quieter tone.

'Damaged?'

'I saw things no man should see.' His face became clouded. 'It is not easy to see your friends die and hear their screams long after the sea has swallowed them.' He put up his hand. 'I've no wish to burden you or have you feel pity for me.

But I find the screams louder when I attempt to sleep in a bed.'

'I want to know. I have a right to know.'

He was silent for a long time. 'I'm not ready to talk about it. I'm not sure if I ever will be. Please don't make it a condition.'

Kara gazed up at the knots in the ceiling beam. She had always envisioned sharing everything, but she had seen Ash's tortured face earlier. She had to give him time. 'When you are ready to talk, I am ready to listen, but until then you are on trial. You can train Rurik, but only if you clear everything with me in advance.'

'Have you thought this through?'

Kara narrowed her gaze. 'Those are my conditions.'

'You did your best, but I want to play my part. I want to make sure our son grows up properly. It is why I am here in this room. It is best to reach an agreement before the sun sets. Isn't that what you always said when you confronted me after a fight?' His lips turned up in a smile which could melt the hardest heart. 'Meet me halfway, Kara. Like you used to do.'

Kara fought against the urge to agree with him. It was so wrong of him to quote her earlier self. She had always made the effort before to smooth over any argument. Ash never had. His way of settling things had been to kiss her into submission...until now. And she did agree that Rurik's supervision needed to be changed. She struggled to take a calming breath. 'You were waiting for me here! The last place I would ever dream of looking for you. I have been looking everywhere for you.'

'It seemed for the best—waiting for you somewhere where you would eventually return and where we could discuss things with a modicum of privacy. Whispers have a way of spreading and forcing people to take sides. The Viken court is a snakepit. Thorkell's queen is poisonous.' He inclined his head. 'Was there something you wished to see me about? You said you were looking for me. Surely it was not to seek another kiss.'

Kara gazed at the tapestries, rather than looking at Ash.

'Two things. I brought you some salve for your leg.' She held out the bowl. 'You should put it on every morning when you wake and at night. It does well for lame horses.'

'And lame men?'

'It may ease your leg if rubbed in regularly. I don't promise a miracle. But in a few days' time, you may find the pain easier to bear.'

He reached out, took the bowl and sniffed it. 'One of your mother's concoctions? It smells strong.'

'I've improved it,' Kara said with real pride. 'If you rub it in with small circular motions, it seems to work better.'

'Thank you for this. I appreciate the gift. Hopefully it will make my leg ease enough that I don't frighten Rurik.' His blue gaze met hers. 'It is why you gave it to me, isn't it? Rather than being concerned about my leg? You hate that I shouted at him. I've apologised.'

Kara wrapped her arms about her waist. She wasn't ready to explore all her reasons for giving it. 'If you understand about Rurik's birth, maybe you will understand why I am overprotective. We both nearly died. In fact, without Gudrun we both would have. She delivered him.'

Ash's muscles tensed. He had never considered that the birth might have been anything but straightforward. Kara and Rurik appeared perfectly well now.

'Your life was in danger? How?' he asked as a massive wave of guilt swept over him. 'Gudrun was never one for delivering babies.'

'Rurik was early. Gudrun found me crumpled in the stables. I had gone to change a poultice on one of the horses' legs and the pain came too sudden and fast. Gudrun supported me back to the house and stayed with me during the birth. She made sure that I had all the strengthening broth I needed afterwards.'

'Rurik was early? How early?' Ash forced his body to remain completely still and his hands at his sides. He wanted to gather her in his arms and check that she was safe. 'Tell me everything.'

'He was very little. My fault. Your father had forbidden me the stables and I was determined to help your favourite horse. I knew I could save his leg and his life.' Kara tucked her head and concentrated on the tafl board, rather than meeting his eye.

'Floki? You went into the stable because of him?'

'He was always gentle about me and I wanted him to be here for you when you came home. He'd hurt his leg. I wanted to try the salve out on it.' She held up her hand. 'Arrogant and reckless, I know. Your father said as much to me many times over, but I knew how much you loved that horse.'

'My unborn child would have meant more.' Ash pressed his lips together. He'd failed her utterly and completely. He really didn't deserve a son or a wife, but the gods were kind and had granted him a second chance. This time, he would do the right thing. 'But I know you and injured animals. If anyone is to blame, it is me. Floki spooked easily.'

'Everything was quiet to begin with. I was

nearly done,' Kara explained. 'And then it happened. A small twinge in my back. I cried out, but it was enough. Floki kicked his leg out. I stumbled backwards to avoid the kick and I landed hard. Then the pain ripped through me and there was blood and nothing I could do but pray to the gods. The gods answered me in the form of Gudrun. How she managed to get me out of the stable I will never know.'

Ash listened to Kara's tale with mounting horror. The debt he owed her grew with each sentence she uttered. When babies were born too soon, the vast majority of them died within weeks despite the best efforts anyone might make. The gods were cruel.

He ought to fall down and kiss her feet. She'd suffered greatly and all he'd done was escape from a dungeon.

'But he has always been a fighter,' she finished. 'I knew I had to fight for his life. It was my fault that the accident happened. Your father nevertheless had the horse destroyed.'

'And what did my father say about our son? Did he demand you expose Rurik?'

'Your father was far from happy, but I told him that you should make the decision. You were the only one who could decide if our son lived or died in that fashion.'

'And my father?'

'He looked at me as if I had grown two heads, turned purple and said I would not get anything to eat unless I complied.' Kara's eyes blazed at the memory. 'I told him I would never abandon my son. And I won't.'

Ash's admiration for her grew. It might not seem like much to defy his father, but Ash knew how frightened she had been of him. Kara hated strife of any kind and felt it deeply even if it wasn't her fault. Her words might give the impression of ease, but it would have been far worse for her than she said.

'He gave way? Immediately in the face of your immovability?'

'Gudrun saved my life a second time. She sided with me and brought me food so that I wouldn't starve. Luckily Rurik thrived and your father relented weeks later. I owe her a debt I cannot repay.'

'You defied my father for weeks?' Ash's mouth dropped open and he didn't even bother to hide his astonishment. 'Kara!'

'I found it easy when we were speaking about my child.' Kara jutted her chin out. 'Hring learnt that I might bend with the wind, but my backbone is flexible steel, rather than brittle straw. I bend, but I do not break and there are some things that I am immovable on.'

Ash heard the warning in her voice. She had

defied his father and she'd defy him over this. His wife had the determination of a thousand men. 'I wish you had told me the truth straight away.'

'I wanted you to think the best of Rurik. I didn't want you to turn your back on him.'

Ash ran his hand through his hair. He'd made so many mistakes today. This time he had to get it right. 'But the fact that you and Rurik survived is down to you, rather than Gudrun. You always refuse to take credit for your skill.'

'It is in the past, Ash.' She clasped her hands together. 'But I want you to understand why I claim the right to have final say on my son's up-bringing.'

Ash's heart thumped. His son's future hung in the balance. Rurik was not going to grow up living in fear. Or trying to do things when he didn't know how to use the equipment properly. Training a warrior properly was a difficult and delicate task, but Rurik had to be one, otherwise he'd lose the estate. Selfishly he didn't want to lose Kara either.

'Rurik is my son. He will inherit these lands and all that entails some day. I mean to make him a good leader of men.' He paused and fixed her with his eye.

Kara backed away, becoming a frightened falcon again. 'I know the sort of training you went through. Rurik won't survive it.'

'Which is why I know how not to do it,' he said quietly. 'You must believe me. I will look after Rurik. Give me a chance. Give me the chance to make it right.'

'He is far too young. Let him have time to grow up.'

Ash moved over towards her. He had made a mistake earlier, rushing her, trying to bend her to his will. He should have bided his time. After all this time he still needed a lesson in patience. 'Kara, trust me. You once said you would always trust me. Trust me in this one thing. Make good your promise.'

'Are you trying to provoke another fight?' She nodded towards the bed piled high with furs. 'So you can kiss me and then we fall into that bed?'

'The last thing I want is to argue with you, but I do want your assurance that you will try to make this marriage work. I know I am giving you time, but please can we work together instead of against each other?'

Asking, not demanding. Kara swallowed hard and her heart pounded. It was far harder to fight against him when he was like this. 'I will try.'

His eyes became hooded. 'I want Rurik to grow up with parents who can work together, rather than who are constantly at each other's throats. See if we can make this marriage work by letting me train our son the right way.'

She gave a hesitant nod, accepting what he said. She, too, could remember the fights her parents had had. Always arguing passionately over something on the rare occasions that her father was home. 'Rurik appears to like you. One of his greatest desires is to be a strong warrior like his father.'

He dismissed her words with a wave of his hand. 'He only knows stories about the old me. Give him time. But let me use that admiration to ensure he knows how to hold a sword, to skate and to swim.'

'You rescued him from near-certain death,' she reminded him with a frown. 'In Rurik's eyes, you are already his hero.'

'Any one of my warriors would have done the same for a child. I happened to be the closest.'

Kara stared at him. The old Ash used to trumpet his success, making it seem like he was a greater warrior than he was. Ash had changed in more ways than she ever thought possible and she found she admired the new Ash. 'Don't ever dismiss what you have done to me again. Making it less doesn't change its importance to Rurik.'

She fancied a bit of respect came into his eyes. 'I had never considered it.'

'Next time do.' She crossed her arms, aware of him and the fact that he was in her room.

'I will ensure he is properly trained, Kara. Not how my father trained me, but with challenges appropriate for his age. It will be risky, but he won't have to do dangerous things.'

'Do…do you truly know how to make boys into proper warriors?'

'I learnt how to do it properly when I was in Viken. I saw the difference between a warrior who men feared and the sort that men followed willingly and for whom they would lay down their lives. A strong leader is respected, not feared. Fear leads to a knife in the back.'

Kara sighed, knowing Ash was correct. Rurik did need to be trained by someone he respected. It was why she'd been prepared to marry Valdar. She would have to trust Ash's words and that he would be here to finish the training. She wanted him to have a reason to stay. 'Remember Rurik is only little. He has big ideas, but his body…'

'You may watch any of the training sessions and stop them if you think they are out of hand, but it is better he knows how to do things properly than to be tempted by a know-nothing like Virvir and get in trouble. Is that a fair compromise?'

Rather than meet his eyes, she reached out and straightened one of the tafl pieces. The stone was cool against her hand. Hring had always forbidden her from the training field. 'You are willing to do that? Let me watch?'

'I won't pretend I will always get it right as I have never trained a six-year-old before, but I am willing to try.'

She bit her lip. She should have listened to Ash before and trusted him about the graveyard. And his men certainly appeared to be well trained with plenty of discipline. There had been none of the usual complaints from the women so far. Normally when any warrior visited, she was overrun with complaints in a short space of time. 'I will trust you to come to me if you are unsure.'

'There is a lot I have to learn about being a parent. You have a head start on me.'

'You do the best you can. I make mistakes all the time.' She looked up at the ceiling and blinked several times. 'I nearly made a grave error tonight.'

His hand caught hers. 'Will you help me, Kara? I want…I want to be a better father than mine was for Rurik's sake.'

He was actually asking her for help. She struggled to remember the last time. Probably when his falcon had broken its wing. Kara swallowed hard. Her fingers tightened about his. 'If I can, I will, but the surest guide I have found is to love him.'

He didn't let go of her hand, but stood up. She was aware of the breadth of his shoulders and the strength in his arms. 'I want to make a new beginning with you, Kara. I want to get to know you better.'

'You already know me pretty well.'

'I know the old you, not the new one. Not the one who has been single-handedly running this estate or who is prepared to argue for better terms for the timber in front of the entire Storting.'

'Who told you that?'

'Rurik. He is very proud of his mother. Protective, as well. I'm not to make you cry again. He looked me straight in the eye and challenged me. Our son is no coward, Kara. I doubt I could have said that to my father.'

'I used to cry on the anniversary of your death. I'm surprised Rurik knew.'

'I profoundly regret I ever made you cry.'

He gave a little tug and her body gently collided with his. Unlike his earlier kiss, this kiss was gently persuasive. Where the other kiss had aroused fury, this one made her want to linger. Under the gentle pressure of his mouth, her lips opened and she tasted the warm interior of his. It was infinitely better than her dreams of the previous night.

He stepped back. 'Good night, Kara.'

'Good night?' She put her hand on his chest and felt the steady thump of his heart. He was as affected by the kiss as she was. So why was he preparing to leave? Why was he rejecting her? 'I don't understand.'

'If I stay, it will go further, much further and would be immensely pleasurable.' He ran his hand down her cheek. A delicious tingling filled her. She fought against the urge to lean into his hand and ask him to stay, but she knew she'd hate herself in the morning. 'But…it isn't what you or I want.'

'Further?' she whispered, her throat parched. Her body ached for his touch and the way he used to play it like a harp. She wanted to sink into sensation again and forget. It was why he was here, surely. He had decided to take the choice from her.

'I want it to go further, but only when you are ready. I want no accusations that I pushed you into it. I want you to take all the time you need.' He smoothed a tendril of hair from her forehead. 'Tomorrow we'll play tafl. With a wager between friends rather than lovers. I intend to be your lover again…when you are ready. I want our marriage to be a true marriage, not something just for show.' He reached out and retrieved the bowl of salve. 'Thank you for this. I will use it.'

'And if I'm not ready for a wager?' she asked through aching lips.

'We play for the joy of playing. I want to get to know the new you, Kara. I like what I've seen so far.'

Kara closed her eyes. Hoisted by her own words. She could try to get to know Ash as he was now, instead of expecting him to behave like he had done seven years ago. 'I suppose we can play but no wagering. We have gone beyond that sort of thing.'

'Coward.' He gave a wicked smile, the sort that made her insides go liquid. 'Aren't you even going to ask what the wager was?'

Kara tilted her head and tried to control the pounding in her heart. Her entire traitorous body longed to know what the wager was and if it involved touching Ash and feeling his skin against hers. It would be so easy to melt into his embrace, particularly if she had no choice in the matter.

She straightened her spine and forced her feet to stay still. 'How am I a coward?'

'You challenge me, but then you run so you can sit up on your lonely mountaintop of female superiority, telling all the world that I forced you into a corner and that was why you surrendered.'

Her cheeks burnt. 'Am I that obvious?'

'No, I'm greedy.' He bowed low. 'I want to

possess all of you rather than simply enjoying your body for one night.'

He was gone before she could utter a word in protest or explain why even one night would be a bad idea.

She lent her fevered brow against the cool panelling as her lips ached. Logic and not emotion. She had to think clearly, rather than consider the shape of his mouth and if the bristles on his chin remained as soft as they had been before.

Rurik needed a father, someone who could properly train him.

She had made the right decision, but she knew what she wanted from her life's partner and it was very different from what she had wanted as a young girl. But she had to give Ash a chance. She wanted to see if it was more than desire or the memory of what had once passed between them. Why had everything become so complicated now that Ash had returned?

Chapter Eleven

'I've brought the tafl board to you,' Kara said, setting the board down next to where Ash sat in the great hall, engaged in an engrossing discussion with one of his men.

The remains of the welcome feast were spread out before him. Kara doubted if Ash had even realised that she had gone from the table. Just before she left, he had seemed utterly absorbed in the conversation about rigging sails. Further confirmation that Ash had no intention of staying here for the long term.

He wanted her to be a custodian of the estate and carry out his orders when he was gone. It wasn't going to happen like that. It was why she had rejected several suitors earlier in the year. She knew what she wanted and all she had to do was to stick to her well-considered plan and keep her heart out of it.

Ash immediately broke off his conversation and turned towards her. His face lit up with some secret amusement. 'You returned, Kara. I thought we might have to send out a search party.'

His friend laughed. 'You've no idea how worried his lordship was, my lady. I've never seen him this perturbed. No, I lie. Once before when he worried about a Ranerike attack. His caution proved right that day. He kept turning his head and looking for you, even when he denied it. Normally he has no eyes for a skirt or a sultry smile. We used to wonder why and now we know. He left a beautiful lady at home.'

Ash banged his fist on the table. 'Saxi! Enough!'

Ash had ignored other women? Kara forced a breath and recited the names of Ash's mistresses before their marriage. Hring had made sure she knew about each and every one.

Had none come after her? She dampened down the sudden spark of hope. She must be realistic rather than grasp illusions of romance. It would be because he had been determined to regain his honour and didn't have time, rather than because he had been pining for her. But she found it impossible to silence the insistent little voice that whispered, *He seems to care now.*

'You did say you wanted a game and this is

the perfect time.' Kara slid back into her place and attempted to control her heart's fierce beating.

It had seemed simple enough in the kitchen where she'd retreated under the guise of checking the stores after she'd checked that Rurik was truly asleep and not watching the feast from some hidden vantage point. Playing the game in front of everyone would ensure that it remained an innocent game, rather than turning into one of wagers and forfeits in the bedroom. Being alone together with a bed nearby would have compounded her mistakes. Falling into his bed would make the situation worse rather than better despite what her body screamed or what her dreams promised.

Trust and mutual regard were the necessary ingredients for a happy marriage. She had made a list after Hring died. Nothing had happened to change her determination to have that contentment. The joining of bodies was simply passion and passion faded.

'Perfection depends on your point of view.' His eyes deepened to a midnight blue. 'I'd hoped for later, but we can play now. Test our skill against each other and see how well matched we are.'

'The skald can sing as we play.' Kara opted for a bright smile as warmth flickered throughout her body. She could remember how well matched they were in bed. It was outside of the bedroom which bothered her. 'Who knows, maybe we can create a tournament and get others involved? We had one three winters ago with your father. He found it very enjoyable.'

A faint smile played on Ash's lips. 'And who was the overall champion? My father again? He always enjoyed being the champion and sulked if anyone else won.'

'I was, much to your uncle's disgust and your father's amusement.'

'My uncle and father were alike in many ways. Both of them hated losing.'

Kara stared at the tafl board, remembering the tournament. 'Your uncle, though, knows when he is beaten. Your father never liked to admit it.'

'My uncle tends to be pragmatic. You have nothing to fear from him.' He put his hand over hers. 'I enjoy playing more when there is a challenge.'

She withdrew her hand. If she wanted to show Ash her skill, she would need all her wits about her. 'Then you agree, we shall play here. In front of everyone.'

His look became one of mock innocence. 'Where else is there to play? You must enlighten me some day, Wife.'

'You are teasing me now because you want to

put me off my game.' She glanced up and tumbled into his dark blue gaze. 'I know all of your tricks, Ash.'

'I hope not all of them,' he murmured. 'Shall we begin and see if I can match your winning form?'

The game started well. Kara rapidly saw that Ash was a skilful tafl player, perhaps even better than his father. But she wasn't worried. She had spent hours in the last few winters pitting her wits against Hring and everyone else. There was something therapeutic about playing, rather than wasting energy worrying about whether they had enough grain or if the trees would be felled at the proper time. And she had missed the challenge since Hring's death. The two times she had played Valdar, she had easily won. Ash was right—there was little challenge in always winning.

She glanced down at the board. His basic strategy was one she had encountered before several times with Hring. His father's son. She made the correct countermove and captured a piece. 'Did you play much tafl when you were away?'

'Once I managed to save a man's life with a tafl game.'

'Was he a good man?' Kara leant forward, eager to know more about his life.

'Better than me.'

'Why? Why was he better?' she asked.

'He had simply been unlucky. He bore no shame of causing other men's deaths.'

'What was he to you?'

'My lord. He had plucked me up from obscurity.'

'Why did you play instead of him?'

'He had a head injury. My shield had connected with his head. But then he was a hopeless tafl player and I knew if I won, I could bargain for our freedom. But if he lost, we were all dead.'

'And you won.' She saw from his face he had. 'Did he forgive you? You saved his life.'

'His wife and two children forgave me when I brought him home. But I had to find another master.' He shrugged as if it was nothing. 'Gudrun appears to be missing from the festivities.'

'Gudrun departed this afternoon. I offered her a cottage.' Kara noted the change of subject. Some day, he would trust her enough to tell her. 'She is grateful for the cottage and has taken Virvir with her to fetch and carry.'

'You sent Virvir with her? Interesting.'

'On reflection, it seemed better than banishing him. He couldn't stay at the hall. He has caused so much mischief since he arrived after his parents' death ten months ago. The roof incident was the final straw.'

'Banishment rarely works,' Ash said, moving his king piece and neatly capturing one of her pieces. 'He will have less time on his hands. Allow Rurik to see Virvir, Kara.'

'Are you giving advice beyond the training ground now?' Kara dropped her piece and hurriedly moved another one. 'You must be joking. You know where his mischief led. They have to be kept separate. I won't have that boy ruining my son.'

'Our son.' He raised his hand. 'Hear me out. Please. Then you decide.'

Kara reluctantly nodded.

'All you will do is to create temptation by forbidding something. Rurik will get used to defying you. Virvir is his best friend at the moment. I used to defy my father to see my friends.'

Kara rolled her eyes. 'You're spouting nonsense.'

He covered her hand with his. A warm current ran up her arm. 'I speak from experience. Rurik needs time to create a new god to worship. In time he will see this Virvir for the false friend that he surely is, but you have to allow him the opportunity to make that discovery on his own.'

'You? You want to be his new god?' she enquired softly, clenching her hands together. She couldn't allow her attraction to Ash to override her judgement. She knew what it was like to have Ash as a god and how he could destroy with casual indifference. 'Do you still need to be worshipped?'

'Hardly.' He shrugged and moved another piece. 'One of my men would be better. Someone he can look up to rather than a father who is lacking.'

'And here you are, the person who saved a man's life with a tafl match.'

'Saxi might do,' he said by way of answer. 'He had children once. Right now Rurik spouts all sorts of nonsense about Virvir says this or that when he is holding his sword or bow wrong. He watched us in training this morning with your woman, rather than helping with the grain, and I took the opportunity to quiz him.'

Kara wrinkled her nose. Thora was supposed to have been keeping an eye on him. She supposed Thora couldn't resist watching the warriors. And Ash had always been one to take advantage of opportunities. 'Rurik doesn't know how to hold a bow.'

'I agree. His fingering is all wrong. He will never be able to kill any prey or hit any target beyond the barn door, if he continues to hold it in that way. But he insists that Virvir has shown him the true way.'

'An accident in the making,' Kara said, pressing her lips together and rapidly moving one of her pieces. Rurik had been using a bow and arrow without her permission. He had climbed without her permission. What else had he done?

'You can see why he needs to be properly trained. He needs to learn not to point the arrow at anyone except if he is in battle.' Ash neatly captured another of her pieces.

Kara frowned. This match was not turning out how she had planned. 'He is too young, Ash.'

'But he desperately wants to be a warrior and he is a boy. He wants to have a hero. A man to look up to. I'm not speaking about sending him into battle or off to sea, but giving him the skills to survive.'

'How do you know so much about boys?'

He laughed. The rich sound warmed her down to her toes. 'I was one once.'

'What happened when your heroes turned out not to be what you thought they were? When they left you?' she asked, concentrating on his face rather than on the board. Ash had to understand how it hurt when it turned out the hero you worshipped was simply ordinary and very flawed. She knew intimately how much that ached.

'Are you asking for Rurik or for yourself?' His fingers cupped her cheek.

'I want to know if you remember the feeling,' she said and kept her head absolutely still, resisting the temptation to turn her lips towards his palm.

'It hurt,' Ash admitted with a long sigh, releasing her. 'You can't protect Rurik from every hurt or sorrow, Kara. You will drive yourself mad. You need to relax and trust your son's judgement. He is an intelligent boy. No one is perfect. It is wrong to make a man into a god and then hate him when he turns out to be a man. Now take your turn.'

Kara's hand trembled on her king piece. It was easy for Ash to criticise. He only saw Rurik as he was now—well and strong. She had seen him struggle for his breath and the terrible colds he suffered each winter. She had nursed him through each illness until even her bones trembled with weariness.

'I've lost interest in this game.' She put down the piece. 'There are a thousand things I need to do before I retire. Perhaps it is best we end it here.'

'Running away won't change the truth. I learnt that lesson long ago.' Ash put his hands behind his head. 'Are you giving up this easily? I never took you for someone who quit at the first sign of losing. It was one of the reasons I wanted to marry you in the first place. You never wanted to quit. Have you changed that much?'

Kara peered at the board. She could win, just.

And he was right. She hated quitting and admitting defeat. 'I've just begun to fight.'

She rapidly took one of his pieces to show that she could.

'Good. Let me try this, Kara.' He leant forward. 'Let me follow my instinct with Rurik. I promise you only good will come of it. Give me permission. Let me fight for our son.'

How very like Ash! Agreeing to one thing and then asking for more. But she could understand why he asked it and at least he was asking.

'The last time I let you follow your instinct, you were gone for seven years.'

'Circumstances beyond my control.' He gestured about him. 'Had I known all this waited for me, I would have tried harder to get home.'

Something inside her melted. Ash had offered her an apology of sorts. And he liked it here. 'I'll take it into consideration.'

The firelight lit the planes in his face, highlighting his cheekbones. His eyes had turned into pools of the summer sea. He wore the identical expression as Rurik when he'd begged to be trained. 'Please, Kara.'

Her heart tugged. She hated that Ash might be correct about Rurik and his hero-worship. And he was abiding by her decision, rather than begging forgiveness after the fact. It was a question of the lesser of two evils. 'Very well, I won't forbid Virvir, but it is up to you to keep Rurik safely occupied.'

'Good.' Ash expertly took her king piece. 'This match is now mine.'

Kara stared at it in dismay. 'How did you do that?'

A smile kissed his mouth. 'My father taught you well, Kara, but I know that gambit that you used. You're far too cautious and seek safety when it is an illusion. I waited for you to make a mistake. I never give up even when things appear blackest.'

'You have no idea how I play.' She raised her eyes to his. 'Not now.'

A muscle twitched in his jaw. 'I've made a careful study over the past few days. You are a fascinating woman, Kara. Endlessly fascinating.'

Her mouth ached to be kissed. She kept her gaze on the board. 'A warning that you don't play fair?'

'I prefer—taking advantage of every opportunity and having the patience to wait for the right one.' He gave a half-smile. 'It makes life easier.'

'Are you trying to tell me something?' Kara ground out. She hated that Ash considered her easy to understand. 'If so, know I, too, learn from my mistakes. I tend not to repeat them.'

'Am I a mistake?'

'I haven't decided.' She saw a flash of hurt

cross Ash's face and remorse went through her. 'However, you gave me Rurik and he could never be a mistake.'

'Then you agree to a match tomorrow night, so you can show me how wise you've become overnight?'

Kara winced. She'd intended to find an excuse. 'I accept your challenge.'

'Good. I look forward to testing your skill to the limit. We are well matched, even if you refuse to see it.' Ash reached for the pitcher of ale and poured a glass. 'The skald should sing other songs. Something a bit more pleasing to the ear.' He mentioned one of the sagas she used to love.

She shook her head. 'The hour is late and the song is long. I need my rest.'

'Then I wish you pleasant dreams. Remember the choice of venue for our match is yours.'

Kara was intensely aware of his gaze on her mouth. Her lips ached as if he passionately kissed them.

'Here will be sufficient. No wagers—I've seen how you play.'

'If I'd truly wanted you off balance, there were other ways. I'll allow you your illusions for now.' His low voice followed her out of the room.

Once Kara reached her chamber, she halted and sunk down to her knees, disgusted at how her body hummed with desire for his touch. She couldn't risk her heart. Not again. Denying the attraction was practically impossible, but her heart shattering again was worse. Ash was far from dependable. She tried to recite the litany of his failings, but kept finding reasons why they no longer applied. She breathed deeply and knew the night would be a fight against dreaming about him and how good they could be together.

'My lady!' Thora burst in the kitchen where Kara supervised the bread-making several mornings later. 'They have begun the training early. Your son has a sword, a proper long sword.'

'A sword? Yesterday it was only a stick.' Kara looked up from her portion of bread dough. Ash should have asked her before he put a sharp blade in her son's hands. She thought he would have discussed it with her first, perhaps during their nightly tafl matches. So much for his easy words about consulting her.

She slammed her fist against the bread dough. Less than a week and he'd reverted to type. Would she never learn—words came easy to Ash and then he did precisely what he pleased. It would be no coincidence that Ash had started the training early. He probably hoped to keep it a secret.

'I thought you'd want to know. It is a pleasure

to watch the sell-swords train. The way their muscles bulge when they fight… A feast for the eyes.'

Kara hurriedly cleaned her hands. 'Yes, thank you. Take over the kneading, please.'

Kara picked up her skirts and ran to the practice yard. The various sell-swords were busy training and several of the women had found excuses to watch. She clapped her hands and immediately they turned away and started to be busy about their tasks again.

In the centre, Ash stood with Rurik. Rurik struggled to lift a sword nearly as tall he was. Its overly sharpened blade gleamed. One false move and Rurik could get cut or worse. She frantically signalled to Ash to halt.

'Ash! Ash! Rurik is too little! Stop this nonsense immediately.'

'Watch and decide!'

'But…!

'You promised to give me a chance! Give it!'

Ash kept his gaze on Rurik, but saw Kara sit down in a huff. His neck muscles tensed. He wanted to get this right not only for Rurik, but to prove to Kara that he could be trusted. If she wouldn't trust him with this, how could he get her to trust the marriage?

It was important that Rurik learn he needed to grow before he could use a sword. This morning he'd discovered his son standing with a sword and spouting nonsense to various kitchen boys. He had no idea where Rurik had found the sword, but Rurik needed to learn that such weapons were not toys and must be treated with the proper respect.

'Reach like this, Rurik, not like you were doing before. You will lose your sword before the battle truly begins.' Ash showed Rurik how to properly lunge with the sword for the tenth time. 'You wanted to use a sword for today's practice. Let's see what you can do.'

The boy's face narrowed with concentration as he copied each of the easy moves that Ash showed him. His entire being glowed.

Kara did not move from where she sat, but watched very move. Every time he glanced over, her face appeared more set. Beautiful, but judgemental and cold. His heart plummeted. Surely she had to see what he was doing—making sure his son knew how to respect a sword. He knew in his heart that it was the correct thing to do. He would beg her forgiveness if it came to it.

'When will I be able to fight for real?' Rurik asked, wiping sweat from his happy face. 'Warriors need to fight other warriors. It is what they do. With proper swords. Hacking each other until the blood comes and I get scars.'

'Who told you that?' Ash enquired mildly, guessing the answer.

'Virvir. He said that I couldn't be a true warrior unless I fought. Scars are the sign of a true warrior.'

'And when did he tell you this?'

Rurik tucked his head. 'Last night. We arranged it. I wanted to show him what I'd learnt. He called it babyish.'

It didn't surprise Ash that Rurik had found a way to see his friend. He hoped that within a few weeks, once Rurik began to properly train, he would see Virvir for the braggart and bully that he was. But he had to go slow. 'Is Virvir a warrior?'

Rurik considered it. 'No, but he knows a lot of special things. He listens when people think he isn't there. What I'm doing is baby stuff. Real warriors use swords.'

'And how did Virvir get in?'

'Through the kitchens. And he told me where to find my grandfather's weapons. It is very easy to take the sword.'

Ash knelt down beside his son, glad of the intelligence. He would ensure the weapons were moved immediately. If Virvir knew, others would.

'The next time he tells you something, you come to me and ask if it is true, before taking a weapon.' He put his hand on Rurik's shoulder. 'I have fought in more battles than he has and no longer have to listen to rumours.'

Rurik blinked. 'You are not angry that I saw him? Mor will be. I wasn't supposed to tell anyone, Virvir said. It was to be our secret and now I've told.'

Ash glanced over his shoulder towards where Kara sat, face thunderous. Her two dogs lay at her feet. The autumn sunlight highlighted her golden hair and kissed her skin. He felt the now-familiar tug of attraction towards her. How could one woman be so attractive and maddening at the same time? What more could he do to show he was worthy of a place in her bed? Each time he got closer, she seemed to slip out of his grasp. He needed the final key to unlock her passion, but he was fresh out of ideas. It had to be something simple.

He glanced down at Rurik. 'If you know you might make your mother unhappy, why do you do it?'

'Otherwise I'd never get to do anything. I'm not a baby. I want to do things and Virvir knows everything.'

'There is more to being a warrior than thirsting after glory or recounting stories. A warrior uses his head as well as his strength. Lift that sword and no complaining. I promised I'd make you into a warrior, but you have to trust me.'

Rurik nodded and lifted the sword again. His small arms trembled with the exertion and he dropped the sword almost immediately. 'I...I...'

'Again, Rurik,' Ash said.

The session would be shorter than usual so that Rurik wasn't completely exhausted, but it would have to be carefully done as the last thing he wanted to imply was that Rurik was too weak. Rurik bristled when anyone suggested that he was sickly or somehow not up to the task. His son was a fighter, which Ash thanked the gods for, but that fight had to be channelled correctly. He had seen far too many men make mistakes in anger.

'Rurik is tired,' Kara called out from where she sat when Rurik failed to lift the sword for the third time. 'Ash, he must come inside and have a rest.'

Rurik shook his head. 'I'm not the baby Mor thinks I am.'

'Rurik needs to lift the sword first,' Ash called back. 'Go on, lift the sword over your head. Show your mother you can do it.'

Rurik redoubled his efforts, planted his feet firmly and lifted the sword. For a heartbeat, it hung in the air as Rurik staggered.

'You did it, Rurik,' Ash called out immediately and Rurik released the sword with a huge sigh. 'The session is over for today. I have other things to do this morning. I have to train, as well. And a good warrior listens to his commander. Think of your mother as your commander. Respect her.'

'Is it done?' Kara called out, coming over to where they stood.

'Why don't you sit here and watch my men train for a treat?' Ash said before Kara had a chance to drag him off. 'You can see that real warriors do use wooden swords.'

Rurik's eyes shone. 'Can I, Mor? Please!'

Kara nodded that he could, but her face was like thunder. Ash gritted his teeth. She had agreed that he could train Rurik, but she was very quick to give Rurik permission to quit. He had to learn that just because a thing was hard, it didn't mean he should give up. Ash had been in control of the situation.

'Please, Kara. It is your choice now that Rurik's training has finished for today.'

Ash looked down at the perfect sculpted brows. Every time he saw her, it amazed him that he had been blind to her promise seven years ago. Or maybe he hadn't wanted to see. She instantly straightened her apron dress. She wore the brooches he had given her as a morning gift after they had married. He remembered how her eyes had sparkled and shone and how he always wanted to have her look at him like that—like he was worth something. He wanted to throttle his younger self for hurting her.

Whatever happened with his uncle, he vowed that Kara and Rurik would be kept safe.

'He can stay,' she said with a sigh. 'When he looks that eager, how can I deny him anything?'

Ash bent down and looked his son squarely in the eyes. 'Your mother allows things when asked. Go on. Talk to Saxi. See if you can pick up any tips from that old warrior. He never tires of talking about the battles he has fought.'

He ruffled Rurik's hair and then pushed him towards his men. Rurik ran off and started chatting with various warriors, including Saxi. Ash gave a satisfied nod. Saxi would give him sound advice combined with an embellished story or two. Virvir and his bloodthirsty tales would soon be a thing of the past. And he could concentrate on Kara.

'Will he be safe with them? You said they were desperate men.'

'Men become much less desperate with a good meal in their bellies and a solid roof over their head.'

'They are no farmers. They are warriors. There is a difference.'

Ash tilted his head to one side, trying to assess her mood. 'Warriors have their place.'

'But I want someone who understands the land.'

'Like you do.'

Her mouth became a disapproving line. 'I only learnt because I had to.'

'It will do him good to observe warriors in action and to talk to them. He can pick up a number of tips.' Ash paused and knew he had to tell her about Rurik's confidences. 'He saw Virvir last night. He was the cause of the earlier trouble. I thought you should know.'

'Virvir!' Her face crumpled. 'Why does Rurik keep defying me? I wish I'd never taken the boy in. He has been nothing but trouble.'

'Boys will be boys. Let me handle this, Kara.' Silently he willed her to compromise. 'See how excited he is. My men will keep him from harm. He will learn that the best warriors respect women.'

'Sell-swords?'

'Men who know how to use weapons properly, rather than bullies who will simply encourage bad behaviour,' Ash corrected.

Kara bit her lip, turning it the colour of autumn rosehips. 'Very well. I suppose I should go and see about the sewing. There is more to getting ready for winter than watching warriors train, despite what my women seem to believe. By the time your men depart, I suspect more than one woman will have a full belly.'

'Stay. Stay and watch me train,' he asked softly, willing her to agree. He used to find excuses to send her away, but now he wanted her there. He wanted to show off for her. She had to be softening a little. 'Like you used to.'

Her cheeks coloured slightly, but she turned her head towards the dogs. 'Why would I want to do that? I've no need of learning swordplay. I have no wish ever to be in a battle and there are a thousand things I need to do.'

'Because I work harder when I know you are watching.'

'Showing off.' Her tongue flicked out and wet her lips, turning them a deeper red than the last of the summer cherries.

'Demonstrating my skill.'

'A warrior's skill has no place in a peaceful farm. Why not demonstrate your skills with livestock or bringing in the grain?'

Ash's jaw tightened. Kara intended on fighting him for every morsel of respect and he knew he could not explain about his plan. If he did, she'd take Rurik away and any hope he had of gaining their regard would vanish. Some day he'd prove to her that she needed him and his unique skills.

'They ensure a farm stays at peace. You have enough men to do the other tasks, but this estate is not very well defended.' He paused, seeing her slightly shocked expression as she lifted her head from the dogs. 'Are you going to deny it?'

Kara tilted her chin in the air, looking the picture of a virtuous lady. It was all he could do to keep his hands at his sides, rather than grabbing and kissing her red lips. He had trouble remembering the last time he'd had to exercise this much self-control.

'I watch only because I want to be able to answer Rurik's questions tonight,' she said with a tiny triumphant smile. 'What sort of mother would I be if I failed to answer my son's questions?'

'I'm sure he is glad that you take an interest.' He lowered his voice for her ears only. 'I know I am.'

'Please stop.' Dipping her head, Kara made a show of brushing the dirt from her gown. 'You overreach.'

He caught her hand in mid-swipe, raising it to his lips. Her flesh quivered under the gentle pressure. 'If I offended you, I'm sorry.'

She withdrew her hand, but her eyes sparkled. 'Your apology is accepted.' She wrinkled her nose. Ash's heart skipped a beat. The tiny gesture was so instantly familiar that he could not believe he had forgotten about it. He used to try and get her to wrinkle her nose for the sheer pleasure of watching her. 'Who am I fooling? Yes, I do like to watch you fight. I always have. It can be very exciting to watch, but mainly it is for Rurik.'

'I always used to try to fight better if I knew you were watching,' he said with a rueful smile. 'I always knew you were there, Kara, even when you hid in the bushes before we were engaged.'

'I didn't… That is… It was only the once and I was returning your falcon.' Her eyes bulged. 'You remember that!'

'I had not thought about it for a long time,' Ash admitted. 'But it is in the back of my mind. It was one of the reasons why I gave your name when my father asked whom I wanted to marry. It felt right. And our marriage still feels right to me.'

'You mean you had other more important things to think about.' Her shoulders shook with barely suppressed indignation. 'I understand. Just remember that my son isn't something to be forgotten or ignored in the way I was. He isn't to be humiliated either.'

Ash struggled to control his fury. She had twisted his words. He had deliberately put such things from his mind. What was the point of re-membering the good times when he was stuck in the horror of unending war? 'I can remember my father yelling at me on this very training ground to be a man, to be a warrior and never to be weak like a woman. Know I will never humiliate Rurik in that way.'

Something new gleamed in her eye. 'I believe you.'

'My son is my future. I want him to succeed rather than feel he will never measure up. I want him to feel that he can always return home.'

'Good, I'm glad. Sometimes you seem more intent on showing off your skill than teaching.' She held up her hand, stopping his protest. 'Only an observation, Ash...from where I stand.'

He winced. He supposed he deserved the rebuke for his earlier remark. 'Your observations are always welcome.'

'That is kind of you and unexpected.'

'It is the truth.' He reached out and caught her hand. 'I will take good care of him, Kara, I promise. He is no less precious to me than you. I simply haven't known him as long, but I like what I see. He is a boy that any man would be proud to call son. And I can never repay you for what you did to ensure his survival.'

Her hand curled around his. 'My pleasure.'

'What are you afraid of?' he enquired softly, watching her mouth.

Her eyes slid away from his and she withdrew

her hand from his. The cool autumn air rushed to fill the space between them. The ease vanished faster than the morning mist. 'I've tarried far too long.'

'A pity. Maybe next time, you will stay.'

'I will think about it.' Silently Kara vowed to find another way to keep an eye on Rurik, something which didn't involve Ash getting the wrong idea about her. Or was it precisely the right idea? a tiny voice questioned in the back of her head. Angrily she silenced it.

Ash was going to leave when the winter snows melted. Seawater and the love of raiding ran in his veins. It was why he trained the warriors so hard. He would go. This time he would not be taking her heart with him. Except she knew her thoughts lied. Each time she encountered Ash, her heart opened a bit more. Kara stuffed her hand into her mouth as she hurried away from him. He was entirely too unreliable to love.

'I surrender!' Saxi put up his shield. 'You have proved your point.'

Ash checked his next move and lowered his sword. Sweat dripped down his face. It felt good to be moving and fighting. 'You are a bit slow today, Saxi.'

'You work too hard, old friend. You will end up injuring your leg again.'

Instinctively Ash leant down and rubbed the knot in his upper thigh. Now that he had stopped, the pain started. But it was easier to work hard, rather than to think about Kara and the way her dress moulded against her curves. 'I know what I am doing.'

Saxi pursed his lips as if he wished to say more. 'You're the man who pays the gold.'

'You will consider staying after...?' Ash tilted his head to one side. He was being pragmatic. Kara seemed further away from him than ever. It was only a matter of time before his uncle made his move and he'd have to fight for real. Whatever happened, he needed to know that someone he trusted would watch over his family.

Saxi drew a line in the dirt. 'You know how much of a life debt I owe you.'

'And you like the look of the area?' Ash lifted a brow. 'Or the women?'

'It amazes me that you waited this long before returning.'

'I had my reasons,' Ash said, looking over to the *tuntreet*. Tall and unyielding. 'You never met my father.'

'And did those reasons include your wife?' the other man asked softly.

'None of your business.'

'It is my business if you force us to work this

hard so that you don't dream about her. You still sleep outside, Ash. It is not good.'

'You are getting soft. Too much ale and feasting. Too many women. I want you all in the best condition.' Ash regarded the empty river. 'My uncle will make his move soon. I want to be ready.'

'You think your uncle will come after you?'

'Our escape from Sand was too easy.'

'Does your lady wife know it was an escape?' Saxi asked. 'She appears more concerned about getting the food stored than about taking precautions.'

'She thought the speed of the journey had to do with my desire to see my son. I didn't bother to enlighten her.' Ash stretched. 'I did want to see him, but I wanted to be in possession of Jaarlshiem when my uncle made his move.'

'Tell her, my friend. Immediately. Women like to make preparations in case of war.'

'I refuse to borrow trouble. It is possibly my instinct gone all wrong. When I was young, my uncle was ever a friend to me.'

'When did you say our ship would arrive? I left my best shield on board.'

Ash shaded his eyes from the glare of the sun and looked out along the wide river. 'I had anticipated it today, but it could be longer. Helgi the

Short won't play me false. He owes me too many life debts and he knows I'd hunt him down.'

'You can be ruthless when you want to be.'

'I prefer single-minded. I refuse to worry until the middle of next week. There will be time enough to tell Kara then if the ship fails to appear.'

He offered a small prayer up to the gods that he could uncover the key to her passion before then.

The grizzled warrior shrugged. 'My wife used to appreciate knowing about such things in advance. You are storing trouble. Trust her instead of looking at her like you want to eat her up.'

'Kara will only panic and take Rurik away. They are safer here.'

'They are safer with you, you mean.'

'Nothing will happen to her or our son. They'll remain here. It is why I brought you lot.' A muscle jumped in Ash's jaw. He knew what he was doing. He had played this sort of game before in Viken, but never for such high stakes and never with anyone he'd cared about. 'Now are you ready to fight again?'

'Bed her and tell her in the afterglow. Women love to feel protected. My wife did. You should have more children. Your son is a credit to you both.' Saxi pushed back on his helm. 'It would give us a chance to recover if you did bed her. Think of it as a favour to us all.'

Ash rolled his eyes. He'd been naïve to think the entire hall didn't know of his sleeping arrangements. But the last thing he wanted was advice on wooing his wife. 'She needs time. Seven years.'

'She is worth fighting for, Ash. The good ones always are.'

'When I need your advice, I'll ask for it.' Ash raised his sword. If he kept fighting, maybe his dreams would cease to be plagued with a beautiful blonde who had blue eyes to drown in. 'Shall we have at it again? Or are you getting too old?'

Chapter Twelve

Kara breathed in the sweet air of the stables. All about her the horses stomped their feet. For once she was all alone.

She did her best thinking when she was around animals. Her dogs sat in the corner of the stable and waited for her to be finished. She picked up a brush and started to work on the nearest horse, a simple enough task, but when she was done, she knew she'd feel steadier and more able to cope with her increasing desire for Ash. Desire rather than deep feelings. It had to be. She couldn't entrust her heart to him a second time.

'Why are you never where you are supposed to be?' Ash asked, coming into the stable as if her thoughts had conjured him. The horse gave a whoosh of air, but continued to stand placidly.

'I'll wait until you are finished, but I do want to speak with you.'

Kara concentrated on brushing out the horse's mane, teasing out several burrs, rather than glancing up towards where he stood in the doorway. When that was done, she moved away from the horse, slightly surprised he remained there. 'I like working with horses. I always have. Thora knew where I was.'

'I didn't.'

She put the brush down on a bench. 'Do I have to inform you every time I change a task?'

'No, it is just...' He rocked back on his heels. 'I missed you and I wanted to tell you that you were right. Your salve has helped my leg. I wanted to wait until I knew for certain. Thank you. I didn't want you to think me ungracious.'

Her heart thumped. He missed her. And her salve had helped. 'I'm pleased. Can I see it?'

He knelt down and slowly lifted his trouser leg. A great scar ran down the back of his calf. The muscle had healed knotted and twisted. 'You see why I said nothing would help. The knee was injured, as well.'

'If I may...' She knelt beside him and touched his scarred flesh. Her fingers worked with sure purpose. She could feel the knots easing under the pressure. 'It will improve further with a regular massage.'

'You do have a healing touch. Are you offering?'

'Perhaps.'

'Then I accept.'

The air hung between them—sweet and still. The temptation to lean into him and lift her lips to his nearly overwhelmed her. Kara rapidly rose and pretended to be busy, picking up her brush again. 'How did you know where to find me?'

'You always used to go to the stables when you were upset.' He rolled down his trouser leg and gave a crooked smile as if he hadn't noticed her pulling back. 'We made love once on a bed of straw because I found you in here after my father had been cruel about a stew you made. It cheered you up. I wanted to make sure you weren't upset.'

Kara laid down the brush with a trembling hand. It bothered her that he remembered that time. She'd cried against his chest until he'd lifted her chin and kissed her soundly. But making love, as enjoyable as it had been, had not solved her problem with Hring. Ash had departed five days later, knowing she wanted a buffer between her and her father-in-law.

'I'm happy. Rurik is doing well. The farm is prosperous. Why should I be unhappy?'

'You failed to mention me being here. Much remains unsettled between us.'

She toyed with the brush. 'Rurik is very glad to have a father, his real father, at long last. He has really blossomed.'

He put his hands on her shoulders and pulled her close. His breath laced with hers. 'But I want to be a true husband as well as a father.'

His mouth descended on hers. Darkness and hunger calling to that banked fire deep within her. The point of his tongue teased her lips, parted them, penetrated deeply and then re-treated.

She gave up her mouth with a sigh. Her hands buried themselves in his hair, holding him there as their tongues indulged. Each touch of his tongue sent the flames inside a little higher until she felt like she was being consumed. His mouth moved slowly over her skin to her earlobe. He captured it and suckled, tugging and pulling.

His hands roamed over her back, pulling her closer so that her body collided with his hard planes, leaving her in no doubt of his arousal. He wanted her as much as she wanted him.

Slowly he lifted her skirt, running his hand

down her white thigh. Then slowly his fingers advanced towards the heart of her fire.

'Ash,' she murmured, not knowing if it was a plea for him to stop or to continue.

He sank to his knees before her. 'Let me…'

Somewhere a door slammed and the sound of shared intimate laughter floated on the breeze.

Kara froze.

'Not here,' she whispered.

'Where, Kara? When?' Ash's voice sounded like he'd run a mile.

She twisted out of his grasp. Her face burnt. She had behaved worse than a mare in heat, worse than whichever of the women lay with the unknown man.

Ash regarded her with a puzzled expression. 'Talk to me, Kara. Tell me what is wrong.'

'I want time, Ash.' She smoothed down her skirt. Her skin protested. 'You rushed me the last time and look where that led us.'

'Where? We married. We had fun together until I left.'

'If you can call it a marriage.' Kara snapped her fingers with greater bravado than she felt. 'A few weeks and you were gone.'

'We'd known each other for years.'

'We had known of each other for years. I was

the girl with stars in her eyes and you were the boy who could do no wrong.'

'I always liked the way your eyes shone and how you made me feel better about myself.'

She concentrated on the hollow of his throat. 'A little over a year and I was a widow as far as anyone knew. You now want to saunter back into my life and turn it upside down.'

He put a finger under her chin. 'You have no idea how deeply I regret that happening. It is impossible to change the past.'

'Didn't being away from your wife bother you? Or did you find some comfort like that man is doing?' She put her hand over her face. 'Ignore that. I promised I'd never be like my mother.'

He put his hands on her shoulders. His hold was different this time. 'Kara, I'll be honest. I tried not to think of Jaarlshiem, Raumerike or even you. It made the horrors of my life easier to bear. Make no mistake, there were horrors as I watched my friends die and then had to survive with only my wits.'

Kara's breath caught and she willed him to say more.

'Returning covered in shame was impossible. You wouldn't have wanted me as a husband. But there were no other women. I was a married sell-sword seeking to regain his honour, not a berserker seeking a few moments of peace between some unknown's thighs.'

Kara rolled her eyes.

'You asked,' Ash said steadily. 'You deserve the truth. I tried not to think about you. But I have come home and everywhere I turn I find memories gathering. I do want to try again when you're ready.'

'Ash,' she said, pushing her hands against his hard chest before his mouth descended again. If she gave in now, there would be far too much unsettled between them. Ash appeared to believe that having sex would settle everything between them. It only complicated things. 'Your father explained about the other women. He had me meet them and hear their stories. He had them list how you made love to them—what you liked and how you seduced them.'

'My father did what?' His face became thunderous. 'It is well he is dead or I would rip his misbegotten heart out. He had no right.'

'He wanted to break my spirit over Rurik.' She shut her eyes, seeing them again—all much more beautiful than she. 'And he nearly did.'

'That was my father using everything in his power to get his own way.' He lifted her chin so she had to look into his eyes. 'He should never have done that. I never married any of those women. The only woman I wanted to marry was you and I married you. I came home to you.'

'But those women told the truth,' she said tonelessly, wrapping her arms about her waist. She wanted to bury her face against his strong chest and cry. Somehow, she'd hoped for more. Somehow, she'd hope he'd deny it.

His arms fell to his side. 'From here on, you will have to be the one to ask for my mouth before I give it.'

'To ask?' She blinked.

'Forcing you is the last thing I desire, Kara. Undoing the past is an impossibility as much as I might wish to. I want you, but I don't want you accusing me of seducing you. It works both ways. If you want to be kissed, you will have to ask, not provoke me or imply, but ask.'

'I am not sure what you are saying...'

His eyes turned serious. 'It is your move in the game we are playing. Make it. Stop hesitating. Stop playing it safe. If you want to make a break from the past, so be it. You take charge. See that it doesn't have to be like it was. You bear some responsibility for our old marriage as well as I. I am willing to change. Are you?'

She lifted her chin and summoned all her dignity but her insides knotted. Ash couldn't be right. She had always tried to behave in the correct manner. She wasn't avoiding her feelings.

She refused to suffer a second heartbreak over the same man. 'I will take your advice under consideration.'

Kara stepped back from the loom she had just threaded. The wool was all spun and now came the interesting part—weaving the cloth. It was time she started taking responsibility rather than mooning over Ash or hiding away with the animals. Ash had been right about that yesterday. She was avoiding her responsibilities.

Thora and the other women were hard at work on their looms or spinning the last of this year's wool. For too long she had neglected her duties in favour of watching Rurik and Ash training. Her dreams last night had been particularly vivid and concentrating on the tasks that needed to be done rather than watching how Ash moved as he trained Rurik was an attempt to get her mind back on a steadier course.

She was attracted to Ash. That much was clear, but she wasn't prepared to risk her heart again. He had carelessly trampled all over it once. She wanted to be certain she could keep her heart safe if she was going to stay in this marriage. Once she'd given everything and had nothing in return. It had to be more than desire on his part.

'There you are, Kara. Hard at work as usual.'

Ash appeared in the doorway. His hair gleamed and the light from the doorway made his shoulders appear very broad and his hips narrow. The sight did strange things to her stomach.

'Have you been looking for me?' she asked, striving for a neutral tone as her heart knocked against her ribs.

'You failed to turn up at this morning's training session.'

'We are behind with the weaving.'

'There was something I wanted to discuss with you about Rurik. It won't wait, so the weaving will have to.'

Disappointment stabbed her. She had to stop thinking he was searching her out because he wanted to spend time with her. He had told her that it was up to her to make the next move, but he was here. She had to take it as a good sign. 'Go on.'

'Tell me first why you didn't show up this morning. The truth this time.'

'Rurik informed me this morning over breakfast that he was a big boy and didn't need his mother looking after him.' She crossed her arms over her stomach. Keeping the subject to Rurik was far safer. She had no wish to continue their conversation from the stables out here where people could hear. 'Six and already he has no time for his mother. I listened to him and stayed away.'

'He needs his mother. He adores you.'

'You are being kind. I dare say your scheme to pry Rurik away from Virvir is working. Instead of quoting Virvir, he has now started quoting Saxi.'

'Excellent news.'

'Is Saxi the right sort of man for Rurik to look up to?'

'Saxi is a good man and a good warrior.' His face became sombre. 'He had three children until they were killed by the Franks. His youngest would have been about Rurik's age.'

Kara concentrated on the loom. She hadn't even considered that the big warrior might have had another life before this one. Ash had done a kind thing. 'I'm sorry for his loss and I'm sorry I doubted you.'

'An apology. Will wonders never cease?' His blue eyes blazed. 'You have done a fantastic job with that boy. He is a son any man could be proud of and I am grateful that he is mine.'

'Was there something else you wanted to see me about? The weaving waits for me,' she said quietly.

'I want to take Rurik hunting. Properly. He needs to learn. Saxi agrees with me. He used to take his eldest at this age, but I need to make sure he is eased into it.'

She put her hand to her mouth. Hunting. She didn't even want to think about the possibilities for Rurik to get hurt. Her father had died in a hunting accident. 'He is far too young. Hunting is very different from the control of a training yard.'

'He must learn.' Ash's face became alive with barely concealed passion. 'He has real skill with the bow and arrow. It needs to be cultivated, rather than ignored.'

'Can't he just shoot at targets and learn that way?'

'He needs a challenge. Something to completely occupy his mind.'

'He has been sneaking off to see Virvir again?'

'No, that has stopped, but some day they will meet and Rurik needs something he can brag about.' Ash put his hand on the loom. 'Leave your weaving and come with me, Kara. Now.'

'An order?' Kara gestured about the room. Hunting and Rurik were two words which sat uneasily together. She knew Ash was correct, but she wasn't ready to allow Rurik. Ever since their conversation in the stables, every time Ash searched her out, it was to do with Rurik rather than their relationship. It was frustrating in the extreme.

'A request.'

'You can see how much needs to be done.' Kara struggled to keep her temper. Why did this have to be settled this instant? 'With Gudrun gone, we are one woman short. Thora is training her niece, but the girl is clumsy with the loom. She is far more interested in discussing the merits of various warriors. Words won't keep men warm come winter.'

'One afternoon. This afternoon.' His tone left no room for objection. 'You will scarcely notice the difference. You always hated weaving, Kara. You complained bitterly about it when you were little.'

Kara put her hand to her mouth. He would have to remember that! After her mother died, her aunt had arrived to look after the house for her father and had insisted that she learn to weave properly rather than looking after animals. 'Do you know how much I have to do? Winter is coming. It waits for no one, not even you.'

'I want to show you what I plan to do when I take Rurik out on his own to ease your nerves. You will get more done if your mind isn't constantly occupied with worry.' His eyes held hers. She made the mistake of looking directly at them and tumbling into their blue depths. 'I want you to feel secure with Rurik's training, rather than having every possibility prey on your mind. I know what a vivid imagination you have. If you are not completely satisfied, then I won't mention the idea to Rurik.'

Kara's heart constricted. The offer was very unexpected. Ash was doing this for her to ease her mind rather than simply taking Rurik or building Rurik's hopes up. She had to meet him halfway. She had to trust him with this small thing.

'You want me to go hunting with you? Alone?'

'Tracking is perhaps the better word, learning to distinguish various tracks and follow the best ones.' He gave a half-smile. 'You used to beg me to take you on every expedition.'

Kara put her hand on her hip. 'You used to delight in taking me the hardest ways.'

'But you never gave up.'

'That's right.' Kara's stomach tightened. Before Rurik, she went along with everyone's ideas and didn't complain. She always tried to see the best in everything. 'I'm a very determined woman.'

'Come with me for the afternoon.' Ash gestured about the room where several other women worked. 'Leave this to the others. Say you will go. You and I, like the old days.'

A tide of warmth enveloped her. Ash wanted to spend time with her. Alone. 'So I can know what you intend with Rurik.'

'Precisely.' His smile spread across his face. 'I promise no harm will come to you. Nothing will happen that you don't want to. I won't make you fire an arrow to kill a bird.' He named several other incidents from long ago when she had been allowed to tag along, only if she did what he said.

'I never complained,' she answered stoutly.

'It would have been better if you had. It is impossible for me to know what you are thinking if you keep it to yourself.'

'You mustn't regret those excursions. I did enjoy them…after a fashion.'

He gave a crooked smile. 'Even though I treated you like a nuisance. My only excuse is the ignorance of young age.'

'A young girl trailing at your heels is hard. You were very good, Ash. I never came to any harm.'

'Saxi will look after Rurik and teach him how to fashion the feathers on an arrow.'

'Thora can take charge,' Kara said, coming to a decision. She wanted to go. Not just because of Rurik, but to spend time alone with Ash. It had been far too long since they had spent an afternoon together. And she didn't have any fears. She was in charge of the situation.

* * *

'See if you can tell what these tracks are,' Ash said, kneeling on a grassy knoll beside a small pond. 'Use the things I taught you today, rather than any long-ago knowledge. Pretend you are Rurik.'

Kara breathed deeply, savouring the feeling of being outside, rather than inside weaving. It was one of the last unexpectedly warm days of autumn. In the mornings, faint ice appeared on the edges of ponds like this, but when the afternoon sun hit, the air was pleasant. She had trouble remembering when she last felt this free. No responsibilities other than enjoying herself.

'I'm pleased you recognised at last that I do know animal tracks,' she said.

He laughed softly. 'I always knew, but I want you to experience how I teach now.'

She peered at the number of tracks in the mud. A wide variety of animals had obviously used this pond. 'Which ones do you want to know about?'

'The ones closet to the pond. They are the most difficult. It is the sort of thing I want to do with Rurik. Do you think you can do it?'

'Of course I can and I am sure, with a little help, Rurik will be able to, as well.' Kara knelt down and examined the various different tracks. It had been years since she had done this and she had forgotten how much fun it could be to be out in the woods with only Ash for company. 'Those are obviously rabbit, being followed by a fox. A deer has muddied the trail, but they were there first.'

She waited with bated breath, fairly confident that she had it right. Somehow Ash's opinion mattered. He had been a patient teacher, unlike when she was growing up and pestering him. He had taken the time and the trouble to explain everything, even when she reminded him that he had reluctantly taught her before.

'Very good. Better than good.' He knelt down beside her, his face wreathed in a genuine smile. Her heart turned over and she wondered how she thought she could do without his smile. 'I'd anticipated it would take several afternoons of intensive work before you'd be able to tell them apart. The fox is particularly unclear.'

'I'm a quick learner. I always was. I simply had forgotten the finer details until you reminded me.' She passed a hand over her eyes. 'How I could have mistaken a moose hoof for a deer is beyond me. You have been very patient, Ash. I can see why Rurik enjoys his lessons with you.'

'You forgetting? I thought you remembered everything.'

Kara looped a strand of hair behind her ear.

If she leant forward, it would be easy to brush Ash's lips. One little taste. But one taste could destroy their growing friendship. 'Obviously not.'

'I won't tell anyone.'

Kara rocked back on her heels and pressed her hands into her thighs. It was far harder than she thought to fight against this growing heat inside.

'Ash,' she whispered.

He reached out and smoothed a strand of hair from her forehead, straightening her head kerchief as he did so. 'It is easier to see if the hair isn't in your eyes. Concentrate and see if you can identify any more.'

His voice sounded strained and husky to her ears.

She knew then that she needed to make the first move. Now. Always before she had waited for him to act, but now she had to make the first move. For both their sakes. He was right about that the other night. This had to be a break from the past.

She looped her arm about his neck and pulled his face to hers. She brushed her lips against his, tasting their faint coolness which quickly gave way to a pulsating warmth. She wanted to linger and delve deeper, but...

She drew back, waiting for him to make the next move, to show her that the kiss was welcome. He watched her intently, much as a cat might watch a mouse hole. Waiting, but not moving.

Her breath caught in her throat. Silence filled her ears. Had she left it too long? Had his desire for her stopped?

'To say thank you for teaching me and all that you have done for Rurik.' She tried to keep her voice light, but she knew her cheeks burnt. She'd made a mistake with the kiss. She'd risked everything on an impulse and had lost. Her mouth tasted of bitter salt.

'No thanks is necessary, I assure you. My pleasure.' His voice held a faint rasp and his fingers flexed into a fist and released as if he were keeping a tight rein on his body.

'But I wanted to.' She drew a deep breath. She had to try once more. 'I want to kiss you again... if you are willing. Out here where it is just us.'

His intake of breath was sharp and sure. 'Don't say things like that unless you mean them. Once we start, there is no going back, Kara. I'm not made of stone.'

She cupped his face between her hands. The soft bristles of his unshaven chin tickled her fingertips and sent little flutters through her body, teasing her and awakening a fire deep within her belly. His eyes became heavily lidded with passion. A sense of power surged through her. 'I mean it.'

This time, rather than brushing his lips, she flicked out her tongue, running it along the outline of his mouth and lingering on the soft curve of his bottom lip. She caught it between her teeth and nibbled.

His arms came around her and roamed all over her back before crushing her to him. Her soft curves met his hard planes and his arousal pressed into her, leaving her in no doubt of his desire for her.

She knew she wanted much more and she was tired of waiting. Going back to the hall with all its people milling about and waiting until dark would take far too long. Even though it was autumn and a distinct chill hung in the air, she knew she wanted to experience it.

All of her hesitation vanished in the security of his arms. His mouth opened to her and she tasted the sweetness of him. Their tongues met and tangled, retreated and advanced.

He lifted his head. His ragged breath fanned her cheek. 'We must stop.'

'Why?'

'This place…it is not what I'd want for you, for us, for the first time since my return.' He put his hands on her shoulders and looked down at her, his face utterly serious. 'If this continues, I will lose whatever small amount of self-control I have with you.'

She laughed softly. A small thrill rippled through her. He wasn't tired of waiting. He was trying to go at her pace. Seven years ago, she'd been forced to go at his. But now they could move together. 'Ash, I am tired of waiting. My dreams have become unbearable. Help me make them real.'

'Dreams? You have dreamt of me. They cannot be half as vivid as my dreams of you.'

'You have no idea.'

'I used not to be able to sleep because of my memories of the shipwreck, and the men I'd killed, but lately I can't sleep because of you and what I want to do with you.' He cupped her cheeks between his palms. 'A soft bed can do wonders, Kara. Out here is hard ground and cold air. Uncomfortable at the best of times.'

Her stomach clenched. If they waited and went back to the hall, something would stop them. She wanted to do this now before she lost her nerve. 'I thought you disliked sleeping in rooms.'

'Did I say anything about sleeping?' He placed a soft kiss on her forehead. He looked down at her face and sighed, putting her from him. 'This is wrong. I'm sorry, Kara, but it is.'

'Wrong?' she whispered.

'Before we make love, you need to know what I went through,' he said slowly as if coming to a decision. 'I want you to know before…so you don't feel bound to me. You need to know everything or our marriage will still be false. I see that now as clearly as I see your face.'

Kara's breath caught. Ash wanting to share was far more important than their joining. He had said that he might not ever feel comfortable sharing his past.

'If you like,' she said cautiously. 'I'll listen with a sympathetic ear. I want to know everything about you.'

'I haven't been able to sleep inside since I was trapped on the ship after the lightning struck. A good captain would have gone down with his ship, but something within me fought to live.'

'You were asleep when the lightning struck?'

'The ship turned over and I was trapped for a lifetime.' Slowly Ash began to recount the story of his survival, including how he'd used the dead bodies of his friends as a shield to get out of the dungeon alive. Kara listened with growing horror at what he'd been through and respect for his survival. He spoke about the men he'd killed and when, leaving nothing out.

'There, you know everything—the bad and the ugly.' He started to turn away. 'We can go back to the hall now. When you make your decision, you can let me know.'

'I've made it.' She leant forward, grabbed his arm before kissing him on the mouth. 'We stay here. No more secrets between us. If anything, your story makes me admire you more. You went through all that and you remained determined not to give up or give in. I've seen you with Rurik and your men. What you went through didn't destroy you, Ash. It made you.'

His eyes darkened. 'If that is what you want.'

She undid her cloak and spread it out on the narrow strip of grass, sure of herself. She gestured about the hushed forest glade. 'We have the rest of our lives for a soft bed, but right now, we have all this beauty and solitude. But if you are unwilling, I'm willing to give you time.'

His rich laugh rang out as he threw an arm about her. 'If you knew how hard it has been for me, particularly in the past few days. I promised you time and I gave it, but I never said it would be easy on me.'

'On either of us,' she confessed to her cloak.

'It's good to know. I worried.' His hand traced a line the length of her back, sending a warm pulse throughout her, enveloping her in its heat. And his touch was better than any dream.

She spun around and he grabbed her hands,

holding them above her head. She glimpsed the vulnerability in his eyes.

'Would you have taken me out today if I'd asked?'

'I wanted to confess my deeds. You were right—you needed to know,' he murmured against her mouth. 'It couldn't hang between us and I wanted it to be out here. I was certain you'd turn from me. All I had was one slender hope, but it was enough.'

'You had hope.'

'Without hope, I'd never have survived. Somewhere deep within me, I wanted to see your face again and feel your skin against mine.' His lips captured hers, slowly moving across her face, raining kisses on her eyes, cheekbones and nose, making a memory.

With each touch, Kara realised her dreams had been a pale copy of the real thing. She moved to touch him, but he shook his head.

'Patience,' he murmured, capturing her hands. 'I intend to enjoy this. You have led me on a merry dance, Kara. It is time you knew a bit of pleasurable suffering.'

Their hands remained intertwined as he eased her back onto the cloak, before he took off his cloak and tunic. The autumn sunlight turned his skin to gold, but she could see a network of scars across his torso and recalled his story about the way he'd battled to return.

She hated to think about the pain he must have borne for each scar. She reached out a trembling finger and traced the nearest scar. His flesh was molten hot to her touch.

'Not the perfection I used to be,' he said, kneeling beside her and taking her hand between his. 'Is that what you are trying to tell me with your serious stare? I don't match your expectations?'

She looked up at the deep blue autumn sky and tried to regain control of her emotions. How could he think such a thing about her? 'I'm sorry you had to feel pain.'

'Take away pain and you take away life.' He lifted her hand to his lips. His tongue made a little circle on the underside of her wrist. 'You've lessened my pain today considerably, the pain I have in my soul.'

She passed a hand over her eyes. The scars might not be visible like the ones on his torso, but they were there. 'Yes, of course.'

Very deliberately she leant forward and placed her mouth on the most jagged of his scars, the one which ran from his right breast down to his left hip where someone once had tried to slice him open. His second battle with the Franks. She ran her tongue along the length of it, feeling its silken smoothness which contrasted with the faint roughness of his unblemished skin.

'May I see you?' His breath tickled her ear. 'Let me feast my eyes on your perfection.'

'Hardly that. I've had a child.'

'You will be perfection to me.'

She leant back on her heels and started to undo her belt, but the knot stuck and refused to work loose.

With nimble fingers he undid her belt before pushing her gown and undergarment up. The cool autumn air kissed her skin.

She gave a faint shiver. He pulled her into his arms. And the heat of his skin slid over her. 'Shall I warm you?'

His body covered hers, providing instant searing heat. His lips made a trail to her earlobe and nuzzled it, pulling and tugging it.

Each touch sent a fresh wave of desire through her, reminding her of the times he had made love to her in the past and how good it had been once. He seemed to know how to play her body and precisely what she liked.

Her body bucked upwards. His hand cupped her breasts and flicked the nipples. A tiny movement of nail against the delicate rose-coloured skin, but it increased her desire to fever pitch. Then he bent his head and his tongue circled her nipples, sucking and exploring.

She made a mewling noise at the back of her throat.

Later they could go slowly, but right now she knew she needed him inside her or she'd die. She tugged at his shoulders and spread her thighs wide.

'Hush now, let me explore,' he rasped in her ear.

His hand slipped down to the apex of her thighs, going between the folds and smoothing her innermost core, stroking and probing until she thought she could bear it no more.

'Please,' she whispered as her body was alive with fire.

He relented and drove himself between her legs. Her body opened and welcomed the length of him. Fully sheathed him.

They lay there, unmoving, adjusting to each other. Then he gently began to rock, going deeper and then retreating. Her body remembered the rhythm, moving along with him.

She knew it was not going to be like her dream and he wouldn't vanish in the mist, but her legs still locked about him, holding him within her, keeping him there as she shuddered to a climax.

Slowly Ash drifted back to earth and raised himself up on his elbows so he could look down on Kara's peaceful sleeping face.

She might be asleep, spent from the passion they had just shared, but he felt wonderfully awake and alive in a way he'd not felt for years. He had forgotten such feelings existed. He had told her the truth about his past and she hadn't pulled away or made him seem less of a man for what he'd done.

He wanted to ensure that nothing ever harmed her. He'd made the right decision to keep his fears about his uncle from her. That was the future, not the past.

He ran a hand down her smooth back, marvelling at the silkiness of her skin. Even the gentle touch made his body harden and he knew it would be a long time before he'd had his fill of her.

Ash concentrated on keeping his breathing even. They had all the time in the world. She belonged to him now. He would be worthy of her. Some day she would see it.

He gave her backside a gentle tap. 'Time to get up.'

'Get up?' Her voice remained slurred with spent passion and sleep. She snuggled further into the crook of his arm. 'I'm far too comfortable here.'

'You might be now, but the temperature rapidly drops when the sun goes in.' He dropped a kiss on her shoulder, rather than gathering her to him. Even the tiny touch was enough to send his heart racing. He'd been seven times a fool to stay away as long as he had. 'We don't want Rurik worrying about us.'

At the mention of their son, she sat up and reached for her clothes. Her cheeks became a delightful pink when she realised the state of them. The pleats of her under-dress were hopelessly creased. 'What will he say if he sees me like this?'

'He will be glad that we are trying to give him a brother or a sister.'

She put a hand over her mouth. 'Of course, I hadn't thought. You want more children.'

'You do want more children?' he enquired softly, trying to understand her change of mood. 'You always said that you wanted a big family.'

'Yes, of course.' The words were far too quick. Her hands tidied her kerchief and neatened her dress. 'I simply wasn't thinking about that. You have only been back a little while.'

'I was.' Ash captured a strand of her hair and ran its silky smoothness through his fingers. 'I'd like a girl with blond hair and her mother's spirit.'

'And what if it doesn't happen?'

'We enjoy each other and the child we do have.' He put his hand on her shoulder and felt her flesh quiver. 'If you want me to be a farmer,

Kara, I'll try. I want to be the sort of man you want for your husband.'

Kara gnawed at her lip. 'That would be good.'

'Is there something wrong?'

'Nothing at all. The hour is late. People will get concerned.' She leant forward and nipped his chin. 'I shall tell whoever asks that I had a lovely lesson in tracking.'

Ash allowed his laugh to ring out and startled several wood pigeons. Things would work out this time. He would defeat his uncle and then he could work at being the sort of man Kara wanted him to be.

Chapter Thirteen

Kara inhaled deeply as she slipped off her cloak in her chamber. Ash had gone to make sure all the equipment he'd brought with him was properly stored, leaving her to make her own way to her chamber. She thanked the gods for a small piece of luck—she managed to get to her chamber without encountering anyone and having to suffer knowing stares or, worse still, questions.

She plucked a stray twig from her hair. His declaration about being willing to be a farmer had unsettled her. It was the last thing she expected from Ash and she had trouble thinking of him being happy, yet he had seemed sincere. It was what she wanted, wasn't it? Someone by her side to share the burden. Her perfect mate. It made no sense. She should be happy, but it unnerved her as if there was something Ash was keeping from her.

'My lady, thank the gods you have returned. Visitors are in the hall.' Thora rushed into the room without knocking. Her kerchief was askew and the relief was etched on her face.

'Have you made them comfortable?' Kara automatically straightened her dress, silently blessing whichever god had watched over her earlier. If she had gone straight to the hall, everyone would have guessed what had happened and it was far too new to share.

'Yes, my lady.' Thora twisted her pinafore.

'What is the trouble, Thora? You appear distressed.' Kara straightened her gown. 'Is it Harald Haraldson? You don't need to fear that his men will behave badly this time. Ash and his men will keep the peace.'

'It's Valdar, my lady.'

Kara's heart knocked. Valdar. She wasn't ready to see him. Her relationship with Ash was far too new. They were still getting used to each other.

'Valdar,' she said, biting the back of her thumb.

Thora smiled. 'Rurik is beyond excited, but considering your recent history and the master being here, do you really want him here?'

Kara hoped her colour stayed normal. The hall traded on secrets and she wasn't ready to share what had happened in the forest with anyone. She and Ash hadn't even begun to discuss sleeping arrangements. He might not want to share her bed because of his nightmares.

'I've no choice in the matter.'

Ash strode in. He glanced at Thora, who blushed, and then purposefully went over to Kara and kissed her lips. Thora hurriedly backed out of the room, stammering. The news would be all over the estate before night fell.

'Problems?' Ash asked, tightening his grip on her waist. 'Whatever they are, they can wait. Let's take a bath together, wash the dust away. I can scrub your back.'

She broke away. 'Visitors.'

'I know.'

Kara froze. He knew and still suggested bathing. Had he known they were near before he took her out into the woods? 'You knew.'

He laughed. 'Hard to miss a half-dozen extra horses.'

Her neck relaxed slightly. There was a logical explanation. 'Oh, I thought…it doesn't matter. But there is no question of bathing, Ash. That would…that would be rude.'

'A suggestion in case you wanted to look your best, rather than like you'd had a delightful tumble in the forest.'

'I…I can't abandon my duties.'

He shrugged. 'Always one for duty, Kara.'

'The honour of the house is at stake.'

'What do you intend to do about him?'

There was no mistaking the jealousy in Ash's tone. She smiled inwardly. After all they had shared this afternoon he should know which man she preferred.

'I will greet him with the usual warmth. Valdar has been a good friend. Only a friend.' She began to walk towards the hall with brisk steps. The last thing she wanted was for Ash to start some unnecessary competition with Valdar where she was perceived as a prize. That was all his suggestion about bathing had been about—a way of presenting her as a trophy to Valdar. She liked Valdar. She'd no wish to hurt him.

'My lady,' Ash called, 'aren't you forgetting something?'

Kara stopped. 'Such as?'

'Your husband. You never know if the visitors will be friendly. One day you may have cause to thank my past life as a warrior.'

Kara's stomach knotted. She hoped Ash hadn't decided to be a farmer simply to please her.

'It is the duty of the woman to greet any visitor,' she replied carefully. 'Valdar is a welcome visitor here. Always. Rurik will be overjoyed to see his old friend.'

'No doubt.' His eyes became speculative. 'I

shall have to make sure Rurik shows some of the moves I taught him.'

'He is a friend. Nothing more.' Kara's heart thudded. 'Rurik likes him because the man took an interest in him. Valdar always brings him something little when he visits and he did visit quite frequently when he was wooing me. Auda even joked that he tried to woo the woman through the son, but I knew the relationship he has with Rurik is based on mutual regard.'

Ash raised a brow. 'Did I ask?'

Kara put her hand on her hip. 'You implied. I want you to know the truth. No secrets, remember? We agreed. A fresh start for us both.'

'Do you know why he has arrived here?'

Kara put her fingers to her temples. 'Let me concentrate.' She counted to ten. 'No, sorry. Nothing. No idea why he is here. I was never a good soothsayer, Ash.'

A muscle jumped in Ash's jaw. 'I can make a good guess, if you won't.'

Kara rolled her eyes. It was gratifying in a way that Ash showed this streak of jealousy, but the last thing she wanted was for the two to come to blows. Valdar had been Ash's friend once. They could be again.

'Why don't we ask him and then we will know the truth? It could be a hundred different reasons, including that he wants to wish us well.

Jaarlshiem is not far from his estate. He might even be able to give you tips on farming.'

'Do you take his tips?'

Kara put her hand to her throat. She had always planned to once they were married. Before then, she had run the estate as best she could. 'They are worth listening to. Certainly.'

'And will you listen to my suggestions?'

Kara tilted her head to one side. 'I listened to you about Rurik. Does that satisfy you?'

'You think he has come to see you, his former bride. To check you are all right and once again make his offer of protection. Will you tell him about us?'

She shrugged and concentrated on the ground. 'As far I knew, he had no plans to come here. I'm shocked that he has arrived.'

'You can be such an innocent, Kara. I am far from shocked. I've been expecting him.' He draped an arm across her shoulders, claiming possession. 'Shall we see him together? He needs to know that while he is welcome as a friend, he needs to look elsewhere for a lover.'

'I am not some bone to be fought over.' Kara ducked under his arm and freed herself. Ash had guessed. She found it impossible to rid her brain of the thought that he had seduced her today. Was that why he made his offer?

His eyes narrowed. 'I gave up fighting, re-member? At your request. I am to be a farmer.'

Her heart knocked. He was doing this to please her, just as he had tried so hard to be a warrior.

'I'm not a prize to be exhibited. I'm your wife and I have always behaved correctly. With modesty and decorum. The entire kingdom will buzz with the gossip, like busy bumblebees.'

'There will be no fighting, I guarantee you that.' Ash's eyes glittered. 'I have won. I trust you to tell him.'

'You could never resist grinding your opponent into the ground.' Kara glared at him.

'I'm not my father or my uncle.'

'Are you coming, Mor? Far?' Rurik called out from the doorway. 'I want to show you what Valdar brought. My very own sword! It is very sharp.'

Ash raised an eyebrow, but Kara shook her head.

'I knew about the sword, Ash. It was to be his present to Rurik for being his new father. Valdar promised that it would not be a full-sized sword, simply one a young boy could be proud of.'

'Rurik already has one father. He has no need of another. Make sure you emphasise that when you greet him.'

Kara didn't bother to reply, but walked with

purposeful strides to the hall where Valdar waited, standing with his back to the hearth and his feet splayed apart. Valdar's face lit up when he spied her. Kara's heart sank. She had hoped he'd be dressed casually, but he appeared to be dressed as if he expected trouble with his broad sword belted to his hip.

'Valdar, what a pleasant surprise. What brings you here?'

'This is far from a social call, my lady.'

Immediately his hand went to his sword's hilt. Without even looking, Kara knew Ash had entered behind her. From the footsteps, it would appear his men were there, ready and waiting for Ash's signal. Ash had made plans she knew nothing about. So much for no secrets. Were his plans to be a farmer also lip service?

'No bloodshed,' she murmured.

'If he draws his sword, I doubt I can control my men,' Ash retorted in an undertone. 'They are loyal.'

'Control them or consider yourself an unworthy commander.'

'My lady has spoken. It seems sometimes she doesn't require a farmer.' Ash's voice held more than a note of irony.

'Valdar Nerison, you are always a welcome friend who comes in peace and friendship,' she said, advancing forward, ignoring that Ash stood behind her glowering at the other warrior. Ash should know after what had just passed between them that she had no feelings for Valdar. She paused and attempted to gather her wits for the rest of the formal greeting.

'For you, my Lady Kara, always.' Valdar inclined his head, but his hand still hovered above his sword hilt.

'I'm sorry we weren't here to greet you,' Ash said, stepping in front of her. 'Kara and I were out tracking.'

'I see.' Valdar's face fell and his hand dropped from the sword.

'Ash took over Rurik's training and I wanted to make sure that what he proposed for Rurik would be acceptable.' Kara was aware that her face had gone bright red. Somehow, her words seemed to make the situation worse instead of better as Valdar paled.

'Kara finds my training more than acceptable.' Ash gave a short laugh, obviously starting to enjoy the situation. 'There again, Rurik is my son. Funny how that works out.'

'Rurik is a son that any man would be proud to call his.' Valdar inclined his head. 'I welcome the fact that the Lady Kara has finally agreed to his proper training. I had hoped she might consent to my services, but I can see the child's father would be preferable.'

'A huge responsibility, but I am more than willing to shoulder it,' Ash commented.

Valdar turned sharply towards her and concern flickered across his face.

'Ash intends to stay, Valdar,' she said quietly.

'I see.'

Kara pressed her lips together. Valdar had known before that it was impossible. Silently she prayed that Valdar had not appeared in the hope that all remained uneasy between her and Ash.

'Rurik has amply entertained me with tales of his training.' Valdar ruffled Rurik's hair. 'You have the makings of a fine warrior. Hopefully we shall see you ice-skating this winter, as well.'

Kara schooled her features. It hurt that Valdar also thought she had been overly cautious with Rurik. 'We shall have to see what the winter brings.'

'Rurik understands why his mother is being careful,' Ash said.

'My mother had only me to look after her. It is different now that my true father has come back,' Rurik piped up.

'Who taught him that one?' Kara murmured, giving Ash a sideways glance.

Ash appeared unrepentant. 'I thought the sentiment had a ring of truth.'

'Indeed.' Kara ground her teeth.

'Did you come merely to see Rurik and how

he fares?' Ash asked in ringing tones. 'Or was there another darker purpose?'

'I came to see you, Ash Hringson, on urgent matters.' Valdar stood and reached into his pouch and withdrew a wooden tablet. 'The king instructed it be placed in your hand. You are to return to Sand immediately. There is to be an enquiry. I have the authority to bring you in chains, if you do not come willingly.'

Kara's stomach roiled. The king had turned against Ash. She had thought everything was settled before they had left. 'Why?'

'My uncle demands my ship plus tribute.' Ash gave the rune-stick the briefest of glances. 'He swears my ship attacked his on its way up the river. An act of aggression against Raumerike on my orders. Unfounded, but effective. My oarsmen had their orders to come straight here. The king takes a cautious approach and wishes to investigate. I had expected it might come to this.'

'You already knew? You expected this?' Kara stared at him in astonishment. He'd kept something so important like that from her! After declaring no secrets! He couldn't be certain his men had followed orders. Sell-swords were notorious for going after easy prey. She sank down on a stool. If the charges were proved against Ash, Harald Haraldson would be within his rights to demand all of Ash's holdings, including this estate.

'I suspected my uncle might make this move. I thought the ship would arrive three days ago, yesterday at the worst. Far better to know my men are safe rather than suffering in a shipwreck.' Ash inclined his head. 'I thank you for being swift, Valdar Nerison. It has eased my mind no end.'

'I felt it my duty to let you and the Lady Kara know as soon as possible.' Valdar straightened his back, giving her a significant look. 'There are other people to think of besides yourself, Hringson or Ash the Untrusted.'

'I am well aware of that name. My father unfairly gave it to me after I fell asleep guarding some sheep when I was ten and had been awake all night. It has not been used for many years.' Ash gestured towards the door. 'You appear dusty and travel-worn. You should have a bath and relax before we discuss all the news. The morning is soon enough to depart.'

'You will go willingly?'

'When my king makes an order, who am I to refuse? I am a loyal subject of our king, regardless of what Harald Haraldson might say.' Ash gave a crooked smile, but his eyes were deadly serious. 'The hour is late. We leave at first light.'

He rapidly gave orders for Valdar's things to

be placed in his bed cabinet and for his men to be treated with respect.

'You should have said something when you suspected that something had gone awry,' Kara said when Rurik had led Valdar off and they were alone in the hall. Her mind whirled. Ash had deliberately kept things from her. 'You should have confided in me about this.'

'Why worry you about something which might not come to pass?'

'We're far from ready if Harald Haraldson should decide to attack Jaarlshiem. The grain and wool will need to be moved.' Kara pressed her hands together to keep them from trembling. 'It was wrong of you.'

'And have you fret and use it as an excuse?'

Kara bit her lip. 'You should have told me.'

'Harald Haraldson will not attack here. He wouldn't dare. Not with my sell-swords guarding it. And he covets this estate. He doesn't want to lay waste to it.'

'How do you know?' Kara glanced at the door. Suddenly Ash's insistence of a guard and men seemed less extravagant. 'He could be on his way right now. Things need to be properly stored. We could be facing a long siege.'

'Think with your head, Kara, instead of giving way to blind panic.' Ash slammed his hand down on the table. 'My uncle wants this hall above all things and believes he will get it through the king. It makes no sense for him to attack if he has taken my ship. He needs to remain in Sand if he wishes to influence the king.'

Kara put her hand over her mouth. Ash was correct. If Harald Haraldson wanted to influence the king, he needed to be in Sand. Ash did know what he was doing, but it didn't make her any happier or feel any less used.

'You weren't sure which way your uncle would move. It is why you brought your men, rather than fearing any threat from Valdar. It is why you have been training them so hard. You expect war. You have been using me like a counter in a game of tafl.'

'War happens whether you expect it or not. It is best to be prepared.' Ash shrugged and began to rearrange the pieces on the tafl board, concentrating on them, rather than looking Kara in the face. He could sense Kara slipping away from him. This afternoon she had been his, but… It hurt that she refused to understand that he was acting to protect her. 'Sometimes you have to wait for the other person in the game to make his move.'

'Who do you think you are playing this game against? The king?'

'My uncle,' Ash said, putting the tafl piece down. Kara deserved to know the truth now that his uncle had acted. Once she knew, she would see that he had done the right thing. 'My uncle seeks me banished or dead. He wants this estate. He is using the king as his instrument of destruction.'

Her face showed her dismay. 'You told me it was all resolved. The king gave you permission to depart. I believed you. It was why I went with you. You used me, Ash. That is unforgivable. You should have trusted me. What is a marriage without trust? Was your promise to become a farmer simply mouthing words?'

He winced. In seeking to protect her, he had lost her trust.

'I want to be with you and our son. I am willing to try, but I have to do this first. I am used to operating on my own.'

'The last time you asked for permission to do something first, you were gone for seven years.'

'It won't be that long. I've taken all the steps necessary. The king did give me permission to return to Jaarlshiem. Until my uncle chose his move, I couldn't counter him.' He forced a smile, but knew it wouldn't fool her. 'I am an excellent tafl player. You know that. I mean to win.'

Her eyes turned sad. 'You should have said something when you first suspected.'

'What could you have done?' He put his hands on her shoulders. 'I know what I am doing. It has been my life for the past six years. Let me prove to you that I am worthy.'

She shrugged off his hands and her eyes flashed. 'You leave for Sand at first light. You won't be here to put things right.'

'Everyone is prepared.' He struggled to understand her hurt. He knew what he was doing. He would return as soon as he could. 'You'll be safe here.'

'Sometimes safety is an illusion. You showed me that with Rurik.' She dipped her head and he could only see the crown of braids. 'I thought Rurik was safe with Gudrun and look what happened.'

'Like you, I'd give my life for our son.'

Her mouth became an O.

'Valdar wanted me in chains, but I suspect he gave me the option for the sake of our son and you,' Ash continued. 'I suppose I should be grateful that he likes my son. It would not do for him to see his father escorted out in chains.'

'Valdar isn't like that. He is your friend.' Her hand played with the chain on her waist. 'It is why we first became close. He was able to tell Rurik stories about you.'

'He was my friend once, but he fell in love with my wife. He'll take pleasure in seeing me humiliated. It is why my uncle persuaded the king that he was the perfect man for the job.

Why he wasn't at court that morning. He is my uncle's man now.'

'Will your uncle win if no one pleads for you?' Kara began to pace the hall. Her skirt swished, revealing her trim ankles, but Ash admired the steel in her backbone more.

'My uncle will have put it about that I am a Viken spy.'

She stopped mid-stride. 'Are you a spy?'

'I was a sell-sword who fights in the open, not a spy who hides in the shadows. I certainly never betrayed my country. I never preyed on Raumerike ships and I would never do so.'

He waited, willing her to understand.

'I believe you, my husband.'

Tension rushed from Ash's shoulders. Kara believed him. She had claimed him. He gathered her in his arms. 'It is a start.'

A tiny frown creased her forehead. 'Can you prove it?'

'Should it come to it, I believe I can. My men will vouch for me.'

'Who would believe the word of a sell-sword? Everyone knows they will say anything for money.' She stuffed her hand in her mouth. 'That sounds dreadful, Ash. But you need others to support you. You can't do this alone.'

'My uncle will overreach. He needs a small push, but he will do it.'

'Would you give up your man if it turns out your uncle is correct and your ship did attack?'

Ash considered Helgi. His oarsman was cautious to the point of inaction. He only attacked if he knew he had superior numbers. The ship had barely enough men to get upriver. Ash had made sure of it. They had not been the aggressors. He knew this in his gut. 'It would go against Helgi the Short's nature to attack.'

'That isn't what I asked! Would you be the one to strike him dead if he turns against you? The king is sure to ask you. Hesitating will only give credence to our enemies.'

He tilted his head. 'Our? Since when did my enemies become yours? A man doesn't abandon his friends or the men who trust him, Kara. Helgi did not do this.'

'Not even to save himself?'

'Especially not then. I'll prove Helgi's innocence and my own, as well.'

'Attacking you through this ship means Rurik's inheritance is in jeopardy. I can't allow that to happen. Promise me you won't put your friend above our son.'

A pang went through Ash. He wanted to be more important than Rurik. He shook his head in disbelief. When had he started to be jealous of his son? He wanted Kara to trust him.

'I want the truth, Kara. If Helgi has disobeyed

my direct orders, then I will be the one to draw a sword and strike his head from his shoulders. But a man should be deemed innocent until proven guilty. I will defend him until I have proof otherwise.' He hoped Kara believed it. If he couldn't convince Kara, what chance did he have of convincing the king?

Silently he prayed to any god who might be listening that he would be able to prove it and he would not be the one to end Helgi's life. He owed Helgi far too many debts. 'If he has betrayed me, I will not hesitate. I haven't in the past. Let me go.'

'To do what? Leave and not come back?'

'To fight for us both.' He lifted her chin so he could stare directly into her eyes.

She slammed her fists together. 'I will return with you. You owe me this, Ash.'

He stared at her, dumbfounded. Hadn't Kara listened to a word he had said? He had made arrangements for her. 'You can stay here, safe and unmolested. No one will doubt Rurik's claim to this place. I will make sure of it. It will be better for you to look after Rurik here.'

'Rurik goes to Sand, as well. We all go or none of us goes.'

He stared at her open-mouthed. 'You are going to risk Rurik in Sand? Why? He is safest here!'

'He will be safer with you than being left here, and there is no one I will leave him with, not after what happened the last time. There, I've given you an excuse if anyone asks, but I want us to be together as a family. We face this together. United against the world.'

Ash gulped hard. Kara wanted to come with him. Once, he'd longed to hear those words. Now they made it worse. This wasn't about proving his worth as a warrior, but saving his family. He had to outthink his uncle and he couldn't do that if he was worried about Kara and Rurik. Here at Jaarlshiem he could leave enough men to protect them. In Sand anything could happen to them.

For the past seven years, he had only had himself to worry about and now he was terrified for Kara and Rurik. He wanted to be able to protect them, not just because he had a duty towards them but because he cared about them.

'Your offer is unexpected.' He ran his hand through his hair, wondering how he could stop her without destroying this new fragile bond that had grown between them in the last few days. And he selfishly wanted her there with him, which was wrong. If he was truly the man he wanted to be, he'd make her stay where she was safe.

'Unexpected or unwelcome?' she asked sharply.

'I'm used to being on my own. Worrying about myself and no one else. I have everything under control.'

She slipped her hand through his arm. 'You are not on your own any longer.'

Ash's stomach knotted. Her saying that made it worse. The walls pressed in on him, making it difficult to breathe. He had planned everything. Kara was supposed to want to stay out of harm's way. She wasn't supposed to volunteer to come with him. 'It could be a trap. My uncle might try to harm you or Rurik to get at me. Think of how that will make me feel.'

'You proclaimed that everything was in hand.' Her mouth turned mulish. 'If it is safe enough for you, it is safe enough for Rurik.'

'It is different for me. I know the risks. You can stay here. I will leave my men to guard you.' He ran his hand down the length of her arm. 'I want to know you are safe. Do this for me.'

Her lashes swept down, hiding her expression. 'You asked for the opportunity to show me that you have changed. I will give you that opportunity. Will you let me come and bring Rurik?'

Ash brushed his lips against hers and tried to dispel his sudden sense of panic. He wasn't a better man. He was a selfish one who would take every opportunity to be with his wife and child. The fact tore at his insides. 'After this afternoon, I've no wish to let you go.'

'Then you agree. I'll come.'

'How can I stop you?' He bowed his head. The walls of the hall seemed to bear down on him, reminding him of his duty and how he'd failed before. Far more was at stake this time. There would be no second chance to get it right. 'I need to see my men and make sure all is ready, including a cart for you and Rurik.'

Kara paced her chamber. She had retired for the night after she had given up waiting for Ash to return from his making arrangements for their departure. Her mind spun with all the worries about the future. Ash was going again and she had no guarantee when he might return. Or if. And had he truly meant his words about becoming a farmer? Or had that been a sop?

After giving a soft knock, Ash entered the room. 'Valdar and his men are bedded down. Safe and secure. And all arrangements are in hand. We leave at first light.'

'Was it that difficult?'

'It took some doing.' Ash ran his hand through his hair. 'He doesn't know you are coming yet.'

She stared at him. 'If you hope to use your power of persuasions with me, I will warn you my mind is made up. I am going.'

He shook his head. 'I know enough about you not to try that. Less chance of objections from Valdar. I wanted to spend tonight with you, rather than countering his arguments. I had to show him the fortifications so that he could test you would be properly guarded.'

'Then he is not entirely your uncle's creature.'

'You have a point, Kara. You are far more than a pretty face.'

Kara frowned at the way the warmth curled about her insides at his hooded look. She wasn't going to fall into bed with him, just yet. She wanted to make sure he understood her terms first. 'I'm sure Valdar will see the necessity and he would far rather I travelled with him and you, instead of making the journey on my own.'

'Stubborn. Just the way I like you.' He moved closer. 'Do I have to provoke another fight before you will kiss me?'

'I'm finished with fighting you.'

He lifted her chin. 'You will see, Kara, I will prove I'm worthy of you. A few short weeks and we will return.'

Her heart panged. The echo of seven years ago rang loudly in his words.

'It will take as long as it takes.' Her voice trembled on the last word. She screwed her eyes up tightly, silently cursing. 'I know that, Ash. I have accepted it.'

She hoped he believed it more than she did.

'I've stopped thinking about the future, Kara. I want to live in the here and now.' He smoothed the hair off her forehead and her entire body tingled with an acute awareness of him and what they had shared earlier.

She wanted that sharing again, that feeling of closeness.

'Can you do that?' he rasped, gently tugging at her earlobe. Little flames licked at her inner core, igniting her senses in a way that only Ash could. It amazed her that she could feel so alive. Like a moth drawn to a flame, she found the movement of his mouth impossible to resist.

She knew it was impossible to explain her feelings for him in words, but she could allow her body to speak.

'I will try.' She looped her arms about his neck. 'Enough thinking for tonight, I want to feel.'

Chapter Fourteen

The early morning mist rising from the lake hung in the valley. Ash glanced up at the hall looming behind. He'd left Kara sleeping. Nothing had felt right between them when he'd made love to her last night—far too frantic and forced, as if they both knew that he might not ever get another chance.

Lying next to her afterwards, he had struggled to breathe and knew he had to escape the airless room. His leg had throbbed, making sleep impossible. He had given her naked shoulder one last kiss and slipped away.

He had dressed quickly and started towards the lake, intending to swim and loosen the knots in his leg. When he reached the *tuntreet* with its now-naked spreading branches, he sank down to his knees and buried his face in his hands.

Somehow he had to find a way to keep the people he loved safe.

Coming home was supposed to be simple. But every time he turned around, he saw other ways in which he could never measure up. A dull pain formed behind his eyes.

'Here I find you, Ash.' Valdar's cold tone rang out across the lake, causing several geese to rise up. 'Thinking of leaving? Or making a stand here? Or are you praying to the gods for a swift and merciful release?'

Ash slowly rose and faced the man who had once been his friend. 'I gave you my word. I will be going to Sand. Voluntarily and not in chains or with my feet dragging. My men have their orders. They will obey them. It should be enough.'

'Does that bother you?'

'Not in the slightest.' Ash inclined his head. He wondered briefly how many battles Valdar had fought or if he ever felt uncertain or afraid. If he failed, Kara would need a strong arm.

Ash pressed his lips together. Now was the right time to begin his move and see if he could separate Valdar from his uncle.

'Kara intends to take Rurik to Sand. Will you allow her to travel with us or will she be forced to travel on her own?' He looked the man in the eye. 'I need to know how to deploy my men.'

The other man's lip curled. 'The Lady Kara

is supposed to remain here. Is this one of your mad ideas?'

'Far from it. It's Kara's. I wish you better luck than I had at persuading her to stay.'

Valdar's eyes widened. 'And you are letting her go?'

'Rurik has never been to Sand before.' Ash bent down and pretended to be examining various pebbles, but in reality he was aware of every movement Valdar made. 'It seemed like an opportune moment to give in to my lady's desire for this to happen.'

'The Lady Kara wanted this?' Valdar's hand went to his sword. 'I took you for many things, Hringson, but not a liar. The Lady Kara would never suggest such a thing. She keeps Rurik here on this estate. She fears for his life.'

'She means to travel with Rurik whether I wish it or not. We quarrelled about it, but I lost.' Ash waited, willing Valdar to understand what he was asking. 'I want her kept safe whatever happens. Will you give me your pledge?'

Valdar pursed his lips. 'Willingly. The quarrel is with you and your ship, rather than with the Lady Kara. Harald Haraldson was quite clear on that point—the Lady Kara should stay on the estate. He gave me his pledge.'

A tiny fillip of satisfaction filled Ash. His uncle didn't want Kara there. Or rather he worried about Valdar supporting his cause if he attacked Kara as well as Ash. And he'd seen the respect she commanded. Kara had been right. She needed to go. He needed her by his side.

'And you believe my uncle's pledges on this matter?'

Valdar bowed his head. 'You don't.'

Ash held out his hand. 'If anything happens, get her and Rurik back here. My men can do the rest.'

'You love her.'

'I think we both love her.'

'Obviously.' Valdar started towards the hall, stopped and turned with a frown. 'How did you do it? You are gone for seven years and she falls immediately for you. What is so much better about you?'

'Not immediately and I have no idea,' Ash said quietly. 'She wants what is best for her son. She has always done so.'

Valdar nodded. 'Yes, Kara Olofdottar refused to look at me until I started paying attention to the boy. He is a pleasant boy, but he talks a lot and is not very strong. I have serious doubts about him ever becoming a warrior. I said as much to your father.'

Ash's shoulders relaxed slightly. 'There is more to being a warrior than brute strength. Give him time. He'll make a fine and cunning one.'

'It is good, then, that you returned home.'

Ash picked up a pebble and tossed it out into the lake where it made ever-expanding circles. 'I like to think so.'

Valdar did the same. 'You always were a lucky bastard, Hringson.'

Ash rubbed the back of his neck. The dull ache in his head began to throb with increased intensity. 'They say you make your own luck, but now I have hope.'

'The Lady Kara is a beautiful woman, even if she is colder than a statue. Or I thought she was until I saw her at the wedding. She possesses a fire when she is around you. You can see it in the way she moves. You make her alive.'

Ash pressed his hands against his trousers. Once he'd have crowed about her responsiveness to him, but now he knew it was private.

'It is more than her physical appearance.' Ash gave a wry smile. 'I underestimated her for years. Now I'm learning her true strengths. What she has done to Jaarlshiem has been nothing short of amazing. And Rurik is a boy to be proud of. He will inherit an estate worthy of its name. I only hope I haven't left it too late.'

Valdar stroked his chin and stared off into the lake where the faint glimmer of sunrise turned the lake's surface to a pale pink. 'What will happen when she goes to Sand? Will you be able to hold this estate?'

Ash gave him a sharp glance. 'Whose man are you?'

'I would have been Lady Kara's until you returned.' Valdar inclined his head. 'But I carry her in my heart. Should anything happen to you, you must not worry about your family. How many men do you want?'

Ash released his breath. He had won a small victory. 'I'm leaving my men here to guard Jaarlshiem in my absence. Saxi owes me several life debts. He'll hold this place until his last breath. Get her here and he will do the rest.'

Valdar nodded. 'I won't pretend I'm happy about this. Something feels off. Kara should be made to listen to reason. Sand will be dangerous for you. She might be caught in something that she doesn't understand.'

'Now that you are standing next to me in the sunrise instead of having my uncle drip his poison in your ear.'

Valdar gave an unhappy nod. 'I gave the king my word I'd bring you back. Your uncle doesn't expect me to. He expected you to fight me. I see that now.'

'My uncle never truly understood me. He underestimates me and that is his mistake.'

The pain receded in Ash's head. He had done

what he could. He had to hope that Kara would not take any crazy chances on the journey and that his uncle would not attack them as they neared the city.

'I am to take Ash straight to the king's dungeon when we arrive in Sand, but you may reside with me until the outcome of the case is known,' Valdar said, bringing his horse alongside the cart where Kara and Rurik sat.

'You are speaking to me again?' Kara enquired lightly, resisting the temptation to roll her eyes at the patronising speech.

'I've no quarrel with you, Lady Kara.'

'My mistake.' Kara eased a pillow behind her back and gave a half-turn in her seat, pleased of the distraction from the incessant jolting of the cart. Her hand sent Rurik's sword tumbling to the floor of the cart. Immediately Rurik gave an anguished cry and picked it up again. That sword had been nothing but trouble since Valdar had given it to Rurik. 'You have barely said two words to me since this journey started. Suddenly less than a day's journey to Sand, you wish to talk.'

'I want this settled between us. The king has no quarrel with you.'

'He should have no quarrel with Ash either,' Kara said, giving a warning look to Valdar as

Rurik's eyes slid shut and the sword threatened to fall out of his grasp again. 'What good will that do? Humiliating him in that way? Ash gave you his word. You prevented his men from travelling. And he has done nothing wrong.'

Despite readily agreeing to her travelling with them, Valdar had not allowed Kara to take any of Ash's men with her, arguing that it would look like an act of war. To Kara's surprise, Ash had given way immediately. There appeared to be a newfound respect between the two, but neither said what had caused it.

Their journey to Sand had taken several days longer than when she had travelled the other way with Ash because Ash had insisted that she and Rurik travel in a covered cart.

'Do this for me, Valdar. For what we once shared. Allow my husband some dignity.'

Valdar's expression turned grave. 'Kara, you do have feelings for this man.'

Kara concentrated. Were her feelings that plain? She had hoped by ignoring it, no one would know. The last thing she desired was pity. 'I know how to keep my heart safe.'

'I consider you a friend.'

'You won't say anything to…to my husband.'

Valdar's eyes danced. 'My lips are entirely sealed. It will do him good.' He nodded. 'What do you think will happen when we reach Sand?'

'I've no idea,' she answered truthfully. 'But I want to be where I can help.'

'And how is having Rurik there going to help?'

Kara leant forward and smoothed a lock of hair off her sleeping son's forehead. 'His father adores him. Rurik will add weight to the argument.'

A sudden shout drowned out Valdar's reply.

The cart jerked to a halt, throwing both Kara and Rurik to the floor.

'Stay down, Kara.' Ash's voice rang out. 'For the love of the gods, keep down.'

Every sinew in Ash's body froze. He had expected the attack for the last few miles. The very air seemed to hold its breath. He had heard the rustling of human movement and had seen the shadowy figures in the woods.

Silently he cursed his folly of allowing Kara and Rurik to travel with him. Thankfully Valdar had chosen to ride near Kara's cart.

'What is going on, Hringson?' Valdar thundered up on his horse. 'Why have you stopped this column and panicked your wife? And why are you retreating?'

Ash nodded his head towards the woods. 'I don't like the way the shadows are moving. Send someone to investigate. I'm going to make sure my wife is safe.'

Valdar gave an impatient sigh and sent two of his men. 'You are in Raumerike, not Viken. Your wife is fine. Your son was asleep. Our conversation was pleasant until you interrupted.'

'Raumerike worries me in ways Viken never could.'

One of the men waved his arms.

'You see—nothing.' Valdar gave a smug smile. 'You go and explain to Lady Kara. You face her wrath. Next time make sure you actually see men rather than—'

'Owls don't screech in the daylight. And animals stay away from men on horseback.'

A strangled scream rent the air and the man fell with an arrow in his heart. Valdar immediately stiffened and dismounted from his horse. Two thralls came and caught the horse's bridle.

'Shall I investigate?' Ash asked, clinging on to his temper. 'Surely, man, you must see. Something is wrong. You need to protect my wife.'

Valdar drew his sword and picked up a light shield. His men formed a ring about Ash.

'Not so fast, Hringson. You will not be allowed to escape.'

'If I had wanted to make my escape, I would have hardly had my wife and child in your protection.' Ash shook his head at Valdar's arrogant stupidity. Even now, the other warrior did not see how he'd been manipulated. Ash wanted to kick himself for not thinking about the possibility. Kara should not be here. Kara should be back in Jaarlshiem where she'd be safe.

A host of men in full armour emerged from the woods and stood before them, brandishing their shields. Ash's heart sank. They were outnumbered three to one and he had no confidence in Valdar or his men to fight their way out of a linen-cloth bag, let alone an ambush planned with this sort of precision.

'Give us Ash Hringson,' the leader who wore his uncle's insignia on his left shoulder thundered. 'Then we will allow you to pass in peace.'

'The welcoming party?' Ash asked in an undertone. 'They are a bit far from Sand. Will you keep your promise and look after my family?'

'I gave the king my pledge. I will not give you up to any other man.' Valdar's face became grim. 'Your uncle had other plans which he failed to divulge. Nep was one of my best men.'

'If you give me up, you may be unharmed,' Ash said in an undertone, watching the man he dimly recognised as the captain of his uncle's guard. 'There again, my uncle might take the opportunity to rid himself of a troublesome neighbour.'

Valdar gave him a telling look. 'And the

heir to the estate he covets. We played straight into his hands. I've been a fool. The Lady Kara should never have travelled.'

'He tricked us both. I hadn't expected this move. I thought we'd be safe until Sand,' Ash confessed. 'I would have warned you otherwise. And I would never have put my wife and child in danger.'

Valdar raised his fist. 'Then we fight! I promised to deliver you to the king and by Thor's hammer that is what I will do.'

'I'd be honoured.'

Ash's heart raced. He wasn't worried for himself, but for Kara and Rurik. Thankfully Kara appeared to have heeded his warning cry and stayed in the cart. 'Do I get a weapon?'

'None to spare. Stay to the back. There will be weapons soon enough.' Valdar started to advance forward.

Ash hated how powerless he felt. All he had was his eating knife. He hated to be here at the back when he was needed up in the front. Every sinew of his being longed for the fight.

'Ash!' Kara's frightened voice resounded from the cart.

'Keep down, Kara!'

'Rurik has a sword. You will need it more than he does.'

Silently he blessed her. He crossed over to

the cart where Kara and Rurik huddled. Kara had her arms about Rurik and his son's face was white. His hand closed about the light sword. It was far from the ideal weapon, but it would do.

He smiled at his son. 'Will you allow me to use this?'

Rurik gave a hesitant nod. 'I would be...I would be honoured, Far.'

'Good lad. Stay there with your mother and look after her. Keep your head down. Wait until the battle has ended.'

Kara gestured towards the noise. 'Go. Do what you have to do. Come back quickly. We... we will be waiting for you.'

Ash nodded. He drank in the picture of Kara and Rurik huddled together.

'My luck will hold. It has done so far.'

'You don't need luck. You are a great warrior. Always remember that,' Kara called back. The same words she had said when she saw him off on his ill-fated voyage. 'I believe in you!'

His throat closed, stopping any more words.

He forced his feet to move. If he stayed, he would be no good to anyone.

When he reached the fighting, Valdar and his small group of men had managed to get his uncle's men on their back feet. He was a far better warrior than Ash had remembered

'Watch your back!' Ash lunged forward and

met the sword of his uncle's captain before the sword hit Valdar from behind.

His sword clashed and clashed again. He turned to his right and mistimed his step. His bad leg pulsed pain. He slipped, going down on one knee, blindly lifting his sword and missing his stroke.

A sharp burn sliced through his face and the salt tang of blood trickled into his mouth. He wiped his hand across his face, seeking to clear the blood. The pain rocked him. It would be easy to fall to his knees, give in and finally admit he had lost. He could barely remember what he was fighting for any more. He had nothing left to prove. He could feel the soft breath of a Valkyrie coming to claim his shade for Odin.

A Valkyrie. Kara. Ash instantly became alert. Kara was who he fought for. He wanted to spend his life with her. He had always been fighting to get back to her. It hadn't been his father's regard he was afraid of losing, but Kara's. He had been a fool. He had to make sure that as long as he walked the earth, Kara was at his side. And he'd left without telling her his feelings and why he wanted to be a better man. He had to have the chance to explain and to make it right.

He redoubled his efforts and stood. His sword met the other's sword and the effort reverberated through his arm. He pivoted to his left, found a tiny opening, blindly thrust his sword forward and connected.

'I owe you!' Valdar called out as the captain's body fell to the ground.

Ash wiped his sword on the grass and turned to face his next enemy. Survive. That was all he had to do—survive. 'This battle is far from over.'

Chapter Fifteen

Kara sat paralysed with Rurik's head in her lap, unable to look away from the raging battle. It was impossible to tell who was winning or indeed where Ash was. Over and over she prayed to any god that Odin wouldn't want Ash, not today, not ever.

She cursed herself for not saying that she loved him before Ash had rushed off. It was wrong of her. She had made mistakes in their relationship as well as him. She could see that now. When they were first married, she had wanted to be the wife of a great warrior. She had encouraged him to go. And when he returned, she had tried to insist on him being a farmer and helping her to run the estate when the person she wanted was Ash with all of his faults. She could easily run the estate on her own, knowing that Ash would be there to back her decisions.

She wanted him to be part of her whole future. She wanted to share her life with him but she wanted as long as he walked the earth to have him as hers. She wouldn't be happy otherwise. And he needed to be Ash, the man she had married, not someone he was trying to be to please her. She was a one-man woman.

'Please let him live,' she whispered over and over again. 'Please give me a second chance.'

The silence fell without warning. Sudden and utterly consuming. Somewhere a pigeon cooed, breaking the oppressive stillness.

'Mor, is it over?' Rurik asked in a frightened voice. 'Have Valkyries taken the fallen to Valhalla? They won't come and get me, will they? I'm not ready to go to Valhalla.'

'It is, sweetheart.' Kara kissed Rurik's head. Her limbs shook. They were safe, precisely as Ash had promised. They were safe, but where was Ash? Surely he should have returned. 'And you are right, the Valkyries will have been, but they are gone now. They are only searching for fallen warriors, not little boys.'

Kara stood up in the cart, craning her head, trying to see where Ash stood. Her heart clenched. If he stood… From the cart, it was impossible to see who stood, but she didn't recognise Ash's shape. She clenched her fists. He had to be there. Alive. She had to be able to say she loved him.

'Did my father win?'

'I think so. No one came close to the cart or the horses, did they?' Kara knelt down so that her face was level with Rurik's. 'I want you to do something for me. I want you to stay here and not move. I'm going to find your father and bring him back to us. Can you do that for me? It is very important.'

Rurik gave a tiny nod. 'A true warrior obeys his mother. Far told me that. I obey your command.'

Silently she blessed Ash's forethought. He had been right about that. She was so afraid of losing Rurik that she kept him too close. Ash's coming back had changed so many things.

'I'll be back as soon as I can. With your Far. Be a good warrior.' She started off, but made the mistake of looking back. Rurik looked far too young and miserable.

'Please, Mor. Please may I come with you? I'm scared.' Rurik's face crumpled. 'I'm not ready to be a good warrior. I still need my mother.'

Kara pinched the bridge of her nose. With a request like that how could she refuse? He'd be safer in the cart, but she wanted him with her. She held out her hand. 'Come, then.'

Together they picked their way past the horses

and scattered gear to where the battle had taken place. Bodies littered the blood-soaked ground. Kara gave a small cry and turned her face away as Rurik gripped her hand tighter.

'I don't like this, Mor.'

'No one does.' Kara steeled herself. If she had to, she'd turn over every corpse to find Ash. Then she'd go into Sand and get justice for Ash. Not to save the estate, but to make sure everyone understood what a good man Ash had been.

Over to her right, she could see the outlines of the hut where they had stopped that first night. Good ground for a battle. The memory of Ash's words thudded through her. She hoped he'd been right and his luck had held.

'Now to find your father.'

She forced her hand to turn over the first body. Breathed again. She didn't recognise the man. 'This warrior has gone to Valhalla, Rurik.'

Rurik's face went white, but he didn't cry. 'We need to find my father.'

'And Valdar.'

'My father first.'

'My thoughts precisely. Your father first, always.' Silently she prayed that she'd figure out a way to keep Ash from fighting again.

The sound of male laughter floated on the air towards her. Someone was in the hut. Relief flooded through her. She started to run towards the sound.

'Ash?'

The laughter instantly stopped.

'Kara! I told you to stay in the cart.'

'Since when do I do as you say?' she asked, putting her hand on her hip, but keeping a restraining hold on Rurik, as well.

Ash sat on the ground outside the hut, resting Rurik's sword on his knee, his face half-turned from her. Blood splattered his tunic and trousers. Valdar stood in the doorway with his helm off and his shoulder bandaged.

'Ash, is there a problem?'

'You should do as I asked.' He resolutely kept his face from her. 'And you should not have brought Rurik with you. It is far from safe. There might be a second wave of attacks. I…I can't risk you both.'

'Let me see you.' She crossed the distance in two strides and stuffed her hand in her mouth. Ash now sported a wide gash on his face. If the blow had struck only a little differently, he'd dead instead of sitting and joking with Valdar. 'Ash!'

'It looks worse than it is.' His hand wiped away a trickle of blood. 'There are others worse than me. I survived.'

'I will be the judge of that.' Kara reached into

the pouch she always wore and withdrew a scrap of linen. She put it on Ash's cheek, noting how close the sword had come to his eye. Ash was right. 'It appears to be deep. Hold that there and I will be back with my healing supplies.'

'I will go,' Rurik piped up. 'I know where it is. Trust me to get it.'

'You are sure?' Kara asked, hesitating. She should go, but she wanted to see how badly Ash was hurt, preferably without Rurik right there.

'Yes! And I can run faster than you because you are wearing a skirt, Mor.'

'Then go swiftly. I will watch you.'

'Should you have allowed him to do that?' Ash asked. 'He is awfully young to be on a battlefield.'

'He is capable of more than you or I think,' Kara answered, shading her eyes with her hand. 'You have shown me that. It will be good for him to have a little responsibility. He is old enough.'

Ash shook his head. 'I do trust you.'

Rurik returned from the cart, dropping the small satchel at her feet. He placed his hands on his knees and panted from the exertion. 'Did I go quick enough?'

'Faster than the wind.' Kara rapidly sorted the various supplies and found the herbs her mother had used.

'These should work. They are good at stopping bleeding. When mixed with a little honey.' She dabbed the mixture on his cheek, brushing the dirt from it. He winced as she worked. 'The wound is clean. I don't think there will be an infection, but you will sport a scar.'

'You brought the right medicine, Kara—you and Rurik,' he said, standing up. 'I feel stronger already. I hope you don't mind a scarred husband.'

'I will take my husband however I can have him,' she said, wrapping her hands about her waist. 'But you should sit and rest. It looks as though you have lost a lot of blood.'

'No, I need to return a sword.' Ash knelt down on one knee. 'A warrior always returns a weapon to its owner. It has been bloodied, Rurik. It has good balance. It is destined to be legendary. Use it wisely.'

'Truly?' Rurik's face broke into a wide smile.

'Yes, truly.' Ash put his hand on Rurik's shoulder. 'Valdar chose the blade well.'

'How is he?'

'A scratch to my wrist and a deeper one to my shoulder,' the warrior said, coming up. 'Rurik, why don't you come with me and see my men? I want to see how badly hurt they are. Your parents can spare you for a little while.'

Valdar led Rurik away, leaving Kara with Ash.

'Are you hurt anywhere else? Your clothes are bloody.'

'Most of the blood is other people's, Kara,' Ash said.

'Can I see for myself?' Kara asked, reaching for his tunic.

'I'll live.' He turned away.

'You're worse than Rurik. I want to know you are fine. There is a difference. You fought without a helm or protection.'

Ash took off his shirt and she saw his skin had no fresh cuts.

'The gods were kind,' she murmured.

'I have been in battles before. Other than this scratch, I will have a few bruises. My knee took a battering, but I can still walk. Valdar took a sword cut to his shoulder though. I have bound it up, but he will need to rest it and not ride a horse.'

'If that is a scratch, I would hate to see what a real wound looked like.' Kara clenched her fists. There were so many things she wanted to say, but Ash seemed different. More alive and at peace with himself. He enjoyed this, she realised. 'Your father would have been proud.'

Ash's face sobered. 'My father was different from me. I don't need to seek his approval. I know how to do my job.' He laced his hand through hers and brought it to his lips. 'I didn't think my uncle would attack us here. Just like I didn't think the lightning would hit the ship all those years ago. I would have insisted you stay in Jaarlshiem. I never meant to put Rurik or you in danger. Will you forgive me?'

'If Rurik and I hadn't come, you'd have been without a sword and I would never have forgiven myself for that.'

He tilted his head to one side, assessing her. 'You say the most unexpected things. I hadn't looked at it in that way.'

Her heart turned over. With great difficulty she held back the words about loving him. Despite the wound, his entire being radiated happiness and contentment. How could she ever hope to deny him if he wanted to go off and fight more battles? And how could she bear the pain of wondering what was happening to him? But equally she couldn't bear him only living half a life. 'It is the truth.'

His eyes assessed her for a long heartbeat. 'And here I worried you'd be furious with me.'

'For saving my life and Rurik's? You must think me very hard. You are the hero of the battle.'

'No, I am a man who made sure his family was protected. I was not about to lose either of you. You are far too precious for me.'

Kara wrapped her arms about her waist. The

full impact of what had nearly happened coursed through her. Ice-cold shivers consumed her. Ash had come too close to death. The world started to turn black. 'I nearly lost you.'

'Breathe, Kara. Concentrate on the now, rather than what might have been. Put it from your mind. It is over. We survived.'

'Your uncle's men attacked.'

'Yes.' Ash shaded his eyes. 'One or two may have escaped during the fighting. I regret I was otherwise occupied. I was not as good as I should be.'

'Escaped?' The full impact of Ash's word hit Kara. This wasn't the end move. This was an opening gambit. They were far from safe here. 'You mean they are on their way to your uncle?'

'They could be. What my uncle does with them is another question. He hates failure.'

Kara slammed her fists together, coming to a sudden decision. 'We need to see the king as soon as possible, preferably before your uncle learns of this. We need to keep him off-balance.'

Ash struggled to his feet. 'I agree with you. We press on. A few hours of daylight remain and there is a moon tonight.'

'Once my men are seen to,' Valdar said, coming back with Rurik in tow. 'We need to wait, Ash.'

'I collected the fallen warriors' brooches.'

Rurik held out a number of insignia before Ash could answer. 'Like you told me, Far. Every warrior should do this—to know who he fought. Can I keep them?'

'You may keep them,' Ash confirmed.

Rurik gave a glad cry and threw his arms about Ash. Instantly he enveloped his son and spun around with him.

'Why should we wait, Valdar?' Kara asked, watching the pair. 'We hold the advantage now.'

'We need an escort. One must proceed with caution, particularly now that your uncle has made his move.'

'Your men can look after themselves and travel at their own pace, but we need to get to Sand,' Ash said, setting Rurik on his feet. 'I hardly want you branded a traitor because you raised a sword against my uncle's men. He will try to twist what happened here today.'

Valdar pursed his lips. 'I see what you mean, but even so one must be cautious. I vote we stay here until we know we have the strength to fight. And I am the one responsible for taking you to Sand. You must yield.'

Kara ground her teeth. Even she with her limited knowledge of warfare and strategy saw that Ash was correct. Sometimes you did have to take a risk. Whatever happened, she knew she was safer with Ash than staying here with Valdar's men.

'Allow Kara to decide. I trust her judgement on this matter,' Ash said. 'Do this for me and I will say your life debt is cancelled.'

An inner glow filled her. Ash trusted her judgement. He believed in her. 'You owe Ash a life debt, Valdar?'

'He saved my life and received the cut to his face for his pains.' Valdar gave a short laugh. 'It improves his looks.'

'What is your decision, Valdar?' Ash cleared his throat. 'Will you accept Lady Kara's judgement? Or do you wish to feel her wrath?'

'Very well. Lady Kara, what do you wish to do? Press on or wait?'

Kara glanced about her. Valdar's men would not be in any fit state to travel for several days. Time they did not have. But travelling on also meant they were at risk if Harald Haraldson should decide to attack them again. Valdar was many things, but he was no tafl player.

'I trust Ash's judgement. He is the expert. We see to the worst of the wounded and then we go. Valdar must ride in the cart with his injured arm—he won't be able to control his horse.'

'Who will ride Valdar's horse?'

'I will ride alongside Ash until we see the gates. Valdar can have his horse back then. There will be fewer comments if you ride your horse in. We want to catch Harald Haraldson unaware if at all possible.'

Ash kissed her cheek, but his lips were cool. Kara's stomach knotted. She was going to have to let him go out to sea again and she wasn't sure her heart was ready for it but how could she not let him go? She wanted Ash, rather than someone else who was steady and always there. Ash was the only man for her. 'That's my woman. Your head for strategy is excellent, but I will ride Valdar's horse. My horse knows you.'

'Then it is settled.'

Valdar bowed his head. 'I hope you know what you are doing, Kara.'

'Not much farther, Kara,' Ash said from his horse. His bones ached with weariness and his facial wound pulsed, alternating with ice-cold numbness and excruciating pain. He had spent most of the night concentrating on riding Valdar's horse. Valdar with his wound to his shoulder rode in the cart with Rurik. There was simply no way Valdar could have controlled the horse with his injured shoulder. Thankfully the warrior had seen sense.

Right now he had to hope his plan would work. All of his battlefield knowledge came down to this moment.

'See, we have reached the outlying farms. We will be at the gates before dawn.'

'The third farm is Auda's. I suggest we rest there until the town gates open in the morning. Valdar is her brother-in-law. She will give us shelter.'

Kara's being radiated tiredness. Her determination to reach Sand surprised him. If they pulled this feat off, people would talk about it for years to come. Once the thought would have pleased him, but now he worried. Fame and glory meant nothing if he didn't have Kara to share it.

'You can stay there if you want. Wait for me until I get this solved. You and Rurik will be safe.'

'I want to see this through. I want to be at your side.'

Ash gave her a sharp look. In the dim light only her proud profile shone.

'Trust me to get this right. I will protect Rurik's heritage. We will get back to Jaarlshiem. I can do this alone, without your help.'

'I will find that too hard.' Kara pulled her horse to a stop.

'Hard or impossible?' Ash asked softly. His heart clenched. He had to know what was in her heart. 'Once I know you are safe from my uncle, Kara, we can talk about the future.'

She ducked her head. 'Hard, but not for the reason you think. I want to be there, Ash. Let me be there. I might be able to help. Don't shut me out.'

'A tangle of my making. I should be the one to put it right.'

'Why do you find it hard to accept help? Why do you always have to be the only hero?' The muscles in her neck tightened. 'There are times when I wish I could strangle your father. You don't need to prove anything to me.'

Ash looked down at her face. He might not need to prove anything to her, but he wanted to prove something to himself. 'I love you, Kara. I don't want anything to happen to you. I want you to be safe.'

'Sometimes, you have only the illusion of safety if you fail to face the things you fear. You taught me that.' She nodded towards where the farm nestled in a hollow. 'We face what lies ahead together. If you love me like you say you do, you will allow me to be there and plead on your behalf.'

His heart panged slightly. He wasn't alone. He had her. She had not given way, but she had compromised. He had to show her that he could meet her halfway. Deeds, not words, were required.

* * *

The gates creaked open and the king's guard rode out. Kara's heart sank as she recognised the leader—a loyal follower of Ash's uncle. They had made it thus far, only for Ash's uncle to win.

'We demand to be taken to the king!' Ash shouted, jumping down from his horse.

'Our orders say otherwise, Ash Hringson. You are under suspicion of ordering an unprovoked attack. You are to be delivered to Harald Haraldson first, for safekeeping.'

'We were attacked on the king's road and demand justice. Have the laws of Raumerike changed that much?' Ash spread his hands. 'See, Valdar the Steady is with us and you know him to be an honest man. Allow him to go to the king and then take us to my uncle.'

'I demand to be taken to the king!' Valdar thundered. 'Ash Hringson was put in my charge. Where I go, he goes.'

The men looked nonplussed and hurriedly retreated to confer. After a few agonising heartbeats, their leader came forward again. 'We will accompany you to the king's hall. We are not at war with you, Valdar the Steady, you may retain your sword.'

Valdar nodded, but he swayed slightly. Kara gave him a hurried glance. The journey had been too much for him.

'Valdar should rest before we see the king,' she said. 'He is nearly dead on his feet.'

The captain smiled. 'He may rest. He may go anywhere he likes.'

'Forgive me,' Valdar murmured.

'And the Lady Kara?' Ash asked, ignoring her swift intake. 'Where are they to go?'

'They are to go straight to Harald Haraldson. He will keep them safe. They are part of his family.'

Kara clenched her fists. She should have thought about the potential to be a hostage. Instead of helping, she had played directly in Harald Haraldson's hands.

'Neither Hringson's son or wife has been accused,' Valdar said, giving a quick glance at Ash, who nodded in confirmation. 'But they are under my protection and need to travel with me. They may reside at my house.'

'They must stay with Valdar Nerison,' Ash agreed.

Kara's stomach knotted. The words and actions were very unlike Valdar. Had they come to some agreement before she had found them by the hut? She went back over Ash's words throughout the journey. He was giving her up.

'Kara,' Ash said. 'Forgive me, but I have to know you are safe. Valdar will look after you should anything happen to me. I will go to meet the king alone. Once you are settled, then Valdar will come to the king's hall.'

His uncle's man nodded. 'I can agree to that. Valdar Nerison is not wanted for questioning. He only needed to bring you.'

'I want to share your fate,' Kara said in an undertone before they led Ash away. 'Let me come with you.'

'You have to think about our son. He needs one parent to look after him if things don't go as I planned. Valdar knows what to do.'

Kara bit her lip. 'I thought it was decided. I want to be with you.'

'I thought it was understood.' He raised her hand to his lips. 'Do as I ask for once. Please.'

'I do trust you, but you need to know I am there to support you in spirit.'

'I don't want my uncle to use you.' His brow creased. 'Valdar and I made the plan in case of this happening. He will look after you…should the worst happen.'

'And you were the one who always said that when things looked blackest, you did your best work. Remember the tafl game? You can do this.'

'Hold on to that thought.'

Kara's heart sank. Despite his earlier bravado, Ash was less certain about the outcome than he pretended. 'Nothing will happen to you. I won't allow it.'

'It is right. Valdar has given me protection through this journey. He will provide it now. He is what you need, Kara. Someone steady.'

She shook her head. 'No, you are wrong. I need you. Never forget that.'

'I will do my best to remember it.'

Ash strode into the hall. Alone. His entire body ached with pain, but Kara was safe. His uncle's men had beaten him and then taken him to the king.

In the centre of the room, his uncle stood next to the king, wearing a triumphant smile. The king appeared older than when he had left Sand, more careworn. Ash struggled to remember that this man had once been one of the greatest warriors that any of the North lands had seen.

'You have returned, Ash Hringson,' the king said. 'Your uncle feared you might be reluctant.'

'And far from willing by the look of him,' his uncle sneered. 'His cloak is torn and his face bruised. And where is the man who was sent to fetch you? Lying in some ditch?'

Ash inclined his head. 'Valdar Nerison proved an adequate escort. However, he was injured in the fighting and rests. He gives his apologies.'

'How did he come by the injuries?' the king asked.

'Be careful, my liege. My nephew was once a sell-sword. The lies spring readily to his lips,' his uncle said.

'We were attacked on the road from Jaarlshiem,' Ash said evenly. His stomach clenched. He knew his uncle's line of attack—how he could fight back.

'Attacked in Raumerike?' His uncle laughed. 'Since when does that happen? Who attacked you?'

'Your men,' Ash answered.

'Do you have proof?' his uncle asked.

'Do you have proof that my ship attacked yours, Uncle?' Ash retorted, struggling to keep his temper.

'I have my captain's word. A man who has never sold his sword to the highest bidder. He is loyal to me because of my birth, not because of the amount of gold I pay him.'

'Where is this captain?' Ash demanded. 'I would like to speak with him and learn more.'

'Bring him here, Harald,' the king said. 'A man should face his accuser. We agreed on this. Ash is Hring the Bold's son. I owe his late father that much.'

'It can be arranged.' His uncle snapped his fingers and the captain of the guard came closer.

'This is my man and you all know him to speak the truth.'

'Where is my oarsman?'

'You needn't worry. You two will share the same fate.' The king inclined his head. 'First I wish to hear more about this attack. Was Valdar Nerison there?'

'Valdar is in love with my nephew's wife. Perhaps there is another reason for his absence. Or perhaps she has addled his wits. Kara Olofdottar is very beguiling.'

Ash clenched his teeth. His uncle was better than he'd anticipated. He should have insisted on Valdar being there. One more mistake. Perhaps a fatal one. 'When he arrives, he will vouch for my word.'

'We will need physical proof.'

'I have proof of whom my father fought.'

Ash looked around and saw Rurik standing in the doorway with Kara. His uncle's men blocked her path. Valdar was nowhere to be seen, but Kara appeared furious. She shrugged off the restraining arm as Rurik darted forward. Ash saw with a smile that Rurik wore his sword.

'And who are you?' the king asked, nonplussed.

'I am Rurik Ashson and I have brought the brooches of the men my father fought. A warrior should always have proof of whom he fought. My mother agreed with me when I reminded her. It is why we have come.' Rurik placed them on the floor in front of the king. 'My grandfather said that you were a fair man and would listen to me if I ever had a boon to ask. He said you would grant it because of the pledge you gave my grandfather at the battle where you won your crown. But it could only be one request. He said I could ask to be a warrior, but I have a different request. Listen to my father.'

'I will listen to him…for your grandfather's sake,' the king said.

Ash peered at the insignia. He had told Kara that he didn't need anyone, but she had come anyway. That alone gave him hope. His hand closed around his uncle's captain's brooch and held it up high.

'Here is your proof, Uncle. Or do you deny the evidence of your own eyes? Your captain attacked me and my family. The same captain who attacked my ship. I can remember his crest from years ago. My father used to make me re-cite the crests as punishment. A snake curled about a raven.'

His uncle's eyes darted about the room. 'I fear I may have been mistaken. My captain acted without my orders.'

'I thought your men always obeyed your orders.'

'I...I...'

The king lifted his hand and motioned to the guards. 'Seize Harald Haraldson.'

For a telling pause, none of them moved. Then one of them grabbed his uncle and pinned his arms behind his back. 'My loyalty is to the king!'

Ash bowed his head. It was over. His uncle had lost.

Kara waited outside the king's hall for Ash. Auda had come into town and had taken Rurik away to play with her sons so that Kara could be alone with Ash. However, the king had requested a private audience, which had gone on and on.

Ash's uncle vanquished, Ash triumphant. Everything that Ash once wanted was coming true. He looked to be every inch the warrior hero, a man other men could admire.

She should be happy for him, but it meant she was going to lose him. She wanted to go back to the ease they'd had in the woods when it had been just the two of them, before any of this had started. She wanted someone with her, sharing her life, but how could she deny him his dreams?

She had been wrong earlier. She had not safeguarded her heart. There was nothing left to safeguard. She had given it to Ash years ago. She wanted to beat her fists against his chest and cry that she wanted him to stay.

Kara hugged her arms about her waist. She couldn't do that to him seven years ago and she couldn't do it to him now. But she could let him know she would welcome him back and she would wait. For ever if necessary. She could take a risk with her heart.

'Kara!' Ash came out of the hall and enfolded her in his arms.

'You must tell me everything.'

He rapidly explained that his uncle had confessed everything, including his plot to overthrow the king. Kara listened with mounting horror as she realised how close they had come to disaster.

'But all that doesn't matter. You waited for me,' Ash said, smoothing the hair from her forehead. 'I wanted to apologise. Your quick thinking and Rurik's saved me. I said earlier that I didn't need you but I was wrong. I do. I need my family.'

'I will always wait.'

He laid his cheek on the top of her head. 'It is good to know.'

She inhaled, breathing in his spicy scent, savouring the moment. 'You're going away again. You need not be gentle with me.'

He loosened his arms and peered down at her. 'Do you want me to go? Will you let me go without a fight?'

'If it is what the king commands, who am I to say no? But you will have a fight on your hands if you don't come home. I will go and search you out.' She squared her shoulders. She had to take the risk and say the words. If she didn't say the words and he went again, he'd never know. 'I love you, Ash the person, not Ash the hero or Ash the warrior or even Ash the farmer if you wish to be that, but they are part of you. They make you into the man I love. And I'd rather have you to love than a thousand other men.'

'But you want me to go. You will find it easier if I'm not underfoot, making changes to your well-ordered life.'

She shook her head, smiling. 'I prefer your chaos to my order. I would like you to stay and be a farmer, but I don't think you would enjoy it.'

He laughed. 'Answer the question. I can always beat my sword into a plough. I'm willing to try.'

Kara sobered. 'I want you to stay, but I saw your face in the aftermath of the attack. You live for adventure. It makes you alive. I've no wish for you to live a half-life. You would be bored at Jaarlshiem, being a farmer. I can carry the burden of the estate, knowing that you will come back to me.'

'You are wrong there, Kara.' He smoothed her hair away from her forehead. 'I live for you. The only reason I am alive is because of you. You are the face I fight for. I didn't realise it fully until we were attacked and I had to fight, but I have been always fighting to return to you. I am not fighting to get away from you. Quite the opposite. I need you in my life. I once selfishly loved you because you made me feel like I could be a hero. You believed in my dreams. Then when my dreams turned to dust, I couldn't face you turning away from me. I still want to be your hero, Kara, but I want to be part of your life more.'

Her heart did a crazy flip. He wanted to be with her. 'Why were you closeted so long with the king?'

'The king has offered me a new position as his advisor.' Ash stood a little straighter. 'He wants someone who has knowledge of today's world. He wants someone who can inspire the younger men and who can tell them where the best markets are. But I don't need to go to those markets. I can tell the men where to go.'

'And you are going to take it?' Kara clapped her hands. 'It is the sort of thing you were born to do, Ash.'

'I wanted to speak to you first before I gave the king my answer. He granted my request.'

'Then what is the problem?' Kara withdrew her hands from his. 'You should take it.'

'You were wrong earlier when you said that

all I was doing was trying to prove myself to my father.' He touched her cheek. 'It ceased to be about making my father proud years ago. I wanted to be a hero in your eyes.'

She closed her eyes, silently cursing her younger self. 'You were, Ash. You have never had to prove anything to me. You still are.'

He put his fingers over her mouth. 'I was wrong. You are wrong. Instead of wanting to be your hero I should have wanted to be your husband. A husband is more than someone to be admired. He is someone you can count on and who is there to share life's ups and downs. I want to share my whole life with you, instead of consigning you to the outskirts. Will you let me be that husband?'

'And that is what you want for us?' Kara stared at him, hardly daring to breathe. 'You want to be my husband?'

'With my whole heart.' Ash knelt down on one knee. 'Will you stay with me always and be my wife in truth? I might not always be the perfect husband, but I will always be the husband who wants you by his side. I love you, Kara, and I'm unafraid of admitting it.'

'I will.' She grasped his hands and raised him to standing. 'Go and take the king's offer. We will stay in Sand for the time you need to be here. Our family will be together.'

He gathered her face between his hands. 'I don't deserve you.'

'I know but you have me.' She cupped his face between hers. 'Just as I don't deserve you. I was so frightened of loving you again, Ash, that I near'y missed my second chance to be loved. I need you in my life because you complete me.'

'As you complete me.' He put his arms about her and knew that he had truly come home.

* * * * *

Author's Historical Note

Researching the early Viking period is like doing a jigsaw puzzle with most of the pieces missing. The period is often referred to as 'the semi-legendary period' as most of the history we know about Scandinavia at that time comes from sagas which were written down long after the event.

The earliest history of Norwegian kings is the Morkinskinna saga, which in its current form dates from approximately 1220 but is reputed to have been first written down in about 1025. *'Morkinskinna'* literally means 'the mouldy parchment' and refers to the condition in which it was first found. We know from that the names of various petty kingdoms of Norway, and can make some guesses as to who was in power then, but there are huge gaps in the historical record.

Because of various ship burials most of the artefacts date from this period, but the exact meaning of the burials and who was actually in them is something that historians can only guess at.

We know a bit from other sources. For example, the Lindisfarne raid is well documented, but the true cause of the raid is a matter of conjecture. One recent theory is that the militant Christianity of Charlemagne's Frankish empire against the pagan Scandinavia caused the Vikings to be more violent than they had been in the past. Certainly there is evidence of some violent conflicts in the years immediately preceding the Lindisfarne raid.

If you are interested in the period, and want to read something other than the Morkinskinna, I have found the following books to be very useful:

- Ferguson, Robert. *The Hammer and the Cross: A New History of the Vikings* (2010 Penguin Books, London)
- Haywood, John. *The Penguin Historical Atlas of the Vikings* (1995 Penguin Books, London)
- Jesch, Judith. *Women in the Viking Age* (2005 The Boydell Press, Suffolk)

- O'Brien, Harriet. *Queen Emma and the Vikings: The Woman Who Shaped the Events of 1066* (2006 Bloomsbury, London)
- Magnusson, Magnus KBE. *The Vikings* (2008 The History Press, Gloucestershire)
- Roesdahl, Else. *The Vikings* revised edition translated by Susan Margeson and Kirsten Williams (1998 Penguin Books, London)
- Wood, Michael. *In Search of the Dark Ages* (2006 BBC Books, London)

A sneaky peek at next month…

HISTORICAL

IGNITE YOUR IMAGINATION, STEP INTO THE PAST…

My wish list for next month's titles…

In stores from 6th June 2014:

☐ Scars of Betrayal – Sophia James

☐ Scandal's Virgin – Louise Allen

☐ An Ideal Companion – Anne Ashley

☐ Surrender to the Viking – Joanna Fulford

☐ No Place for an Angel – Gail Whitiker

☐ Bride by Mail – Katy Madison

Available at WHSmith, Tesco, Asda, Eason, Amazon and Apple

Just can't wait?

The World of Mills & Boon

There's a Mills & Boon® series that's perfect for you. There are ten different series to choose from and new titles every month, so whether you're looking for glamorous seduction, Regency rakes, homespun heroes or sizzling erotica, we'll give you plenty of inspiration for your next read.

By Request
Back by popular demand!
12 stories every month

Cherish
Experience the ultimate rush of falling in love.
12 new stories every month

INTRIGUE...
A seductive combination of danger and desire...
7 new stories every month

Desire
Passionate and dramatic love stories
6 new stories every month

nocturne
An exhilarating underworld of dark desires
3 new stories every month